A MATTER OF TIME

A MATTER OF TIME

BOOK 1

Tony Edwards

Illustration by Victor Guiza

outskirts
press

Outskirts Press, Inc.
http://www.outskirtspress.com

Paperback ISBN: 978-1-9772-4767-4

Library of Congress Control Number: 2021919411

Cover Illustration by Victor Guiza © 2022 Outskirts Press, Inc.. All rights reserved - used with permission.

Outskirts Press and the "OP" logo are trademarks belonging to Outskirts Press, Inc.

PRINTED IN THE UNITED STATES OF AMERICA

To my loving grandparents, Edward and Nina Emanuele,
to whom I dictated my very first story
—before I even knew how to write.

For want of a nail the shoe was lost.
For want of a shoe the horse was lost.
For want of a horse the rider was lost.
For want of a rider the message was lost.
For want of a message the battle was lost.
For want of a battle the kingdom was lost.
And all for the want of a horseshoe nail.
— **Benjamin Franklin**

PROLOGUE

Aguila de Oro, Cantina and Lounge: it was a place where few people wanted to be, especially during the wee hours of a Wednesday morning. A moth fluttered alongside the flickering Christmas lights that terraced the dimly lit dining room. The odors of stale cologne and cheap tequila filled the air. A cockroach scampered about a plate containing the remains of *carnitas flautas.*

Only two customers remained in the restaurant, both men dressed in business attire. One was middle-aged with olive skin, a mop of white-streaked dark brown hair, and a healthy five o'clock shadow. He wore a circular pin on his lapel adjacent to a salsa-stained silk tie. Across from him sat an older man, his shiny bald head bordered by a smattering of wiry gray hairs. He gazed at the younger man with his piercing hazel eyes.

The middle-aged man broke the silence. "We need to hurry the hell up," he uttered, munching on a chip. "If the media saw me here, they'd cause a frenzy."

The old man smirked. "What would they think you're doing talking to Keith Byrd at some run-down taco joint at three in the morning in a part of the city where the sun don't shine? Not plotting to take over the world, I would assume."

"True," the middle-aged man replied, forcing a laugh. "But we still have to act fast before he figures anything out.

You know, they say that ignorance is bliss."

Byrd grinned. "Precisely. William Shakespeare once said, 'He who is robbed not wanting what is stolen, let him not knowt and he is not robbed at all.'"

"Look at Mr. Blue Collar quoting Shakespeare."

"That *Bard*, or whatever the hell he was called, had a point. The kid ain't gonna know what hit him." Byrd locked eyes again with the other man. "Your job here is simple, Moose. We went over it too many times. You already know what to do. Bring him to me *alive*."

Byrd stopped and grabbed his shot of tequila from the chipped wooden table. He downed it and then smashed the empty shot glass on the ground. The shattering eerily echoed for the next few seconds.

Then, Byrd continued. "Bring him to me, Moose. Once he's mine, the plan will go off without a hitch."

Moose nodded with approval. "The Golden Eagle will fly."

Byrd's face lit up. "*Soar*. The Golden Eagle will soar."

PART ONE

1

SENIOR YEAR

My mom always used to tell me that high school was the best four years of her life. She told me stories of how she was elected Rayburn High's student body president. High school was also where she met her best friend, Cassie Ferguson, who became the mayor of Fresno—and her boss. And, of course, it was where she met my dad. I heard the tale a thousand times. She was a popular senior who took a photography class where he was a student teaching assistant. It was love at first sight, and the following summer, they were married. Of the four grades in high school, my mom always spoke glowingly about senior year, the "cherry on top of the high school sundae." After seventeen years of waiting in the shadows, I was hoping this would finally be the time for me to show the world who Charlie Henderson *really* was.

You see, I never knew my dad. He died from leukemia when my mom was eight months pregnant with me. He was only twenty-one years old. The only real memories I have of him are from the numerous pictures and videos he took during my parents' countless excursions to Yosemite National Park, Mount Whitney, Kings Canyon, and the other wonders of the American West. God may have given him a short life, but it was at least one filled with excitement, adventure, and novelty.

My mom remarried a year and a half after my dad passed away and right after that gave birth to my half-sister, Maddie. Everybody described my sister as pretty much a clone of my mom in both appearance and personality—beautiful, outgoing, energetic, ambitious, spunky. I, on the other hand, was quiet, shy, and awkward. Although I had my fair share of bullying during my first three years of high school, I was essentially *invisible*. Due to Maddie and I having different dads and different last names, most popular kids who were friends with her didn't realize that I was her brother—if they even knew who I was at all. And believe me, my sister definitely liked it that way.

But that year, I was determined to finally break through and move up the high school social ladder. Call me stubborn, but I didn't only have a chip on my shoulder—I had a whole *bag* of chips.

I knew it was do or die. I had two options. I could let senior year pass me by and look back on my high school career as an adult, saying, "Boy, I was such a loser." Or I could seize the moment, *carpe diem* as I learned in Latin class, and finally break out of my shell. I had a vision. After serving as the lowly tech guy for the drama club, I would work up the guts to try out for the football team. I would for once be invited to the wild house parties Maddie always bragged about attending— but most of all, I would get a girlfriend. Gone were the days I was embarrassed that my *little sister* had a boyfriend, while I had not even experienced my first kiss. *Enough was enough.* I knew very well that I could fail in my pursuit of popularity, but I sure as hell was not going down without a fight.

My first day of senior year began with a bang. I awoke at 5:59 a.m. sharp. I sprung out of bed and quickly showered, got dressed, brushed my teeth, and made my way downstairs. As I walked into the kitchen, I saw my mom cooking breakfast. She was dressed in her navy business suit, and her long blonde hair was tied back into a ponytail.

"Hi, Mom!" I exclaimed happily, partly because I was so excited to start senior year, partly because my mother was making breakfast, something she did not usually do on a school day.

"Hey, Charlie Bear!" Mom answered while whisking eggs. "I'm surprising you and your sister with my 'back to school special'!"

"Gee, thanks, Mom! You really didn't have to do it," I said. "I would've been fine with just a bowl of Reese's Puffs."

"This is better," my mom said as she placed some more bacon in the frying pan. "You guys need protein for the new year, not sugar and carbs. Plus, I did grow up in the restaurant business, so I know how to make a thing or two."

"I'm just excited for this year. I have a feeling, Mom. Just like you tell me your senior year was when you met my dad, this is gonna be the year I finally step outside my comfort zone."

"Good for you, Charlie. But whatever you do, don't forget to be yourself. Just remember that."

Just then, Maddie strutted into the kitchen. She was wearing a Dolce & Gabbana designer T-shirt, denim short shorts, Converse sneakers, pearl earrings, and of course, her prized possession—the Gucci watch she received as a gift the previous Christmas. Her naturally straight blonde hair was slightly curled. Without saying a word, she set her leather Louis Vuitton purse under the chair, took her seat, and began texting.

"Hi, Princess," Mom greeted Maddie.

"Hi, Sarah," Maddie snarked back at her, not wanting to be interrupted from her phone.

"Madeleine Elizabeth Thomas. For the ten thousandth time, please do not call me by my first name," Mom scolded.

"Okay, Sarah," Maddie chirped back, still refusing to look up from her phone.

I did not want to let my kid sister ruin the first breakfast of my senior year, so I confidently chimed in. "It looks like you woke up on the wrong side of the bed, *Madeleine*."

Maddie laughed at me. "LOL, you dweeb thinking you can talk to me like that." Yes, Maddie had a habit of using text speak in an actual *sentence*.

"Charles, Madeleine, would both of you quiet down, please?" our mom interjected. "This is supposed to be a happy occasion. Both of my babies are beginning a new school year."

"He started it!" Maddie shouted, pointing her index finger at me.

"Look," Mom continued, "we're not going to fight anymore this morning. It's a new year, and we start with a blank slate. Understood?"

"Understood," both of us replied.

"Good," said Mom as she began to serve both of us eggs, sausage, bacon, and potatoes.

I scarfed my breakfast down. Coming from a long line of cooks, my mom surely knew well how to prepare food, even though she chose a career in politics.

Maddie remained glued to her phone. Taking the occasional nibble, she picked at her food with her fork.

"Maddie, did everything come out okay?" Mom asked. "Did I cook the eggs enough for you?"

"I mean, they're like cooked," my sister responded, "but they taste, like off."

Mom smiled. "So, I'll let you guys in on a little secret. Yesterday, the mayor visited a duck farm on the north side of Fresno, and she brought back fresh eggs for all of her staff. That's what you're eating now."

Without wasting a second, Maddie spit out her food. "Duck eggs? Ew, Mom! Gross!"

Mom shrugged. "Sorry, I thought you'd like them. Plus, I heard they're healthier than chicken eggs."

"What's the matter with you, Mom?!" Maddie yelled. "Ducks swim in those disgusting ponds, plus they eat grass and poop everywhere!"

"Sounds like pigs and cows," I replied. "I guess you're going to stop eating them too."

Maddie rudely cackled. "Literally no one asked what *you* had to say."

"Guys, enough!" Mom yelled, clapping her hands at us. "Did you listen to what I said before? I have a long day ahead of me. I woke up extra early to make breakfast for you two, and this is what I get!"

"Sorry," I replied.

"Sorry, I *guess*," Maddie said halfheartedly.

"I'm going to be home late tonight," stated my mother, "so I have to trust both of you to take care of yourselves after school. The mayor is holding a town hall downtown, and I must be there for the entire thing as I'm her chief of staff. Then I have a date with Brad." Brad was my mom's first boyfriend after finalizing her divorce from Maddie's father a year earlier. She continued. "Please be on your best behavior. Leftover meatloaf and pizza are in the fridge."

"Dibs on the pizza!" Maddie exclaimed in a singsong voice.

I shrugged in resignation. "Day-old pizza doesn't taste that good anyway."

I then heard a loud rustling noise. The school bus had just pulled up in front of my house. I placed my now-empty breakfast plate in the sink and grabbed my backpack. I gave my mom a hug and a quick kiss, and I was on my way.

Maddie and I made a beeline onto the bus. It was the same boring and dilapidated vehicle I had ridden in past years. Its chipped mustard-colored coat of paint still looked like it was going to fall off any second. The dim gray foam and rubber seats were still in dire need of repair. The bus had the same number, #85, and the same driver, Duncan Heinz, who, as he would say, was "not the cake or ketchup guy." But this year, I knew something was different. It was my attitude. I was *totally* ready for my senior year—or so I thought.

As we boarded the bus, I nodded hello to Duncan.

"Hey there, Charlie!" he said. "How was your summer?"

"Pretty boring," I answered honestly. "How was yours?"

Duncan smiled. "Crazy. Remind me not to sign up to drive for Wild Mountain Scout Camp ever again. There was a bear on this bus. A big one with fangs and claws and everything. Enough said."

"Wow," I replied. "Hope it didn't hurt anyone."

"Yeah, don't worry. Everybody made it out of there unscathed. And, to be honest, I can't complain. My picture of that thing chilling in the backseat got two hundred likes on Instagram. I'll take it."

"I guess it was *bear*-ly a problem," I replied, slightly cringing at my terrible joke.

"You're damn right, son." Duncan chuckled.

Maddie completely ignored Duncan, still texting even as she walked. As the doors of the bus closed, the two of us shuffled to snag our seats. While Maddie headed straight toward the back to sit with the rest of her popular clique, I found my best friend, George "Pasta" Patsatzoglou, seated alone in the middle of the bus.

Pasta and I had been close friends since kindergarten—after I told on another boy who threw Pasta's favorite toy dinosaur in the toilet. The two of us shared an interest in technology, and he taught me pretty much everything I knew about computers. We were always there for each other when one of us was bullied or overlooked by our peers. To put it simply, Pasta and I were inseparable. We would do almost everything together. We enjoyed camping out in a tent in his backyard (he was too much of a scaredy-cat to go to the woods), hunting for Pokémon in the City Hall as my mom worked, and going door to door pretending we were *Star Wars* characters. Since he was such a regular at my house, he was the only person my age who was allowed to call my mom by her first name, Sarah. After he fixed the government database used by all administrative employees of the City of Fresno, she figured it was the least she could do for him.

However, there was one significant difference between Pasta and me. Unlike me, he was *proud* to be a geek. He always wore an argyle sweater to school (even in the early fall and late spring, which could get quite hot in Fresno) that fit snugly on his chubby frame. Also, he wore suspenders every Monday and Thursday. Why he chose those exact two days remained a mystery to me. His thick, curly red hair was always piled high on top of his head in a "style" that he termed the "Pastafro." Pasta would always talk about his plans after graduating high school. He would move up to Silicon Valley, attend Stanford, and found a start-up tech company that would eventually grow to rival Apple. He would call it "Pear."

I gave Pasta a healthy fist bump as he quickly got up to allow me to have the window seat. I plopped back down next to him.

"I just led a sick raid last night," my friend gleefully boasted to me, of course referring to his beloved *World of Warcraft*, which he seemed to play every second he wasn't studying or fixing a computer. "My guild left that fortress as empty as a zombie's skull."

"Nice! So, are you excited to be a senior?" I asked.

"Not really," Pasta replied with an anxious look. "Not looking forward to seeing *him* again." He quietly pointed to Rick McCreery, a football player, and the resident bully. McCreery happened to be sitting a few seats away from Maddie, where the popular kids were congregating.

"Just ignore him," I responded. "Remember, it's a new year. A blank slate. It's a final opportunity for us to make a name here."

"Jeez, would you stop?" Pasta asked, visibly annoyed. "Enough with this positivity nonsense. You sound like your politician mom right now. We're social outcasts. High school is supposed to suck for people like us, but that's okay. We're the ones who will actually make a difference once we're out of this place."

"But why do we have to wait?" I was disappointed that the person who was supposed to be my *best friend* doubted my dream of social mobility.

"Because," Pasta opined, "once a nerd *always* a nerd."

"Come on, man. Don't you want to go to parties? And get

a girlfriend? And you know, have fun?"

"Dude, we have loads of fun right now. My definition of 'fun' is just way different from *theirs*." Pasta pointed at Maddie and her group of friends in the back who were loudly gossiping about someone's Snapchat story.

"Say whatever you want about her, but my sister *loves* school. She *loves* her life. So did my mom. Why can't I?"

"You don't have to give up who you are, Charlie. So what if we get bullied? So what if girls don't notice us? When we're adults, no one will care what clique we were in, how many friends we had, how many girls we made out with, and whatnot. Don't you see that pretty much all of the most successful people *ever* are nerds? Steve Jobs—nerd. Bill Gates—nerd. Jeff Bezos—nerd. Elon Musk—nerd. The *nerds* are the ones who *make it* in society. *They* are the ones who get all the money, the good cars, the hot girls. The jocks grow up to be losers who are *working* for nerds like *us*. Some even become drug addicts."

"Pasta, I hear what you're saying, but I disagree. *Why* can't I be successful now *and* later?"

"Suit yourself." He shrugged. "You do you, but I, for one, am perfectly happy with my current life."

At the moment Pasta said that, a mammoth teenager furiously stormed over to our area. It was McCreery. He leaned over my friend face-to-face, placing his right arm on the back of the seat so he couldn't escape. The bus was still moving and just about to pull into the school's entrance.

"So, I hear you were saying something about us jocks

being *losers*." McCreery snorted. "What a pathetic dumbass you are."

"I—I." Pasta froze.

McCreery laughed hysterically. "Oh lookie at his little computer brain, it's—it's m—m—malfunctioning!" He placed Pasta in a headlock before continuing to torment him. "Imma teach you, *nerd*, about something called social hierarchy. You may have heard of it. People like me pick on people like *you*. You will *never* be nothing more than a bottom feeder."

The bus hit a speed bump, and Pasta's head bobbled inside of McCreery's arm, only prompting the bully to tighten his grip. The whole time, I sat next to my friend, motionless and terrified, leaning against the window. At this moment, a crowd of McCreery's friends began gathering around the scene, egging him on. I didn't say a single word the entire time.

"What a moron," one other jock jeered. I recognized him as Dwayne Samuels, Rayburn's star tight end and basketball power forward. His younger sister was one of Maddie's best friends.

"Do you have anything to say for yourself, *geeky geek*!" McCreery taunted.

"Nh-mh-nh-nh-mh" was all Pasta could manage as McCreery's beefy arm was blocking his face.

"That's what I thought," the bully said with a smirk.

I was still frozen, trying the hardest I possibly could not to move a muscle.

As soon as the bus came to a halt, Duncan hastily opened

the doors. He rushed down to the aisle where McCreery was accosting Pasta. "Knock it off, Mr. McCreery," he barked. "Before I tell your dad. You know, my brother's the president of his union."

McCreery reluctantly released his grasp on Pasta's neck at this command. My redheaded buddy's head mercilessly banged against the back of his seat one last time. I quietly thanked God for letting me off the hook.

After McCreery strolled back to join his friends who were starting to disembark, I turned over to Pasta. "Sorry, man," I said, "that was rough."

Pasta would not even look at me. Instead, he sat paused in silence, facing as far away from me as possible.

"Pasta?" Worried, I tried to get his attention.

Still no luck. Refusing to make eye contact with me, he joined the line to get off the bus.

That morning was certainly not the way I wanted my senior year to begin.

I was not ready for what was to follow.

2

WIDE RECEIVERS AND WHITE RETRIEVERS

I sat apprehensively in Mrs. Alvarez's homeroom class, tapping a mechanical pencil against the bottom of my desk. Pasta, who always sat next to me in every class, grabbed a seat in one of the back corners of the room, far from me—and everyone else. He still had not spoken to me since we got off the bus.

Alvarez, a lively brunette in her late twenties, walked into the room. She was flanked by two people I had never seen before.

To her left was a stunningly beautiful, statuesque young woman. She had platinum blonde hair—much lighter than my mother's or sister's, which fell in waves like ears of wheat. She was remarkably tall as well, standing at least six feet and a couple of inches. She wore a short dress that stopped before her knees, tan leather sandals, and Fendi sunglasses. Her skin was pale white like frost. A well-behaved, snow-white

Labrador Retriever accompanied her, which she kept leashed tightly against her body. The dog's harness displayed the words "State of California Service Animal." It was then when I realized the girl was blind.

To the right of Mrs. Alvarez was an equally tall and handsome African American man. His hair was crew cut, reminiscent of a U.S. Marine's. He sported a stubble goatee and a silver necklace with two attached dog tags. He also wore khaki pants and a faded University of Alabama football T-shirt that looked like it was likely a hand-me-down from a relative. His bulging muscles made it clear that he spent some serious time in the gym—he was probably there more in a week than I had been in my whole *life*.

Alvarez spoke. "Good morning, class. Welcome to a spectacular new year here at Rayburn High. It is my pleasure to introduce to you two new students joining our Rayburn Coyotes family this year." She motioned over to the blonde girl. "We have Kristin Magnusson here as an exchange student all the way from Uppsala, Sweden."

"It's pronounced 'oop-sa-la,'" Kristin interjected with a heavy Swedish accent, "as in 'oops, you said it wrong.'"

The class laughed.

"Sorry," Alvarez continued, embarrassed. "The Krikorian family is hosting Kristin during her time in the States. And since she is legally blind, she will be with her guide dog, Olaf."

Olaf barked as if on cue.

Alvarez resumed speaking. "Anyone with allergies?"

A sheepish red-faced boy raised his hand high.

Alvarez marked her seating chart. "Okie dokie," she said, "I'll make sure you guys sit as far away as possible. We sure don't need another repeat of 'bring your pet to school day.'"

The teacher placed the chart back down as Kristin, with Olaf in tow, took a seat next to Steve "Krix" Krikorian, Rayburn High's star quarterback. The Krikorian family was the most prominent and wealthiest in all of Fresno. Their dad, Congressman Jesse Krikorian, a son of poor Armenian immigrants, served as a captain in the United States Marine Corps and then worked his way up to become an extremely successful dairy businessman in California's Central Valley. Due to bold investments in several technology companies, he eventually became a billionaire and, during my sophomore year, "bought" an election to represent my home area in the U.S. Congress. Jesse's wife, Andrea, was a well-regarded interior designer-turned-socialite. In addition to Krix, the Krikorians had a younger son named Leo, the junior varsity quarterback—who just so happened to be Maddie's boyfriend. I was all too familiar with the dominance the Krikorians had on not only Fresno but the state of California as a whole.

Alvarez then motioned toward the boy on her right. "And we also have Lawrence Travers joining us as a transfer from Tuscaloosa, Alabama. Young man, do you prefer Lawrence or Larry?"

"Larry is fine," he answered with a slight southern twang. "Just don't call me late for dinner."

Alvarez smiled. "And I must mention, Larry, it says on your

file that you were an all-state wide receiver in Alabama. Is that correct?"

"Yes, ma'am," replied Larry.

"That's awesome! Maybe with your help, our Coyotes can finally beat Desert Valley."

The entire class, apart from Pasta, who never cared about football at all, applauded.

"I'm not promising anything, but I'll try my best," the new student said.

Since he was a jock, I expected Larry also to take a seat near Krix. But, to my surprise, he instead grabbed the empty desk next to me—where Pasta would have sat any other day.

Alvarez proceeded to take roll. When she finished, we had a two-minute wait before the announcements would come on the TV. I was at first nervous to talk to Larry, as he was a football player, but I quickly remembered that since he was brand-new to the school, he had no idea what clique to which everyone belonged. I recalled something my mom once told me, "There is never a second chance to make a first impression." It was one of the several esoteric mantras she learned from all those years working in politics. I may have only had this one opportunity to step outside of my comfort zone, and I figured I had nothing to lose, especially since my longtime best friend was giving me the silent treatment.

I turned toward Larry, who was scanning the classroom and taking in the new environment. "Hey, Larry, my name's Charlie," I said, reaching out to shake his hand.

"Hello, Charlie," he said while giving me one of the firmest handshakes of my life—like one my grandpa would give me.

I stumbled to say the first thing that came to my mind. "So—uh, you're from—uh, Alabama?"

"Yes, sir. Alabama born and raised," Larry replied, pointing at his shirt.

"Pretty cool," I responded. "I've never been to Alabama before. So—uh—Larry, what brings you here to Fresno?"

"Oh, I transferred here for football reasons. My uncle Bill lives here, and he offered to let me live with him for my senior year so colleges can scout me better. It has always been my dream to play college ball for Stanford or Cal."

"What about the University of Alabama?" I asked, pointing at his shirt.

"Well, 'Bama is obviously a great football school, but I want to go somewhere I can get a quality *technology* education as well just in case the NFL doesn't work out for me. I'm specifically interested in IT, and both Stanford and Cal have amazing tech programs."

When Larry mentioned that he was into tech, my eyes lit up. So maybe talking to him was not so hard after all. "That's awesome," I replied, "I'm a big techie as well."

"Cool. Most people don't realize how fast-growing the tech industry is," Larry remarked. "You see all these kids on their phones today—it's crazy. You didn't see that forty, fifty years ago. So, imagine what it would be like forty or fifty years from now. We'll all have computers in our brains at the rate things are going!"

When Larry said this, I immediately thought of Maddie

constantly being on her phone. "I don't want to imagine that, *at all.*"

The television in the front of the room began to flicker. Finally, it was time for the morning announcements. Two of my unusually perky classmates from Student Government flashed onto the screen.

"Welcome back to school, Rayburn High! This is Student Body President Josh Baumgartner!"

"And this is Student Body Vice President Eva Gallegos! Hope you had a phenomenal, fantastic, totally amazing summer!"

Yeah, my morning announcements were that cheesy.

"That's right, Eva!" Josh continued. "Today is Wednesday, September 7, 2022. It is a *purple* day today, so freshmen, please do not go to your *gold* classes by accident."

"Trust me," Eva remarked. "We all made that mistake ourselves! I want to give a huge shout-out to the Class of 2023. They are beginning their senior year today!"

The entire class, who happened to be seniors, cheered—except for Pasta.

"Today's cafeteria lunch special is chicken a la king. Yum! Fit for a king!" continued Eva. "And now it's weather time! Josh, what you got?"

"It's going to be a high of eighty-seven today!" Josh exclaimed. "A beautiful, bright, sunshiny day. Summer is thinking she is not over. But she is!"

"Wow," Eva said. "Today's a perfect day to spend some time outdoors, which brings us to an extraordinary guest—

Rayburn Coyotes Football Coach Pat Snyder!"

The scene switched to the football field, where Coach Snyder, a jolly, gray-bearded man, clutched a football in one hand and a microphone in the other.

"Thank you, Eva!" Coach shouted. "Welcome back to school, all you Coyotes and Coyotettes! Today after school are football tryouts! Who's got what it takes to beat Desert Valley?"

Larry enthusiastically tapped my shoulder. "You trying out too?" he asked me.

I always did want to try out for the football team, but part of me was afraid of being embarrassed by my lack of athleticism. On the other hand, I did tell myself I was making an effort to break out of my shell this year.

"Yep," I told Larry. "You better believe I'll be there!"

"Awesome!" He fist-bumped me.

I watched the rest of the announcements. The drama club was advertising auditions for their fall play, which was Shakespeare's *Richard III*. The robotics club promoted their fall tournament as well. The student government also performed a skit advertising Heritage Day. Since I was a quarter Polish, I was sure my mom would make her famous pierogis for Maddie and me to bring in.

The announcements finished, and the bell rang to start the first period. I breezed through my first four classes: English, Calculus, Physics, and Local Government—an elective my mom made me take so I would more appreciate what she did for a living. Then it was time for lunch.

After waiting in line for what felt like forever, I grabbed my tray of chicken a la king, rice, a Dole pineapple and peach fruit cup, and a carton of chocolate milk. I was making my way to sit at my usual table of outcasts with Pasta, wondering if he would even talk to me, when I heard a voice call out.

"Hey, bro! Come sit with us." It was Larry, and he was gesturing for me to sit with him—at the popular senior table. I cheerfully followed. *It was happening.*

I took a seat next to Larry. Krix was seated across from him next to Kristin, his new housemate. Olaf was loyally waiting next to her chair. Also sitting at the table were many other varsity football players and cheerleaders, all of whom I was never properly introduced to during my three years of invisibility.

"How's it going, dude?" Krix reached out to give me a fist bump. I fist-bumped back. "I don't think I met you before. Larry says you're trying out for the team today."

I was shocked that Krix had no idea who I was. He *had* to have seen me plenty of times before.

"Hi. I'm Charlie," I unabashedly said to him. "My sister is dating your brother."

"That's awesome! All this time, I had no idea Maddie had a brother," Krix responded. "Hey, we're practically brothers-in-law!" He gave me a playful shoulder rub. "Anyways, the name's Steve, but they call me Krix 'round here. I used to tell people it meant 'captain' in Armenian—it doesn't. But I am the captain of the varsity team, so if you need anything, I'm your guy!"

22

"Nice to meet you, Krix!" I exclaimed. He was surprisingly nice to me. Maybe the "popular" crowd wasn't as bad as I'd thought.

"There are a few other players I'd like you to meet," Larry said. He pointed at two athletic boys with identical curly dark brown hair. "These are the Garcia twins, Jeremy and Sebastian."

"Jeremy is our strong safety-slash-fullback. Sebastian is our free safety-slash-halfback," Krix added.

"Wassup," Jeremy greeted me, giving me what looked like a Boy Scout salute.

"Howdy!" shouted Sebastian, "slapping" me an air high-five.

"Seb, what did I tell you about air high-fives?" Jeremy playfully scolded.

"That they're so *2019*?" Sebastian answered.

"Think of something else. Like a finger pistol. Or a lightsaber."

"But I actually *liked* 2019. You're just sad because that's the year that hot Instagram influencer completely ignored you when you tried to slide into her DMs. She broke your sorry little heart."

"She didn't break my heart—well, maybe she did," Jeremy corrected himself. "But that's beside the point, bro. No more air high-fives."

"Air *low*-fives?"

"He doesn't learn."

Krix pointed to a tremendous student with a buzz cut

sitting next to him. This guy had already finished his plate of chicken a la king—and I had barely started mine. "And this is Alang Khang," he said. "He's our center-slash-nose tackle. We call him The Electric Pillow because, well, he has that effect against the opposing teams' run games. Alang's dad owns literally all the Taco Bells and KFCs in this area of Fresno, so if you're still hungry after a post-game party, he'll hook you up."

"What's shaking," Alang said with his mouth still full.

"Nice to meet you all," I said.

"So, Krystal," said Jeremy to the new girl.

"It's Kristin," a visibly annoyed Kristin corrected him.

"My bad," Jeremy continued. "So, Krist*in*, what was it like living in Sweden?"

"Is there like an IKEA on every block?" Sebastian added.

"What's with Americans and IKEA?" said Kristin, still annoyed. "Like seriously. It's a cheap furniture store."

Sebastian shrugged. "They have good meatballs there."

"Come on, bro," said Jeremy. "It's a furniture store. You don't go there for the meatballs."

"So, Kristin, tell us about Sweden," Sebastian continued. "Like, did you ride a reindeer to school? Do you know PewDiePie?"

"What kind of questions are those?" Kristin replied, having pretty much lost her patience with the twins. "I rode a bus to school, just like you. And no, I don't personally know PewDiePie. Most of the other *ten million* residents of Sweden don't either, FYI."

Trying to diffuse the hostility mounting between Kristin and the Garcias, Krix stepped in. "Hey, Kristin," he said. "You can tell them about how you lost your sight."

"If you insist," Kristin relented. "So, last winter, I was shoveling snow, and a lynx came out from nowhere and dug its claws into both of my eyeballs."

"No way!" Jeremy exclaimed. "Can I see what your eyes look like now?" He motioned for Kristin to take off her sunglasses.

"I'd rather not." She coldly brushed him off. "So yeah, that's how I became almost totally blind. But don't worry, I had my trusty sword on me at the time—so I had the last laugh. In case you're wondering, that lynx is a coat now."

I winced in disgust.

"Poor kitty," replied Sebastian. "And one more question. Since your dog's name is Olaf, like the snowman, have you ever thought of changing your name to Elsa, like the princess? You kind of look like her, you know."

"Gee, I don't think anyone ever told me that before," Kristin answered sarcastically.

"I try to be original," remarked Sebastian, completely missing the sarcasm.

I then heard the sound of heavy footsteps. I turned my head, and I saw McCreery, Dwayne, and two of their friends saunter over to the table. *Well, there goes my fifteen minutes of popularity*, I thought. They pulled up four chairs and took their seats.

"You gotta be kidding me," McCreery said, pointing at

me and then looking puzzledly at Krix. "Who let that *geek* sit here? With *us*?"

"I did," said Larry, immediately coming to my defense. "You got a problem with that?"

"Well, *duh*," said McCreery, like he was stating the most obvious truth in the world. "He's a *nerd*, a *loser*, a *lowlife*. He belongs over *there*." He pointed at the outcast table where Pasta was sitting.

"Too bad. He's one of *us* now," Larry emphasized.

"You're the new kid. Who are you to say who's one of us?"

Krix jumped in to defend me as well. "Richard, knock it off!" he chided. "Quit giving my man Charlie a hard time, or I'll tell Coach to move you down in the depth chart!"

An infuriated McCreery responded, "Don't you dare call me Richard!"

"This is my team. I can call you whatever the hell I want! Charlie is my brother-in-law, and if you mess with my brother-in-law, you mess with me! Am I clear?"

McCreery threw up his arms in defeat. "Fine, fine. Have it your way, *Steve*. I'll leave the kid alone if it makes you happy."

"You better!"

"My bad. I guess dweeb-face *is* one of us now. I didn't know things like that could change, but whatever."

McCreery and his friends obeyed Krix and left me alone for the rest of the lunch period. I spent the rest of the time continuing to get to know the football team. Alang told me about some of the secret menu "hacks" at Taco Bell. Jeremy and Sebastian enlightened me about their so-called "audition tape" for SNL. Krix shared the time he met the president in a bathroom—his dad was a U.S. Congressman, after all. However, the person I seemed to bond the most with was Larry. I had known him only for a few hours, and he was already becoming my new best friend.

Speaking of best friends, I quickly glanced over at Pasta one last time. Then, after a second, I shifted my focus back to the popular table. I was finally getting the new start I had always craved.

It was best not to live in the past.

3

FOOTBALL 101

After we finished all of our classes, Larry and I changed and began to walk out to the football field, where tryouts were taking place.

"I can't wait for this," Larry said. "Football is my life. I put my first pair of cleats on right after I learned to walk, no joke."

"That's sick," I responded, hoping Larry didn't ask me about my athletic history, or in my case, my lack thereof. I quickly changed the subject. "So, what do you think of the rest of the team?"

"They're pretty cool—except for that Richard kid. What he said to you was not cool at all."

"Yeah. McCreery's always been a jerk."

"Just ignore him," Larry told me. "Every school has its bullies. Some people are just gonna not like you for no reason whatsoever. That's just the way life is. There are two ways to handle it: you choose to be a victim or a victor. Which one are you gonna be?"

"Victor," I confidently replied, with a smile on my face. *I was sitting at the popular table now.* McCreery and his buddies simply had to learn to *deal* with it.

"Now that's what I want to hear, Charlie, or should I say, *Victor.*"

I beamed. I was so happy that I had a friend who actually supported my goals and ambitions—unlike Pasta.

Larry continued, "So, Kristin, or whatever her name is—she's hot."

"Yeah," I responded in agreement. "She's way out of my league, though. She's also like an entire half foot taller than me." I couldn't imagine having a girlfriend *that* tall. I was embarrassed that at age seventeen, I was *still* shorter than my mom. I was barely an inch taller than Maddie—a fifteen-year-old girl.

Larry laughed. We then passed Rayburn High's infamous darkroom. Larry excused himself for a minute to check on his pictures from his photography elective earlier in the day. For a split second, I thought of the photography class where my parents had met.

Larry opened the door and revealed Krix and Kristin, right smack in the middle of an intense make-out session. In the corner of the room, Olaf lay curled up with his snout tucked into his body.

"Okay—" Larry whispered, closing the door with a mixture of embarrassment and queasiness. "That's officially the shortest crush I've had in my life."

"Same here," I replied. "Like, doesn't she live with his family?"

"Yup. She's kind of like his sister for the time being. Gross."

Putting this experience behind us, Larry and I continued to make our way to the field.

When we arrived, we saw all the players lining up for a scrimmage. Derrick Stokes, the junior backup, was in as quarterback. Krix was obviously nowhere to be seen—but Larry and I knew *exactly* where he was. Further down the field, Coach Snyder was standing, holding a clipboard, next to a crowd of nine or ten boys, all much larger than me.

"Coach!" Larry called out, running up to him. "We're here for tryouts!"

Coach grinned from ear to ear. He was wearing a bucket hat, and his beard was dripping with sweat. "You must be Lawrence Travers." He acted as if he had just met Jerry Rice.

"Yep, that's me," Larry responded, self-assured.

"It's an honor and a pleasure to meet you," Coach said as he firmly shook Larry's hand.

"Pleasure's all mine."

"I was thrilled when I found out you were transferring. I've been doing pretty much nothing but reading your scouting report the last few days. We haven't had a five-star recruit since, like ever. We already had a decent squad this year, but you're gonna put us over the top to beat Desert Valley!"

"Thanks, Coach, but football's a *team* game. I'm just here to make the team better."

"And humble too! I love this guy!" Coach then looked at me. "And you are?"

"Uh—Charles Henderson."

"You're new too?"

"No, sir," I responded. "I've been here forever. It's just my first year trying out for the team."

Coach's face showed an even more perplexed look than before. "Okay." He sized me up, trying to see if I had any muscles—I didn't. Measuring five-foot-eight on a good day, and weighing in at 130 pounds, I was pretty much all skin and bones.

Was I deluded to want to play football? Maybe I wasn't cut out to be anything more than a hopeless nerd. *Could Pasta have been right?*

"I guess I'll see what you can do at slot receiver," Coach finally said after examining me for nearly twenty seconds. He then signaled for Larry and me to walk over toward the skinnier, more athletic kids while the bigger kids trying out for lineman and linebacker formed another group. I was the most scared I've been in my life since ringing the bell of a "haunted house" on Halloween my freshman year.

Coach called us the "skill position group," which was very ironic to me since I had no football *skills* at all. He called on us one by one to try out.

First to go was Larry. At this point, Krix was *still* missing in action, and therefore, Stokes had to throw him passes. Since Larry making the team was pretty much a foregone conclusion, his "tryout" was more or less a showcase of his skills—a mere formality. And boy, Larry had them skills. Stokes threw him a short bullet pass that he caught effortlessly. Then, he unleashed his stiff-arm, pretending that there was a safety or linebacker in the way.

Wow, I thought. Larry reminded me of another football player with his name—Larry Fitzgerald, who I remembered from the very first Super Bowl I watched. He was *that* good.

Stokes continued by tossing a medium pass with extra spin. Larry quickly hauled it in and continued down the field at blazing speed. Stokes kept throwing to him, steadily increasing the distance after every reception. Larry did not miss a single catch.

On the final pass, Stokes wound up his arm behind his head. From the start, it became clear to me that it was a Hail Mary pass. As Stokes launched the ball, Larry followed its trajectory through the air. For a second, it looked like Stokes's throw was going to be way off target—he was the *backup* quarterback. Despite all odds, Larry managed to extend his left arm far out and miraculously grabbed the ball one-handed. "Got it!" I heard him cry out in celebration.

He strutted back to where Coach, I, and the others were standing, trading astonished looks on our faces. "Twelve for twelve, baby!" Larry chanted to us.

"That was amazing!" I said to him.

"Just what I do." Larry smiled. "Now it's gonna be your turn soon."

Oh great. I tensed up, wondering if it was too late for me to back out.

The other players in the "skill" group took the field one-by-one. Although some flashed serious talent, none were, by a long shot, anywhere near Larry's caliber. After everyone else had already gone, the coach called my name.

"Saving the best for last!" Larry yelled in support as I took my position. I looked utterly lost. Coach noticed, and he rushed over to give me pointers.

"Kid, this is gonna be a short slant route. Just make a sharp cut to the left, and Stokes will throw you a quick pass."

"Got it, Coach!" I said. In reality, I didn't have it at all—not in the slightest.

Coach blew his whistle, and I took off, trying my best to copy Larry's routes. *Just like Madden,* I thought to myself, as I envisioned playing the football video game. When I saw that Stokes was about to release his throw, I cut to the left. I watched as the ball sailed past my head—three feet in front of me. I glanced over at Coach: he didn't look too happy. He made his way back to me, shaking his head as he walked.

"Let's try something different," he said as patiently as he could. "We're gonna have you run a post route." He motioned toward the goal post. "Just run that way and cut slightly to the left in a few seconds."

"You got this in the bag!" screamed Larry. "The post route is one of the easiest routes in the book!"

"You're not helping," I replied.

Coach again blew his whistle, and I darted ahead. After a few seconds had elapsed, I cut to the left again, this time at a forty-five-degree angle. I saw the ball coming cleanly toward me. I was just not going to let it hit the ground without touching it—and I didn't. I extended my hands to make the catch, and the laces grazed my fingertips. I tried to hold the ball steady, but its oblong shape slid out of my hands and onto the turf.

"He's got butterfingers," complained Stokes as he proceeded to join the rest of the team in the scrimmage.

"Okay," Coach said after I botched the second catch. "Wide receiver is not for you, son. Let's get that through your head." He paused for another ten seconds, placing his hand on his forehead. "What we could try is running back. I'm going to have Sebastian play more defense this year because that's where he stars, so we can use more backups, especially at the halfback position."

"So, you're giving me another chance?"

"Just do what I say." He pointed to two cones stationed near the end of the field. One was at the forty-yard line, the other at the goal line. "You're gonna stand at this cone at the forty, and when I say 'go,' run in a straight line to the other cone, *as fast as you can*. You don't need to catch anything. All I want to see right now is how fast you are."

"All right," I said as I made my way over to the closer of the cones. It seemed easy enough to me. It certainly wasn't rocket science. Coach stood by the far cone holding out a stopwatch.

"On your mark—get set—GO!"

I plowed ahead as fast as my legs could carry me. It almost felt like I was running for my life from an evil gangster. Finally, I leaped across the goal line and into the end zone with a feeling of victory—it didn't last very long.

Coach held out the stopwatch, which displayed my time: 7.15 seconds.

"That's fast?" I asked, out of breath. "Is it?"

Coach looked at me with disbelief. "That's slow if you're a *lineman.*" He pointed over at Alang, who was on the sideline eating a donut while the rest of the team was taking a water break. "In our running backs, we look for forty times in the fours, five seconds *tops.*"

I was defeated. It seemed that my longtime dream of playing high school football had just gone down the drain.

Coach looked me sincerely in the eye. "I don't know what to tell you, kid. You can't catch. You're too slow to be a running back or defensive back. You're too small to be a tight end, linebacker, or lineman. When exactly was the last time you played football?"

"Uh—" I stammered, knowing that I was exposed. "I—uh—played a little bit in summer camp when I was in middle school."

"Not summer camp. Those are just scrimmages. I mean an organized game of gridiron football, with X's and O's and whatnot."

I couldn't lie. "Never."

Coach laughed. "Look, kid, I appreciate the effort, but this ain't a flag football team. You're just not good enough. I recommend that you play some pick-up games with your friends who *did* make the team, practice your forty-yard dash, and try out next year."

Larry, who observed the entire debacle, came to my defense, yet again. "Coach! Give the kid a chance. He's a senior. There is no *next year* for him. You must have some role he can fill."

Coach was not budging. "No can do," he said. "He would be nothing but a liability for us."

"Can't you at least make him team manager?"

I appreciated my new friend's support, but I wanted to be part of the *team*. I wanted to wear a jersey with a number on the back. Manager just didn't cut it for me.

"We don't need no manager. We have *me*." Coach was not having it. He took a few seconds to gather his thoughts. Then, he spoke again. "Wait a minute. I might have an idea." He pointed to me. "I know you never played organized football before, but what about other sports? Soccer? Martial arts?"

My ears perked up. "Yes, martial arts," I replied. "I did Taekwondo for a while." I was telling God's honest truth. I took Taekwondo lessons for a few years in elementary and middle school and made it to brown belt. I only quit because my mom could no longer drive me due to her hectic work schedule.

"All right then," Coach said. He looked at the rest of the team and blew his whistle. "Kylie, come over here!"

Suddenly, a beautiful Latina girl wearing a #5 jersey ran over to the tryout section of the field. If I didn't know she was a high school football player, she would have easily passed as a teenage pop star. She had long black hair that stretched down to the middle of her back, which she wore in a braid. Her skin was flawlessly clear, very rare for someone my age, and her white teeth sparkled in the sunlight, complementing her chocolate-colored eyes. Her body had a slim, athletic build.

"Yes, Coach," the girl said.

"Charles," Coach said to me, "this is Kylie Hernandez. She is the star striker on the girls' soccer team. She is also our kicker." He turned to Kylie. "Kylie, this is Charles Henderson. He's trying out to be your backup."

"I am?" I asked Coach, confused.

Coach glared at me for a fraction of a second. "Listen, son, do you want to be on this team or not?"

"Yes, I am!" I quickly said to Kylie. "I'm trying out for backup kicker! And you can just call me Charlie. Charles is what my mother calls me after I eat all her rice pudding from the fridge."

Kylie chuckled. "Okay! Charlie, it is!" she cheerfully replied.

Damn, even her laugh was gorgeous. I had to focus on the game and not *her* if I was to make this team.

"Charles!" Coach yelled, ignoring my request not to be called by my given name. "What you're gonna do is watch Kylie kick a field goal. Pay close attention to *how* she kicks said field goal. You're then gonna do the exact same thing yourself. Is that hard?"

"No, sir," I answered. I was scared before, but now I was terrified. If I messed up, I didn't only risk making the team, but I would also be embarrassed in front of a pretty girl.

"Good," Coach said. "I'm glad we're on the same page."

Coach, Kylie, and I lined up on the twenty-yard line in

front of the goalposts. I watched as Coach held the ball in place, and Kylie kicked it into the air. It soared high into the ether, evenly splitting the uprights on the post: a textbook kick.

"Do that, and you're on the team," Coach told me.

Kylie quickly retrieved the ball and held it in place at the same spot from where she had just kicked it. I took a deep breath, said a short prayer, and used my foot to smack it as hard as I possibly could, dead in the center. I nervously watched as the ball flew toward the post in a similar direction it took when Kylie kicked it. However, toward the end of its journey, it veered sharply toward the left.

Oh, no, I thought. *Please go in.*

Then somehow miraculously, the ball vaulted over the crossbar and stayed to the right of the left upright by what was probably a few inches.

I couldn't believe my eyes. Finally all those years of Taekwondo paid off. My kick was good.

Kylie high-fived me. "You did it!"

Coach mustered a small smile. "Kylie, what do you think about him? Does he make the team?"

Kylie thought for a second. "Well, it was a little rough, but at the end of the day, a made field goal is a made field goal." She turned to me. "You have the distance. Just a little practice, and your accuracy will be there too."

I was still without an answer. "So, am I on the team or not?" I asked Coach.

"It's up to her," Coach responded. "She's the *de facto*

special teams coordinator here, so I defer to her on those matters. Believe me, offense and defense keep me busy enough."

"Yep, congratulations," said Kylie. "You're now backing up a girl."

Coach gave me a thumbs-up. "Well, lookie at that. You made the cut, Charles."

I was elated. It was still my first day of senior year, and after being a nerd for practically my entire life, I could now officially add "jock" to my high school resume. I was very generous with the definition of "jock," by the way.

I pulled Coach in for a bear hug, which he was definitely not expecting. "Thank you, thank you, thank you!" I cried out with joy.

I then noticed that nobody was looking at me. So, I turned in the direction everyone was staring, only to see a very disheveled-looking Krix.

"Look at what the cat dragged in," Coach said.

"Sorry I'm late, Coach," Krix replied. "I was helping one of the new students find her way around the school."

"Sure you were," Coach said. "You're an *hour* late. Drop and give me *fifty*."

"Yes, sir." Krix proceeded to do fifty push-ups on the turf.

Any other player would have been, at the very least, suspended one game for showing up an hour late to practice without a valid reason. But Krix wasn't just *any* player—he was a Krikorian. If you can buy an election to Congress, you can certainly buy your son special treatment from his high school football coach.

When Krix finished his push-ups, Larry told him that I made the team—as backup kicker.

"Better than nothing," he said, high-fiving me. "You're a Coyote now, and it's time to work hard. But don't worry, there will be plenty of time to *play* hard too."

"What do you mean?" I asked.

"Since you made the team, you're invited to my party on Friday, after the game against Desert Valley, of course," Krix told me. "It's gonna be *lit*. Literally half the school will be there. There will be a live band and everything."

"This is not your average high school house party," Kylie added. "It's a Krikorian party. Since Krix's dad is a congressman, he goes *all out* when his kids have friends over. There are Jacuzzis, exotic pets, food cooked by a five-star chef, and who knows, maybe even Tom MacDonald will make an appearance like he did at the last party at Krix's house."

I was stunned. Kylie said this without even knowing how much of a Tom MacDonald fan I was.

My final year of high school was shaping up to be fantastic, beyond my wildest expectations. I was hanging out with the popular kids, I made the football team, and now I was invited to what was billed to be the craziest teen party this side of the Sierra Nevadas.

What could possibly go wrong?

4

LATE TO THE PARTY

The day kept getting better. Larry drove me home in his cobalt blue '72 Corvette Stingray convertible. In my seventeen years, it was the first time I had ever been in a sports car. It was a *very* different experience than my mom's Honda Pilot.

I walked into my house, and I was surprised to see my mom home. She was sitting at the kitchen table, answering emails on her laptop, still dressed in her work clothes.

"Mom? What are you doing home now?"

"Brad canceled our date," she responded, sounding both shocked and frustrated. "He said he had to 'work late.' He's a dentist. How late can he possibly work?"

I shrugged. "Maybe one of his patients had a root canal or something."

Mom changed the subject. "So, how was your first day of senior year, Charlie Bear?"

I smiled. "Amazing."

I heard Maddie rudely stride into the kitchen—with her phone in hand, of course. "Mom! Is it dinnertime yet?!" she yelled. There was no reason for her to raise her voice. My mom was literally three feet away from her.

"Pizza's in the fridge. Go heat it up yourself!" replied Mom.

Maddie groaned and proceeded to place the pizza in the toaster oven. She then turned to me. "Leo told me that Krix said that *you* somehow made the football team," she said. "I guess they made you water boy."

"Backup kicker," I proudly corrected her.

Maddie giggled. "Didn't know that was a thing. And isn't the kicker a *girl*?"

"Yes, and her *name* is Kylie," I said.

"So, you mean to tell me you're backing up a *girl*?" Maddie giggled again.

"Madeleine, knock it off," my mom chided. "And that's great news, Charlie. Just make sure you play safe and don't get hurt."

"Will do," I said.

My mom smiled at me. "So, tell me more about your day!"

"Where do I begin? Well, I made a new friend. His name is Larry, and he's a transfer student from Alabama. He's also on the football team with me."

"How cool! I always love when you make new friends, Charlie! What about your other friend, Pasta. What's he up to?"

Just when I was in the middle of telling her about my new, reinvented self, my mom *had* to bring Pasta up. I tried the hardest I could to avoid discussing him. "Uh—I haven't really been talking to him today."

"Charlie and Pasta had a fight!" Maddie blurted out.

"It wasn't really a fight. It was more of a disagreement."

"I saw it with my own eyes," Maddie attested. "It was a fight."

I scowled at my sister.

"Cut it out, the two of you!" Mom screamed.

Dead silence permeated the room for the next few minutes. I used the time to microwave my meatloaf. All that football trying out made me hungry.

The three of us sat down to eat dinner. My mom grabbed a salad for herself, which she brought home from the City Hall cafeteria. Maddie was, per usual, fixated on her phone screen, cackling to herself.

Mom broke the silence. "So, this Friday night, the Tomato Farmers' Association of the San Joaquin Valley is sponsoring the Third Annual Fresno Tomato Festival. The mayor is asking me to help set up pretty much everything for her. Would you guys be free to come help out?"

"Can't come, got a party," Maddie rudely uttered in her infamous singsong voice. My ears hated when she did that.

Mom looked at me hopefully. Since I didn't have much of a social life before, I could always help her with city events on Friday nights and weekends. I was such a regular at them, Mayor Ferguson herself had nicknamed me her "Junior Chief of Staff."

This week, however, was different. "Sorry, Mom," I said, "I'm actually going to the same party myself."

Maddie almost choked on her pizza. "Say what?"

"You heard me. Krix invited me to his party today—and I'm going. So, I believe you'll see me there."

Maddie glanced at me, baffled. "So what? You barely made the football team, and you're going to the Krikorian party. So is half the school. That's nothing. It's not like you're sitting at the popular table."

Maddie and I had different lunch periods, so she didn't know yet. I grinned. "About that—you better believe I'm sitting there. Larry asked me to sit there today."

Both Maddie and my mom were speechless. Neither of them could believe my transformation. As McCreery had said earlier, social status in my school wasn't supposed to change. Someone going from outcast to popular overnight was, well, unprecedented. I was in uncharted territory. This was real life, not an early 2000s teen drama movie.

"Well," Maddie finally replied, "as Post Malone says, congratulations. You made it."

"Thanks."

"You're late to the party," Maddie continued. "I've *always* been popular. I didn't have some random guy named Larry swoop in and save my ass."

"Madeleine, watch your language," Mom scolded her.

I smirked at Maddie. "Better late than *never*."

After we finished dinner and cleaned up, my mom called me into the living room to have a "chat." Maddie was already upstairs, sequestered in her room, probably making dumb TikTok videos.

A MATTER OF TIME

I sat next to my mom on the couch. She undid her ponytail, and her hair fluttered onto her shoulders. There was a vaguely worried expression in her sky-blue eyes.

"I *am* proud of you," she said. "You've stepped outside of your comfort zone today, and I'm thrilled that you're making new friends."

I knew that there was a "but" coming. My mom would never call me to talk, just to congratulate me. The last time she and I had a "chat," she broke the news that she and Mark, Maddie's dad, were getting divorced. That was almost two years before my senior year began.

"But," Mom continued, "I don't want you to sacrifice who you *are* for the sake of popularity."

"What do you mean who I *am*?" I started to get annoyed. "I'm *loving* the new me."

Mom's concerned look intensified. "You don't understand. I'm in the fortieth year of my life—I have experienced way more than you."

"But Mom, you're only *thirty-nine*. Let's not get ahead of ourselves here."

My mother wasn't in the mood to argue over trivial matters. "I am thirty-nine years old, so that means I'm now in year forty of my life," she quickly corrected me. "I was very popular when I was in high school. Pretty much, I was the 'queen bee' if you want to call me that."

"So, like Maddie."

Mom laughed slightly but maintained her worried demeanor. "Maddie *wishes* she was in my league. I was the girl everybody wanted to be."

This wasn't news to me. I already knew that my mom was a hot commodity in her youth. She even embarked on a brief modeling career that she gave up after my dad got sick.

"Get to your point," I impatiently said.

"So, I would always hang out with my group—well, clique—of friends. I was the leader and my two best friends, Cassie and Erica, were always at my side."

Of course, I knew who Cassie was—she would become the mayor of Fresno, and my mom would become her chief of staff. However, this was the first time I ever heard my mom mentioning a friend named Erica. I assumed they must have lost contact through the years. Maybe she didn't agree with my mom's political views or something.

"We seemed to have fun every day. We would always go to the mall as a group and buy all the trendiest clothes. God forbid any of us wore the same outfit twice. We would go to Backstreet Boys and NSYNC concerts all the time. We'd have the craziest parties. And we'd go out with all the cute boys. Your dad was the one they all wanted—and he was mine." Tears welled up in my mom's eyes. The following spring marked the eighteenth anniversary of his death.

"That all sounds great, Mom."

"Yes, it all *sounds* great. But it wasn't. It was a *façade*."

"A what? Speak English."

"A *façade*. It's when something, or someone, looks wonderful on the exterior but is, in fact, fairly miserable on the interior. Kind of like a ripe, Red Delicious apple that you bite into only to find out it has a worm inside. All of us were very unhappy. We were having 'fun' and being clique-ish to conceal the fact that we were just a bunch of kids who did not like who we *really* were. We relied on the media and stereotypes to govern our lives." My mom took a deep breath. "The most important thing is that you be *yourself*."

I was ready to lose it. I'd had enough of these clichés. "I am *being* myself, Mom. What don't you get? *Myself* wants to be popular."

"But why do you want this so-called popularity so bad? Is it because you need the approval of others?"

"Well, duh," I answered, thinking that my mom was being Captain Obvious. "I want to get invited to parties. I want a girlfriend."

"See. You just proved my point. You want to be popular for *superficial* reasons. Do you know what the word 'superficial' means?"

"Uh—stuck up?" I've heard the word many times before, but I never thought about what it really meant.

"No." Mom went into full lecture mode. Before becoming the mayor's chief of staff, she taught some political science classes at Fresno State. It definitely showed sometimes. "Superficial comes from Latin, meaning 'existing only at the surface.' You think so much about what other people think and how they look at you on the outside, but you forget about what makes you *you*. Do a lot of popular kids become successful in life? Absolutely. But a lot more fall victim to this dangerous mindset and vanity. Thank God I didn't go down that path, but a few of my friends weren't as lucky."

"What do you mean?"

Mom paused for a couple of seconds. "My good friend Erica. She was always very pretty, but the way she looked was never good enough for her. She always wanted to look *exactly* like the celebrities on TV and the magazines. As a result, she developed an eating disorder and severe depression. She began to abuse drugs as well. When I started to model professionally, she suddenly became very jealous of me, and that was pretty much the end of our friendship."

I wondered why my mom never told me about this person. "So, what happened to her?"

Mom started to cry again. "A few years after I stopped talking to her, I got a call. Erica was found dead in her apartment—she had taken her own life. It was right after your dad passed too."

"Wow," I responded, "thank you for sharing, Mom. But I don't see how this has anything to do with me."

"Erica's case was an extreme, but being superficial *always* does way more harm than good."

I just didn't want to hear her sermon. I had a fantastic first day of senior year—I certainly did not want my mom to ruin it.

"Whatever," I said lackadaisically. "It's funny you're saying all this because it's very similar to what Pasta was telling me this morning on the bus."

"So, Maddie was right. There was a fight between you two."

I shrugged. "I didn't fight with him. All I said was that I

wanted to be popular and reinvent myself, and he started giving me crap and telling me that nerds are better than jocks. And the funny part was that he got bullied right after he said all that. He proved my point all along."

"And you did nothing?" Mom asked, knowing the answer.

"Well, yeah. I didn't want to risk getting bullied too."

My mom's gaze narrowed. "I'm very worried about you, Charlie. You and Pasta have been best friends since *kindergarten*, and now he's nothing to you? I completely understand why he's giving you the cold shoulder. You see, Pasta might be a social pariah now, but at least he's comfortable in his own skin. Unlike you."

I was done. It felt like *everyone* wanted me to stay a nerd and a social outcast. It seemed that the people who were supposed to care about me the most—my supposed best friend, my only sister, my *mother*—were the same people who were the most against me.

"I see how it is!" I angrily proclaimed. "It's a double standard. It's okay for Maddie to be popular—just like *you* were—but not me? I guess she's the mini-you, and I'm just a *mistake* from your first marriage."

"You're missing the point of our talk," my mom answered. "It's just—"

I cut her off. "I'm going to bed." I exited the living room and started my trek upstairs.

"Good night, Charlie Bear!" my mom called out to me. I didn't respond.

I locked myself in my room for the rest of the night. I

plopped onto my bed and quickly thought over my present situation. I had two options. I could give in to what my family—and Pasta—wanted and go back to my previous nerdy life or continue to have fun reveling in my newfound popularity. And in what was probably the easiest decision of my life thus far, I chose the latter.

I pulled out my Madden 23 disc and placed it inside of my PS4 console. As I played my virtual football game, of course controlling my beloved 49ers against the rival Seahawks, I thought about the actual game I would be playing in, in just two days. I still couldn't believe I was a *real* football player. Everything seemed surreal to me.

The old Charlie Henderson was dead. A brand-new one had taken his place.

5

A KINGDOM FOR
A HORSE

The following morning, I was eating a bowl of Reese's Puffs when I saw a blue convertible pull up in front of my house. It was Larry's.

"Yo, man!" he called out to me.

I was confused why he was here this early. It was a full forty-five minutes before the bus was supposed to pick me up.

"You forgot we have morning practice!" Larry yelled.

"Sorry, Larry! I'll be out in a minute."

This whole "jock" thing sure took some getting used to. I threw on my #8 jersey and raced out to Larry's car. I leaped into the passenger seat, and he gave me a fist bump.

"Thanks for coming to get me," I said to my new friend. "It's greatly appreciated."

"No problem," he answered with a smile. "I didn't wanna leave you hanging. We're a *team*."

Larry floored the gas pedal, and the two of us sped off to school. At practice, I spent some time working with Kylie on perfecting my kicking form. Although I was improving on each kick, my skills still required *a lot* of refining.

When practice ended, Larry and I changed back into our school clothes and headed to homeroom. While we were on our way, we just so happened to spot Hannah Preston, who was, without a doubt, the prettiest girl in the whole school. She possessed the most vivid sea-green eyes I had ever seen, glimmering like two emeralds against her clear, porcelain skin. They were so bright I'm sure they could have lit a dark room by themselves. Her medium-to dark-brown hair ran just past her shoulders, curling at the end. She had complemented her beautiful face with a sparkling diamond necklace and delicately placed silver chandelier earrings. In addition, Hannah wore a teal T-shirt from the Central California SPCA, where she had volunteered. It had the text "Be a Hero, Save a Life" under the silhouette of a Labrador, which looked like Kristin's dog, Olaf. She wasn't only marvelous to look at; she had a heart of gold as well.

I'd had a crush on Hannah for a few years. Being the tech guy for the drama club, I was well acquainted with her as she always played the female lead in school plays. Hannah was more than a talented actress. She was a surefire Broadway star in the making—if not Hollywood bound. Hannah portrayed her characters with a vibrant passion that made them come to life on the stage. For example, when she played Desdemona in *Othello* the previous year, Hannah Preston wasn't on the scene for those three hours. Desdemona herself was—with all of Hannah's beauty, of course.

Larry and I walked closer to Hannah. She noticed us going by, and she gave us a big, warm smile. I was surprised that I didn't instantly melt.

"Hey, guys!" Hannah said in her dulcet voice. We stopped in our tracks. "I just wanted to let you know that auditions for Rayburn High's production of *Richard III* are today." She handed us both a flyer advertising the play. She then looked at me and continued, "Hey, you're our tech! Corey, isn't it?"

"Charlie," I corrected her. I was a little ashamed that she barely knew me after three years of being in the drama club with her. But I guess that was just life backstage.

"Oh, I'm so sorry," Hannah sincerely said. "I'm terrible with names. Which is very ironic because I'm an actress, and memorizing is kinda what I do."

"It's all good, Hannah," I said. I was trying hard not to blush, and I probably was epically failing. Larry noticed me.

"At least you didn't call me Desdemona." Hannah laughed. "I heard that joke way too many times. So anyway, are you joining drama club as tech again?"

When I was about to say "no" and explain that I had made the football team instead, Larry jumped in.

"My man Charlie here is going to *audition* for a part in the play," he boldly stated.

Thanks a lot, Larry. Why the hell did he have to embarrass me in front of the girl of my dreams? I had no choice but to play along.

"That's right!" I forcefully said.

"Awesome!" Hannah replied. "See you at 2:45, right after school!"

When we passed Hannah, and I was sure she couldn't hear us, I glared at Larry. "Why did you have to do that? Not cool. Not cool at all."

Larry smiled. "Why do you think? You obviously have a thing for her. I'm just trying to be a good wingman and help you shoot your shot."

"I mean, who doesn't have a thing for Hannah Preston. She's so hot it's ridiculous that God even created a woman as beautiful as her."

"Like I said. *Obvious.*"

"But now I actually have to audition for the damn play! What if I mess up badly? She'd think I'm nothing but a joke, especially since I've been the stupid tech guy for all this time."

"Relax, bro. You're overreacting. You won't know until you try."

"True. But how am I gonna do this *and* football?"

"It's funny you say that. Krix told me yesterday that Coach is secretly a *huge* theater fan, a *thespian*, and he lets players act in the play, as long as it doesn't interfere with their results on the field. Jeremy and Sebastian are always in it. Sometimes Alang is too. Think about it, who else is gonna play the funny characters?"

It seemed like I had no way out. "Fine," I said to Larry, "I'm trying out for this play on one condition. *You* have to as well."

"Fair enough. You got yourself a deal."

The school day was very uneventful. It was Thursday, so the cafeteria served General Tso's chicken, which was really just bland chicken nuggets tossed together with slimy green beans, topped with a gelatinous orange sauce. It tasted nothing like the *actual* General Tso's chicken I would get at the local Chinese restaurant. I sat at the popular table again, and the entire conversation was about the big game and Krix's party, which were both happening the next day. McCreery and his lackeys were shockingly benevolent to me, for pretty much the first time *ever*.

When the final bell rang, Larry and I headed straight to the auditorium for auditions. There, we were greeted by Hannah and Franz, the drama club's student director. He was dressed head to toe in his full hipster garb, complete with a checked flannel shirt, bow tie, and boat shoes with no socks. His nose was wedged between his horn-rimmed Warby Parker glasses and mustache. His beard was patchy, but since he was a hipster, he probably liked it that way. I used to think that Hannah and Franz were dating but had heard from another student in the drama club that they were just friends—although Franz had planned to change that as soon as possible.

The Garcia brothers and Alang had also come to audition. "Egads!" Sebastian chirped to Larry and me. "Fancy seeing you guys here."

Egads? That's like something Pasta would say to me, I thought. *Could it be that Sebastian is secretly a nerd?*

"I had no idea *you* were into acting," Jeremy said to Larry.

Larry smirked and pointed at me. "It was his idea we do this together." He then turned his focus to the group. "Since the game against Desert Valley is tomorrow, Coach gave us thirty minutes tops to audition. We have to go to afternoon practice as soon as we're done."

Franz rudely chuckled. I guess he was listening to our conversation. "Who do I think I am to give you *jocks* special treatment?" he snarked in a slight Austrian accent. "We have serious *thespians* here. You have to wait in line and come up when I call your name, just like *everyone else*."

Hannah rushed to our defense. "It's not their fault those are the rules," she said.

Franz blushed. Just like it was obvious that I had feelings for her, it was more than apparent that he did as well. "Uh— we're gonna have to do what Teach says."

He turned toward Mr. Messmer, who was standing in the corner. A tall, bald man, he was my junior year English teacher and the drama club's faculty advisor. And yes, Franz probably thought it was cool to call him "Teach."

I overheard bits and pieces of what Messmer was saying to him. Something along the lines of "rules are rules, and we can't risk getting docked funding by the school board," and also, "the last thing we need is to piss off the varsity football boosters."

After talking with Messmer, Franz returned to us in defeat. "The Teach has spoken," he relented. "The meatheads can go first."

For the first, and probably last, time in my life, I, a 130-pound weakling, was called a *meathead*.

Since the Garcia boys were alphabetically before me, I was third to audition for the play. Jeremy read for the part of Ratcliffe, and Sebastian for Catesby—the king's two minions. It was a match made in heaven for them. Then it was my time to *break a leg.*

Hannah handed me a sheet with some dialogue written on it. "You're gonna read the highlighted lines the best you can," she directed me. "Good luck!"

I stepped onto the stage, clutching the script in my right hand. I quickly glanced at it. I knew it was English, but it wasn't anywhere *near* the language I spoke. Hell, Maddie's text speak was closer to English than *this* was. Then, I saw I was not reading for any old character—Hannah had given me the part of King Richard III himself, the lead. I swallowed hard.

I belted out the highlighted lines, channeling my best impression of Robert Baratheon from *Game of Thrones.* From what I remembered about Richard III from European History class, they were essentially one and the same. "A horse! A horse! A kingdom for a horse!"

Messmer read the following unhighlighted line. "Withdraw, my lord! I'll help you to a horse."

"Slave, I have set my life upon a cast," my voice boomed, "and I will stand the hazard of the die: I think there be six Richmonds in the field." *Seriously, what is a Richmond?* Trying not to overthink, I continued. "Five I slain to-day instead of him." *Again, why is there a hyphen in "today"?* This was getting weird. "A horse! A horse! A kingdom for a horse!" I summoned all my energy and bellowed the line for one final time.

Everyone exploded with applause. I was stunned at how well received I was.

"You did amazing!" Hannah cheered, giving me a double high-five.

Even Franz was clapping. Well, to be exact, he was *snapping,* as hipsters do. On his face was the closest thing to a smile his lips could probably form. "Bravo," he remarked. "And no, I'm not trying to be ironic. That was actually pretty good."

I guess I had a knack for acting. I never would've thought. I waited for Alang and Larry to finish their auditions and then triumphantly marched to football practice with the rest of the group. When we arrived, the coach sternly looked at his watch.

"You took thirty-*three* minutes," he yelled. "Drop and give me fifty, all of you."

I hit the turf and did my best to eke out fifty push-ups. And yes, you heard me right. Coach gave the five of us the same punishment for being *three* minutes late that he gave to Krix for being an *hour* late.

When I finished, I met up with Kylie in the corner of the field where our two-person "special teams unit" was practicing.

"Show me what you got, kiddo," she said. "Let's see if you learned anything from this morning."

I eagerly set up at the fifteen-yard line. Kylie held the

football for me, and I kicked forward, pushing it with the ball of my right foot. Unfortunately, it sailed wide left, entirely missing the goalpost.

Kylie was disappointed. "Try again," she instructed.

I did try again. This time—wide right. And again. Closer than my first two attempts, but still no cigar. I kept missing. I finally made a kick on my *seventh* attempt.

Kylie shook her head at me. "Do what you did yesterday," she demanded with a frustrated tone. "This should be easy. We were on the *twenty*-yard line yesterday. This is from the fifteen."

I froze. I didn't remember what I did differently the day before when I hit my tryout kick from twenty. I assumed it mainly was beginner's luck.

I inhaled deeply and attempted three more kicks, missing two and barely making one.

Kylie was not happy. "Two out of ten. That's borderline pathetic. You need to do better than *that* if you want to back me up."

"Yes, ma'am," I replied. I needed to focus. I tried ten more kicks from fifteen yards out, this time making five. It was an improvement, but Kylie still wasn't impressed.

"Watch me," she stated as she grabbed the ball. One of the other players held it for her as she attempted five field goals from the twenty. She made them all with ease. I just couldn't pinpoint what she was doing differently from me.

I tried my last batch of kicks from the fifteen, making seven out of ten. As my mom always told me, "It's not how you start;

it's how you finish."

Kylie wouldn't give me a high-five. She spoke candidly to me. "Look, Charlie. I took a chance on you because I saw you had potential that Coach didn't see. He didn't want you to make the team, but he trusted *my* decision. Don't make me regret it."

My muscles got tense. Did this mean I was getting cut from the team without even playing one game?

Kylie resumed. "Today's practice was rough, but I *know* you will use this as a learning experience and bounce back. Remember, I also play soccer. If I get hurt for some reason, *you* are the team's kicker. They will need to rely on you in clutch situations."

"I won't let you down again," I told her. I breathed a sigh of relief. My job was safe for now.

After practice wrapped up, I joined Larry, Alang, and the Garcia twins and headed back to the auditorium. The drama club's bulletin board displayed the results of the auditions. I anxiously searched for my name. When I found it, I was in utter disbelief. Next to "Richard III," there it was—*Charles P. Henderson*. My jaw dropped—the part was somehow *mine*. I was astounded. In two days, I went from being a nerd to now a football player *and* an actor. *Anything is possible*, I thought.

I turned around, and standing there was Hannah, looking beautiful as ever.

"Congrats on getting the lead!" she exclaimed, embracing me. I kid you not; this was the first time I'd ever been *hugged* by a girl, other than my mom, grandma, or aunts, of course. It felt amazing.

"I just can't believe it," I honestly put it.

"It was an easy decision. We were blown away by your reading of that scene. None of the other male auditionees conveyed the level of intensity that we got from you."

I glanced back at the board. Lo and behold, I saw the name "Hannah Preston" next to the part of Queen Anne— Richard III's wife.

Was I dreaming? I subtly pinched my hand. Nope, this was definitely real life.

It turned out that we all got parts. Jeremy and Sebastian were cast as Ratcliffe and Catesby, respectively—which was because they were the *only* people to audition for those roles. Alang was selected as Tyrrell, something we all thought was funny as the character was a murderer, and Alang had a reputation for being a gentle giant. Larry surprisingly got a big part in King Edward IV, Richard III's older brother.

"We're brothers!" exclaimed Larry as he patted my shoulder.

"This play is gonna be epic," Sebastian burst out while high-fiving all of us.

Soon, the other football players-slash-actors left, leaving just Hannah and me in the corridor in front of the auditorium. Larry couldn't drive me home that day, as he "had to go somewhere."

I turned to Hannah. "So, what do I need to know about acting?" I asked her. Although I had been her acquaintance for a while, this was the first *real* one-on-one conversation we *ever* had.

"Well," she responded, "I would say the golden rule of acting, if there is one, is always to take a risk when you can. I mean, what's the worst thing that can happen? You get booed? You definitely won't die."

"I certainly took a risk when I auditioned today."

She gave me another big smile. Damn, she was perfect. "And it sure paid off!"

Hannah was right about risk-taking. Until I started my senior year, I would always take the safe route in life—staying boxed in my comfort zone. But, now that I was being bold and embracing the unknown, I was more than pleased with the results. I was on the football team, the lead for the school play, hanging out with the popular kids, invited to insane parties, and most of all, my longtime crush was finally noticing me.

I smiled back at Hannah. "So, what got *you* into theater?" I asked.

Her eyes lit up. "I've loved the stage since I was a little girl. I am originally from New York City, so my parents would take me to Broadway all the time. I still have the playbill from my first show—it was *The Lion King*."

"I've always wanted to go to New York. What's it like?"

Hannah smiled again. "There's a lot of action there. They don't call it 'The City That Never Sleeps' for no reason. It's not like downtown Fresno, where pretty much everything is closed by nine or ten."

"The furthest east I've ever been is Chicago," I said, somewhat embarrassed by my lack of traveling. "That's where my mom is from. She moved here when she was eleven."

"You're kidding me. That was the same age I was when *I* moved here."

"Nope. I'm not kidding. You can ask her if you want." I suddenly remembered that since Larry had already left, I had to text my mom to pick me up.

"I'd love to meet your mom. We can debate what's better, New York or Chicago!"

"Well, California blows *both* of them out of the water." It was the only place I had ever lived. Then, Hannah's mentioning my mom gave me an idea. "Do you have a ride home?" I asked.

"No," she replied, "I was going to call an Uber."

"My mom's picking me up." I had just texted her, and she was on her way. "She'd be very happy to drive you home if you want."

"Are you sure?"

"Yeah, of course. You're my *co-star,* after all."

I quickly texted my mom again and told her that Hannah needed a ride too. She agreed to pick us up. Mom was probably glad I was finally having an actual conversation with her and not just "admiring her from a distance" as I had in years past.

When I slid my phone back into my pocket, I noticed another iPhone 13 Pro Max lying on top of the auditorium windowsill. It was similar in appearance to mine but had a gold case. I turned it on and noticed that the lock screen was the Alabama Crimson Tide logo. Clearly, it belonged to Larry. *He is probably going nuts looking for it right now*, I thought. Modern high schoolers can't function without our phones—case in point, Maddie. If only I knew Larry's address or his home phone number.

Luckily, I did know a trick. "Hey, Siri," I said into the phone, "whose phone is this?"

Siri responded, "I believe this iPhone belongs to Larry Travers." His address popped up on the screen: 2008 N Swearengin Street, Fresno CA, 93711.

I was grateful for being a tech nerd *sometimes.*

Hannah and I walked out to the front of the school and hopped into my mom's Pilot. We both sat in the back. As much as I loved riding shotgun, I knew I wanted to be seated next to her.

"Hi, Mrs. Henderson," Hannah said as she got into the car.

My mom turned to look at her and smiled. "You can call me Sarah," she said.

Now that was peculiar. My mom *hated* when people my age, aside from Pasta, called her by her first name. Maybe she felt bad about our "talk" the night before, and she wanted to get on Hannah's good side to make it up to me. *Who knows?*

"So, Charlie tells me you're from Chicago," Hannah said.

"I sure am," my mom proudly stated.

"What was it like moving to Fresno?"

"Well, I'll be honest. I was bored at first, but then I began to appreciate the quieter, more relaxed quality of life."

To say that Hannah and my mom hit it off was an understatement. First, they talked about what it was like to move out West as a kid. My mom then asked her about plays she acted in, and Hannah proceeded to go through her credits like she was reading them off an IMDb page. Before long, my mom was even telling her about our family's world-famous pierogi recipe. It was almost like they forgot I was in the car.

My mom pulled in front of Hannah's house. "Is this it?"

"Yep, that's the one!"

"See you at the party tomorrow," I told her. I didn't even have to ask if Krix invited her. I knew a girl as good-looking as Hannah Preston was a shoo-in to be there.

"Can't wait!" She gave me a quick hug and got out of the car.

"She's a keeper," my mom said to me.

"Mom!" I screamed, slightly embarrassed. "She's just a friend."

"She's your *co-star*." My mom winked at me.

I gave her Larry's address, and she drove to his house. It was a quaint bungalow with tan wooden shingles. I rang the bell. An older man with wire-rimmed glasses and a heavy white beard answered the door. He was wearing a baseball cap with the words "U.S. Air Force Veteran" emblazoned on the front. I knew it was Larry's uncle, Bill.

"Hello, sir," I said, holding out his nephew's phone in my hand. "I'm Larry's friend. I'm just here to drop this off for him.

He left it at school."

Bill took the phone from me. "Thanks. I'll give it to him."

"Is he here?" I asked.

"No, he's out running errands. He'll see you in school tomorrow."

"Thank you for your service," I said to him before leaving.

When I got home, Maddie was in a reasonably good mood, and by that, I meant she spent the entire night texting her boyfriend, Leo. At least she was leaving me in peace. For dinner, my mom made *gołąbki*, cabbage stuffed with chopped meat and rice—another secret family recipe. It sure made up for the terrible cafeteria food I had for lunch.

I plopped down on my bed, exhausted and with a full stomach. I had a busy day between school, auditioning for the play, and football practice.

I began playing another game of Madden. I found it odd that Larry still hadn't texted to thank me for finding his phone. So, I messaged him instead: *ur welcome for finding ur phone lol*, I wrote. I waited five minutes. No reply. Ten minutes. Still nothing. Twenty minutes. Not a word. I went to bed.

———— • ————

The next day was Friday—the day of the big football game *and* Krix's party. I couldn't wait.

I looked at my phone to see if Larry had texted me back from the night before. He hadn't. I texted him to ask if he was driving me to morning practice. When he didn't respond in twenty minutes, I became worried. Was he mad at me? Did I say something that rubbed him the wrong way? I tried calling him, but it went right to voicemail.

Since I didn't want to risk missing morning practice, I had my mom drive me. When I arrived at the field, I saw all the players huddled around Coach—all except for one. My suspicions were confirmed.

Larry was nowhere to be seen.

6

WHERE'S LARRY?

"**D**o you have any idea where Larry is?" Coach barked at me.

"No, sir," I answered timidly.

"Who saw him last?" A combination of anger and panic colored Coach's voice.

"All four of us did," said Jeremy, pointing to me, Sebastian, and Alang. "We were outside of the auditorium, when we found out what parts of the play we got."

"What was the last thing you remember him saying?" Coach did not quit interrogating us. "Anything that would give you any indication of where he might be?"

"He just said he had to go somewhere," Sebastian replied. "That was it. He didn't specify where this 'somewhere' was. Could've been over the rainbow as far as I'm concerned."

"That doesn't help." Coach looked defeated. "All these years coaching at this school, I finally get a five-star player, and this crap happens right before the start of the season. Unbelievable."

I had no choice. I had to pipe up. "Wait!" I cried. "I—uh, went to his house yesterday evening at about six. He left his phone at school, and I was returning it. He wasn't there, but his uncle answered the door, told me he was running errands, and left it at that. I texted him last night and again this morning but didn't get a response."

"We could try texting him again, now," Krix said.

Krix, Sebastian, and I each sent Larry a message. None of us got a reply. We then called him, and it went straight to voicemail again. His phone was probably off or dead.

"I only knew him for a couple of days, but Larry *cared* about us," I noted. "I don't think it's in him to bail on the team, especially before the big game against Desert Valley."

"Exactly," agreed Kylie, who was standing next to me. "Something must be up."

Coach turned to us. "Look, we're a team, and even though we may be without our star player tonight because of God-knows-what, that shouldn't stop us, because we play as a *team*."

"We lost the last *twelve* games we played against Desert Valley," Alang stated. "They have our number. I'm the first to say football is a team sport, but let's be honest with ourselves. We're not the same without Larry."

"I disagree," proclaimed McCreery. He and his friend Dwayne were the only players on the team who didn't seem saddened or bothered by Larry's disappearance. "We have enough talent already. We don't need his ass."

"Who needs your receiver when you got your tight end?"

Dwayne remarked, flexing his right bicep. It is worth noting that before Larry transferred, Dwayne was the Rayburn player who was receiving by far the most attention from college scouts.

Coach regained everyone's attention. "Look, Larry or no Larry, we're winning tonight." He had everyone put their arm into the center of the huddle. "I want to hear 'Coyotes' on three! One—two—three!"

"Coyotes!" we screamed in unison.

We then dispersed and started to practice. I somehow did fairly well, compared to my abysmal performance the previous afternoon. Kylie and even Coach were pleased with the progress I was making.

But everything was overshadowed by Larry's absence. It left a gaping six-foot-three, two-hundred-pound hole on our team's roster.

After practice, part of me was holding out hope that Larry had just overslept, he would show up in homeroom, and things would go back to normal. However, this was not the case. There was still no sign of him, and the seat next to me remained empty.

As I sat there watching the several announcements advertising the kickoff game against Desert Valley, I was overwhelmed with anxiety. *What if something terrible happened to him when he was running errands?* I thought. Maybe he was in a car accident—or he was kidnapped. I kept imagining the worst-case scenario. I felt personally responsible as I was one of the last people to have seen him *and* I had been to his house as well. Before that day, I was stoked to play in the big game. Now, the game didn't seem to matter at all. I just wanted my *friend* back.

Larry and I were in the same English and Physics classes—and he didn't show up to those either. It is hard to focus on *The Great Gatsby* or Newton's laws when your new best friend vanishes without a trace.

Soon lunchtime had come. Since it was Friday, the school was serving pizza—Maddie's favorite food. It happened to be the only thing the cafeteria made that was halfway decent. I grabbed my tray and made my way over to the popular table to sit. An aura of fearfulness replaced the usually lively atmosphere at the table—the rest of the football players were worried that Larry being missing meant their chances of pulling the upset over Desert Valley were doomed.

"I can't believe he'd do this to us," Krix said.

"Do what?" a familiar voice called out from behind. We all turned around at once. Not one of us could believe our eyes. There, standing with his #1 jersey on, was Larry.

We all applauded. Yes, we were relieved that he was okay, but I'm sure more people were happy that Rayburn again had a legitimate shot at winning the game that night with Larry playing.

He pulled up a chair. "You really thought I was gonna leave y'all hanging?"

"Where were you?" I asked, still concerned.

Larry brushed it off. "There was something I had to do."

"Like what?" Krix questioned. "What could be more

important than going to morning practice the day of the game against our archrival?"

"You don't understand." Larry was extremely vague. He finally relented, "I was helping a sick friend if you *really* need to know."

Jeremy chimed in. "I, for one, don't care where you were. I'm just happy that you're here now, you're fine, and you're gonna help us win. So, who's with me?"

"Coyotes!" we screamed.

With Larry back, we could all finally focus on the game. Between that and the Krix party, we had quite the night ahead of us.

7

GAME TIME

After school let out, the team held a brief afternoon practice. Coach, who was beyond thrilled to have Larry back, gave us a pep talk. We didn't really need it, to be honest. Larry's return was enough to lift our spirits to an all-time high.

Soon, the spectators began pouring into the bleachers. My mom was unfortunately not able to come as she was on duty for the Tomato Festival. Uncle Bill wasn't there as well.

Then, the Desert Valley Scorpions arrived, looking even more menacing than I had expected. They marched out of their bus and onto the field like a swarm of angry hornets.

In particular, one Desert Valley player closed in on me. He was a large, muscular redhead with a bevy of freckles dotting his face. He was wearing a #50 jersey in the Scorpions' black and tan. The player pointed and laughed hysterically at me and then moseyed over to Krix.

"Hey, Steve!" he scoffed. "I see you let a *nerd* play with

you." I knew he was talking about me. "What's the matter? No one wanted to be on your losing team, so you lowered your standards?"

"Marty McLoughlin! Stay the hell away from my *brother-in-law!*" Krix said, highly agitated. It was clear that the two of them had some serious beef.

Marty smirked. "It's not like he's actually gonna see the field." He turned to me. "What position are you, *geek*?"

"Kicker, second-string," I responded, somehow unfazed. I had dealt with bullies all my life. This Marty guy was nothing new to me. For all intents and purposes, he was a skinnier version of McCreery.

"Second-string kicker?" Marty burst out laughing even harder than he was before. Then, he turned back to Krix. "Why did you even waste a jersey on this kid? He would've been more useful as the mascot."

At that moment, Marty saw Kylie and turned his attention over to her. "Hello, sweetheart," he crooned. "You look a bit lost. Cheerleading is over there." He pointed to the sideline where the Rayburn cheerleaders were getting set up.

"Go to hell, you asshole!" Kylie shouted.

Other Scorpions players crowded around Marty in taunting Kylie.

"You think we're intimidated by a *girl*?" Desert Valley #63, a rotund lineman, scoffed.

"Yeah! Get off the damn field and make me a sandwich!" jeered #42.

I had enough. "Leave my friend alone!" I screamed at

them. "She can kick all of your asses!" That was probably a true statement. Kylie was one tough cookie.

"Whatcha gonna do, nerd?" Marty mocked. "Lower my HP?"

I glared at him. Marty knew what "HP" meant—he must have been a gamer. Who was he to call *anyone* a nerd?

It was clear that by becoming popular, I was also becoming more confident and less afraid to assert myself and protect my friends. *If only I were like that when Pasta was getting bullied on the bus.*

Desert Valley's coach blew his whistle, and the entire Scorpions team, including a reluctant Marty, huddled in their corner of the field. Coach similarly gathered us.

Kylie gave me a half-smile, although anguish still marked her face. "Thank you for defending me," she said. "Marty pulls this crap every time we play against each other. He's relentless."

"We're gonna show that *pig* who's boss!" I exclaimed.

"I don't know," Kylie continued. "Marty's their star inside linebacker. He's only the *best* player on that team. Scratch that. He's virtually *unstoppable* at times."

A few minutes later, Krix and Coach assembled around midfield opposite Marty McLoughlin and the opposing coach. The referee stood in the center of the two groups. Finally, it was time for the coin toss. Since we were the home team, we called "heads," but the ref flipped the coin, and it came up tails. Desert Valley chose to defer, giving us the ball to begin the first half. They did this so that when the second half started, they would receive.

I sat on the bench, watching the game unfold.

Desert Valley's kicker sent the ball down the field and into the hands of our returner Todd "Zippy" Jones. He searched for any sign of breathing room but found none—Marty quickly brought him down at our eighteen-yard line, knocking the ball out of his hands. At that moment, I saw exactly what Kylie meant about Marty being unstoppable. Then, to add insult to injury, Desert Valley #42, the player who had told Kylie to make him a sandwich, scooped up the fumbled ball and ran it back to the end zone for a touchdown. Just a few seconds in, Rayburn was already down nothing to six. Desert Valley then kicked the extra point, making it nothing to *seven*.

We had to respond and respond quickly. Rayburn's offense immediately kicked into high gear, with Larry being the much-needed difference-maker. A few plays later and we were leading a death march down into opponent territory. However, as our offense approached the red zone, Marty and the rest of the Scorpions' defense came to attack. On first down, Krix's throw was knocked incomplete and nearly intercepted. On second down, Krix tried to step back to throw the ball out to Dwayne, the tight end, but the pocket collapsed, and a Desert Valley lineman sacked him for a ten-yard loss. It was third down with twenty yards to go. Alang hiked the ball to Krix, and he pump-faked, evading three defenders before unleashing the ball deep to a wide-open Larry. He seized it and propelled forward into the end zone for a Rayburn touchdown.

"That's how you do it!" he exclaimed as he held up the ball defiantly for the world to see.

Kylie subsequently connected for the extra point, tying the score at seven apiece. *Now* we had a ball game.

The contest was back-and-forth for the rest of the first half. Both offenses and defenses brought their A-game. By halftime, it was a tie game: 21–21. The Coyotes and Scorpions regrouped into their huddles. The marching band played our Alma Mater while the cheerleaders piled into the center of the field to perform a routine. Our school mascot, Carlos the Coyote, was busy entertaining some of the players' younger siblings in the bleachers.

"Good work so far, team," Coach said to us. "Though there are still some things we need to iron out in the next quarter. Especially the O-line." He singled out McCreery. "Krikorian has been knocked around the entire first half."

"But those linebackers are just too fast! They're coming out of nowhere!" McCreery complained. As our starting left tackle, it was mainly *his* job to protect the quarterback's blindside from oncoming defenders.

Coach stared at him. He was utterly fed up. "Enough with those baby excuses!" he barked. "Or I'll have no other option than to bench you! Play better, or we lose!"

"Yes—yes, sir," McCreery stumbled to say. It was the first time I had seen *him* that distressed.

Coach took a breath. "Remember, we're Coyotes! And what do coyotes do to scorpions?"

"Eat them!" the entire team called out together.

"You're damn right they do!" Coach exclaimed. "Let's get 'em this half!"

Unfortunately, the mounting hope we had coming into the new period quickly evaporated. The third quarter began with Kylie kicking the ball off from the forty-yard line. Then, just three plays into the opening drive of the new half, Brock Holderness, Desert Valley's quarterback—a tall, lanky boy with long, dirty blonde hair partially covering the #6 on his jersey—gunned the ball deep down the field, into the hands of his receiver, #12. Jeremy Garcia and Larry, now subbed in as cornerback, tried their best to track him down—but it was not enough as #12 broke away for another Desert Valley touchdown. With the extra point, we were now trailing our archrivals 28–21.

When Rayburn received the ball again, our offense struggled to put something together. McCreery *certainly* was no help allowing *two* sacks on the drive. We went three plays and out. Kylie punted the ball back to Desert Valley, who continued to play red-hot. A few minutes after, Holderness had connected with #12 again for yet another Scorpions touchdown. It was 35–21 Desert Valley, going into the final quarter.

And that was when Larry became superhuman again. With time winding down, Krix kept chucking the ball to him on throw after throw. Once the pair had gotten us back into the red zone, Krix called an audible, ordering Larry to shift out wide to a quick corner route. The improv worked as Desert Valley's secondary was confused, and Larry stormed into the end zone for his second touchdown of the game. With Kylie smashing the point-after, the Rayburn Coyotes were trailing by only a touchdown—down 35–28. We were right back in this.

Our defense stepped up as well and smothered a would-be promising drive by the Scorpions' offense. Alang proved to be crucial in this pressure-filled moment. I saw just how he earned his nickname "The Electric Pillow," as he clogged pretty much Desert Valley's entire running lane with his three-hundred-plus-pound frame. He even caused their running backs to *lose* yards. The drive finally ended with Desert Valley punting the ball back to us.

Krix and Larry continued to make magic together by rocketing the ball down the field. For a while, it looked like the drive would end in another Rayburn touchdown. However, when our offense was five yards away from the goal line, Marty and the other Desert Valley linebackers went on the prowl like a pack of wild dogs hunting a wildebeest. On third down, Krix fired a short pass to Dwayne, who appeared wide open in the end zone—but as the ball entered his hands, Marty collided with Dwayne's shoulder, causing the ball to fall harmlessly to the ground. The ref ruled the play "incomplete," bringing up fourth down. Kylie came up to kick the chip-shot field goal, which she effortlessly nailed—she probably could have made *that* kick with her eyes closed. Although we closed the gap, it was a huge missed opportunity for us to tie the game. We still trailed, now 35–31.

With Desert Valley's offense back in action, it became clear to our defense that they were trying to eat the clock as much as possible by sticking to safe running plays. Alang, and the rest of our defensive line, became obsessed with dominating the point of attack. Larry even stepped in and played some linebacker himself. What couldn't that guy do? It worked, and Rayburn got the ball back with the Scorpions failing to add to the score. But only three minutes remained on the clock.

I was sitting on the edge of my seat—both figuratively *and* literally. With all the massive linemen hogging the space, my comparably tiny body could barely remain on the rail-thin metal bench.

Rayburn's offense needed to make something happen—and fast. Things were going very well until one third down when Marty and another linebacker teamed up to tackle Sebastian Garcia, in as running back, one yard short of picking up the first down. Coach had no choice but to call Kylie out to attempt a forty-yard field goal—a distance she had never hit from before.

"You got this!" I screamed to her in support as she walked up to the field.

Kylie smiled back at me. I knew she was nervous, but she tried her best to hide it. The entire school was counting on her. We were all aware that if she missed, the game was over.

Alang snapped the ball to Stokes, the backup quarterback, who was the holder on the play. Marty attempted to break through the offensive line in hopes of blocking Kylie's kick. However, she hit the ball on target, and it flew beautifully into the goalpost. It was perfect. Now Rayburn trailed by only one point. The score was 35–34 Desert Valley.

The referee put his arms above his head in a "U" shape, signaling that the field goal was good. But Marty wasn't finished. The brutish, red-faced linebacker sailed through an unsuspecting McCreery and took a cheap shot on Kylie's shins, tackling her down onto the turf. I watched, sick to my stomach, as she helplessly landed square onto her knees. From the bench, I could hear them buckle as they hit the ground.

"Noooo!" I cried out from the bench. "Kylie!"

8

DESPERATE TIMES

The ref vigorously blew his whistle and ran to the line of scrimmage. "Illegal roughing of the kicker!" he yelled. He grabbed Marty and permanently escorted him back to Desert Valley's bench. Per our division's rules, deliberately hurting the kicker resulted in the offending player having to sit out for the rest of the game. But the damage was already done.

Luckily, Kylie's injury was not severe at all. Coach carefully looked at it and determined that she had merely sprained her right knee. It could've been a lot worse. However, this meant that she definitely couldn't kick for the rest of the game—and probably the next week or even two.

But one thing was for sure—for now, Rayburn's kicker was *me*. I guess that desperate times really called for desperate measures.

We still needed a miracle even to get another chance to score. Desert Valley was still up, although by only one point, and they had possession. It also looked that their offense wasn't going to let up anytime soon. Brock Holderness was *still* making plays this late in the game, and it appeared that he would lead his team down the field for *another* touchdown, putting a win out of reach for Rayburn. Holderness stepped back. He spotted his trusty receiver, #12, in the end zone, and there was a clear path between the two players.

That's the play that's gonna finish us off, I quietly said to myself. *We just lost.*

But right when I thought the game was over, Larry, who was back in the game as a cornerback, snuck up on #12, placed his hands in front of his body, and acrobatically diverted the trajectory of the ball into them—unbelievable.

Larry had just picked off Brock Holderness in the end zone. Rayburn took possession at the twenty-five-yard line.

The good news was that the Coyotes now had a chance to win the game with just a field goal. The bad news was—well, there were *two*. First, there were only twenty-three seconds left on the clock, and we were three-quarters the field's length from the end zone with no timeouts left. And as if that weren't enough, *I* was the guy who had to kick that field goal. Things looked very bleak, to say the very least.

Before I could do *anything*, the rest of the team had to get into field-goal range. Krix first targeted Larry deep, but he didn't muster enough arm strength, and his pass fell well short of its target. Krix tried again, this time to Dwayne, but he was well covered, and his pass again fell to the ground. Those two incompletions had cut the clock in half. Now only *eleven* seconds remained.

Krix was gasping for air. Sweat was visibly streaking his dirt-encrusted purple and gold #14 jersey. He had to have been sacked at least a dozen times during the game—no thanks to McCreery. But, being the son of a self-made billionaire, he was not one to give up.

"Blue forty-two!" Krix yelled hoarsely, signaling to the rest of the offense. "Blue forty-two! Red eighty! Green seventeen! Hut! Hut!"

Knowing he was his only option, Krix again tried for Larry, who was running at blistering speed down the field. Due to my "experience" playing Madden, I recognized it as a flag corner route. Larry hauled in the pass and continued full speed ahead. However, as fast as he was, the defense was catching up. When he was about to be brought down by a Desert Valley safety, he jumped out of bounds, stopping the clock.

There were only *three* seconds of the game remaining.

Coach called my number, and I stepped out onto the field, grasping my helmet underneath my right arm. *Three seconds left,* I thought. I had sat for the first 3,597 seconds, but it was the final three I played that would end up making the difference in who won and who lost. *No pressure.*

"Let's see what you can do, nerd!" Marty shouted from the Desert Valley bench.

That bastard. I'm gonna make him pay for what he did to Kylie.

Stokes, the holder, motioned over to me. "Hey, bro. This

one's gonna be from thirty-three yards out. Good luck."

I was in over my head. *Thirty-three yards?* That was three whole yards longer than the longest field goal I ever kicked—and I still don't remember how I made *that* one.

I said a quick prayer. *Whatever happens, happens,* I thought. *Worst-case scenario, we lose, I get blamed, and I go back to being a nerd again.*

I heard Kylie call out to me from the bench, "Charlie! You can do it!" The other Coyotes players, including Larry and Krix, joined her in cheering for me.

Kylie, I'm doing this for you! She easily would have made this kick I was about to attempt. There was no doubt about that.

The attempt began. *Here goes nothing.* Alang snapped it into Stokes's hands. I swung my right foot back, pretending I was sparring during my Taekwondo days. The ball of my foot made contact with the pigskin and sent it flying through the air. My eyes glued themselves to its path.

My kick definitely had the distance. I had sent forth all my strength, every ounce of my being, into that one football. Its problem, though, was the angle. My accuracy still wasn't all that great, and the ball veered to the left.

The clock hit triple zeros.

The football collided head-on with the left upright.

I shook my head in apparent defeat.

It then bounced off the upright—and in.

The ref held up his arms. It was official. The final score was 37–35 Coyotes.

I couldn't believe it, but *I did it*. I had just kicked the game-winning field goal.

The crowd went ballistic. Rayburn always played Desert Valley twice a year and had beat them last in 2015—when I was ten.

The entire team started to chant my name, "Charlie, Charlie, Charlie!" Even Coach and McCreery joined in. Soon after, the cheerleaders, marching band, and spectators lauded me as well. It was pure jubilation.

Now, this is what it's like to be popular. I was elated.

The rest of the victorious team formed a huddle around me. The chants continued. "Charlie, Charlie, Charlie!" Alang reached out and scooped me up, hoisting me up in the air and showing me off to the fans in the bleachers. It almost reminded me of when Rafiki held baby Simba during the opening scene of *The Lion King*.

"This is the kid that did it!" he shouted. But, of course, no one could hear him, as the loud cheers easily drowned him out.

Alang passed me off to the other players. It was my first experience crowd-surfing.

After about thirty seconds, they put me back on the ground. The chants of my name had finally subsided and faded into regular applause.

Kylie ran up to me and gave me a big hug. "That was awesome!"

"Thanks. How are you feeling?"

"My knee's a little sore, but it will be better in no time," she replied. "I want you to know that you did me proud today, and if I'm not cleared to kick next week, I fully trust you to get the job done."

"Thanks," I said. "I owe it all to you. You've been an amazing teacher!"

I then turned to Larry and gave him a high-five. "Those catches and that pick were unreal. They should be chanting *your* name instead of mine."

Larry grinned. "That's what I love about football. It's such a team game. Sure, I made all those plays, but if it weren't for *your* kick, our team would've lost. So, we're thanking you, my man."

I was grateful to have Larry as a friend. I still couldn't believe that just a few hours earlier, I thought he was gone forever.

I walked over to where Krix was standing. Next to him was his brother Leo—and Maddie.

"There's the man of the hour!" Krix greeted me. "You don't know how good it feels to *finally* beat Desert Valley after all these years." He glanced over at Leo. "Take notes, little bro. You're gonna need 'em when you're on varsity next year."

Leo smiled at me. "Good work, brother-in-law."

Even Maddie was proud of me. "For once in my life, I am not *completely* embarrassed to have you as a brother." Since that was the closest thing to a compliment I was ever going to get from her, I took it in stride.

I rejoined Larry, and when we were about to get going

to Krix's party, I saw Hannah dash over to me. She wore a blue and white Margo shirt dress from Vineyard Vines (one of Maddie's favorite clothing companies) that brought out her emerald eyes and showcased her attractive figure. I assumed that she had picked it out for Krix's party later on. I had no idea she was watching me in the bleachers the entire time.

"Charlie!" she exclaimed, pulling me in for a hug. "You're our hero!"

I blushed. "Thanks, Hannah. I did what I had to do. I didn't know you were into football."

"Yeah, I've always loved it. I grew up a huge New York Giants fan."

"Cool," I responded. "We have a lot in common then."

Being a die-hard, lifelong San Francisco 49ers superfan, I've hated the Giants since they beat my Niners in the 2011 NFC Championship Game. But I wasn't gonna let sports get between me and the girl of my dreams.

I noticed Larry was looking at me eagerly. I knew he was waiting for me to "shoot my shot," as he always said. It was as good a time as ever.

"So, Hannah," I confidently continued. "Do you have any plans tomorrow?"

"Uh—no," she answered. "Other than sleeping in and practicing my lines. Why do you ask?"

You can do it, Charlie, I thought. "Uh—I was thinking about maybe going to see a movie."

She gave me a big smile. "That sounds like a lovely idea. Which one do you want to see?"

I wanted to see the new Gina Carano movie, but I didn't think it was her cup of tea. "You pick," I said. I honestly didn't care if she chose the sappiest chick flick ever made. Her company was enough for me.

"Okay. Let's see the movie that came out today. I forgot its name—it's the one where Gina Carano plays a Russian spy. I *love* action movies. Don't judge me."

I was over the moon. I guess she was my soulmate. "Okay, so I'll meet you at the theater at seven?"

"Sounds like a plan," she replied. "Unless you want to grab dinner before. What about The Brown Cow, the new gourmet burger place that just opened right next door to the movie theater?"

"We'll make it six then," I said. "I can't say no to a good burger and fries."

Did that really happen? I asked Hannah Preston out on a date, and she said *yes*. I had gone from zero to hero in three days. I was feeling on top of the world.

While I was leaving the football field, my eyes scanned the bleachers, and I saw a familiar face in the AV booth filming the game. It was Pasta.

I moved closer to him. "Pasta! How's it going, buddy!"

At the sound of my voice, he immediately turned his face away from me; all I could see of him was the mane of curly red hair protruding from the back of his head.

Once a nerd, always a nerd. I didn't know why I even bothered being nice to him anymore.

9

WHEN IN ROME

Larry and I rode past the school in his Stingray to one of the most exclusive neighborhoods of Fresno. We were in "multimillionaire-ville," as my mom called it. It was unreal how some of the houses looked—they were more like *hotels* than houses to me.

We made a right into a gated community and came across a locked gate. Larry punched in the passcode Krix had given him, and the gate opened. As we continued down the private drive, the houses kept getting bigger and bigger—and farther and farther apart. Finally, the road came to an end. At its terminus stood an enormous mansion—an Italian-style villa flanked by limestone columns and various trees. Its breadth was utterly remarkable. It appeared to be the size of *ten* normal houses, at least. The exterior walls were comprised of sleek coral stucco and surrounded by seventeenth-century stone arches and a pristine slate roof. An exquisite, delicately forged iron gate guarded the property. The mega-house reminded me of the resorts where contestants on *Wheel of Fortune* stayed after winning the "Prize Puzzle."

"Don't tell me this is where the party is tonight," I said, staring at the mansion in disbelief. *So, all along, this is the place where Maddie went when she said she was going to her "boyfriend's house."*

"It's where my GPS took me," Larry remarked, also reveling in the house's beauty. He rechecked his phone just to make sure. "Yep, 435 Cypress Grove Parkway. It *has* to be it. There are no other homes for at least a quarter of a mile."

Larry cautiously parked on the side of the road, sandwiching the Stingray between a Maserati and a Rolls-Royce. We got out and sauntered toward the mansion's entranceway.

A large security guard stood on the opposite side of the gate. He was wearing a jet-black police outfit, including a baggy coat, which I assumed doubled as a bulletproof vest. His hat displayed the seal of the U.S. House of Representatives. An AR-15 rifle hung tightly across his chest, juxtaposed with the iPad he clenched in his hand. Another armed, identically dressed guard stood off to the side, a few feet away from his colleague. *Of course Congressman Krikorian uses his official Congressional security detail at his sons' house parties.* I wondered if it was just to keep the nerds out.

"Names and IDs?" the guard asked Larry and me in a no-nonsense tone.

We both carefully stated our full names. Larry handed the guard his license, and I passed him my learner's permit through a small gap in the gate.

He studied both of our IDs and faces for at least fifteen seconds each to verify that we were the people we claimed to be. The guard then checked his iPad for our names. He looked back at us with approval.

"Mr. Henderson and Mr. Travers, you are all set," he stated. He passed us back our IDs and tapped the iPad's screen. The gate opened wide.

Larry I and walked onto the estate filled with awe.

"Welcome to *Domus Tempus*," the guard said as we walked past him. "Enjoy your stay."

Wow, the house even has a name—a fancy Latin name.

Larry and I followed the circular cobblestone-paved driveway. A babbling brook and a wild orchid garden lay off to our sides. A peacock fanned its tail feathers a few feet away before shuffling off to join the rest of its flock.

Kylie did mention exotic animals. Krix's house was its own undisturbed paradise.

The driveway ended at a flight of Spanish-style steps, leading to an ornate walnut door. The door looked like it would be more of a fit guarding a castle, much like the one where the real Richard III lived. Another Congressional guard, also holding an iPad, was stoically standing on the top step.

Without him having to say anything, Larry and I obediently handed him our IDs. He checked the list *again* before giving us the green light and returning them.

The door swung open, revealing a colossal room marked by teak floors and a spiral staircase at the far end. The ceiling was a minimum of twenty-five feet high and was graced by an elaborate Renaissance-style mural that reminded me of the Sistine Chapel, which I learned about in art class—or, as Maddie had called it, the "sixteen chapel." Antique French chandeliers hung in the stairwell. A long alabaster table, small compared to the rest of the house, was placed close to the entranceway. Next to it stood a well-dressed woman and man greeting the guests. The woman was attractive with long, straight dark brown hair. She looked to be around my mom's age. The man was a few years older than she was, with a similar Mediterranean complexion. I had seen him plenty of times before, but never in person. It took me a few seconds, but I quickly recognized who he was. I was standing face-to-face with Congressman Jesse Krikorian.

The congressman shook my hand. "You must be Charlie," he said with a warm grin.

"Yes, sir," I replied. It seemed surreal that a man I had only seen on the news and C-SPAN addressed me in person *by my name.* "Steven told me a lot about you," he continued. "He wanted me to personally thank you for making that kick today. That victory meant a lot to him, the team, and the entire community."

"Thanks." I still couldn't believe how big of a deal people were making about me *barely* booting the game-winning field goal.

"Well, I don't believe I've introduced myself. I'm United States Congressman Jesse Vachagan Krikorian. And this is my lovely wife, Andrea." He pointed to the woman standing next to him, and I shook her hand. "I know your mother very well.

Both she and the mayor were big parts of my campaign two years ago. Any son of Sarah is a son of mine."

I noticed he specifically said "son" and not "child." Maybe he was not too pleased with the influence Maddie was having on Leo.

I thanked the congressman for his hospitality, and he proceeded to offer me something to drink. I thought for a brief moment that he was going to grab me a soda from his fridge, like Pasta's mom always did when I stayed at his house. However, he instead motioned toward an array of about a dozen cherrywood kegs perched on the other side of the alabaster table.

Okay, I thought. *When in Rome, do as the Romans do.*

A butler handed me a crystal goblet he had just wiped down with a handkerchief. I placed the shimmering glass underneath the third keg from the left. The wooden barrel was stamped with the words "Local American India Pale Ale 7.8% ABV." I pulled the spigot, and the bubbling straw-colored liquid splashed into the goblet, filling it to the brim. As the foam began to settle, I promptly took a generous swig of the hoppy craft beer. It had citrus and pine notes—tasting nothing like the watery light beers my mom drank during our summer barbeques. Its tangy flavor almost reminded me of grapefruit juice, my grandpa's breakfast drink of choice.

I finished my glass in record time and tried a glass of beer from another keg. This one, a wheat beer, boasted flavor hues of peach and apricot. I hadn't even tasted the food yet, and it already felt like I was dining at one of Gordon Ramsay's restaurants. In no time, I was on my third—or fourth glass. I couldn't exactly remember to be honest.

Unbeknownst to everyone at the party—except for Maddie, of course—this was the first time I ever had more than a sip of alcohol in my life.

I mingled with the students in attendance. I had seen most of them before, but none of them had any clue who I was, other than being the guy who had just seemingly single-handedly helped Rayburn defeat Desert Valley. I realized just how *invisible* I was during my first three years in high school. With beer in hand, I walked out of the great room and into a corridor. I continued following guests outside to where the action was happening.

When I opened the sliding door, I was beyond stunned. The *backyard*, which went on for at least ten acres, was somehow even more magnificent than the house itself. It made my own backyard, as nice as it was, seem like a potted plant. To my left, an olive orchard flourished in all its splendor. A sprawling grassy field lay to my right. It must have been *some* place for the Krikorian boys to practice football. And smack-dab in the middle was the main attraction—a hundred-foot-long inground swimming pool—which I could've easily mistaken for a natural tropical lagoon. An expansive travertine stone deck encased the crystal water. The patio's vivid ivory color made the sapphire blue pool look even brighter, if not fluorescent. The water was inviting me to jump in. It was a far cry from the dirty public pool my mom took Maddie and me to as kids. Good thing Krix had reminded me to bring a bathing suit—I wore mine underneath my shorts.

I made my way toward the pool. It was bordered on its left side by two large jacuzzi hot tubs. On the opposite end of the pool, a small pond flecked with Japanese koi bubbled as a manmade waterfall funneled water into it. A large stone grotto lay sandwiched between the lagoon and pool. Inside, a live band was performing atop a small stage. Behind the pool stood a sizeable two-story pool house that could have easily passed for a house *on its own*. The sunset illuminated a dozen bronze statues of Roman gods and goddesses.

It must be nice to be rich.

Outside the pool house, a chef was serving the party's food. And no, this was not your typical house party fare of chips and dip, pigs in a blanket, or shrimp cocktail. Krix's party's spread was complete with filet mignon, lobster tail, imported French cheeses, sushi, and even Ossetra caviar straight from the Caspian Sea. I filled my plate high with the multitude of delicacies and sat down on a chaise lounge, looking out at the pool. I was in heaven.

Larry met up with me and claimed the seat to my right.

"Kylie was right," I said. "This party is *sick*."

"*Sick* doesn't do it justice," he agreed.

Krix and Kristin—or "Krixtin," as Maddie had nicknamed them—walked up to us. Kristin was walking Olaf, who seemed timid, attempting to stay as far away from Krix as possible.

I quickly saw why Olaf was so scared. The quarterback was holding what appeared to be a giant kitten—but I knew it wasn't.

"Just wanted to introduce you to Dakota," he said, "our new snow leopard cub."

Some families had dogs as pets. Some had cats. The Krikorians had a *leopard*. I'm sure that was illegal in California, but so was underage drinking, and I don't think the congressman cared about either. The law just didn't seem to apply to him.

Even though Dakota looked harmless, I knew that she would grow up to be a vicious predator one day. For that reason, I was terrified.

"You can pet her," Krix offered. "She doesn't bite."

Since I didn't want to look like a wuss for refusing to pet a *baby* animal, I reached out my finger and gently stroked Dakota's fuzzy body.

"Mwrrr," she cooed, baring her tiny teeth at me. I pulled my finger away at that instant.

"She likes you," Krix said.

Sure, she likes me. She likes my index finger, for dessert.

Maddie and Leo then ran up to the four of us. Maddie was nursing a lime-green apple martini. Leo's face was covered in Maddie's Charlotte Tilbury lipstick.

"Wanna play Truth or Dare?" Leo enthusiastically asked.

All of us agreed. I mean, one simply does not say *no* to Truth or Dare when asked to play.

It was my first time playing the infamous teen party game. I had no idea what to expect.

10

TRUTH OR DARE?

When Larry and I finished eating, we joined the others inside the pool house. Most of my new friends were also there, including Hannah, Kylie, the Garcias, and Alang. I made sure to sit as far away as possible from Maddie to avoid her asking me a question or giving me a dare—at all costs.

Sebastian went first. He chose "dare," and Larry dared him to belly flop in the pool.

He joyfully made a break for the water, dashing out of the pool house and onto the travertine before finally faceplanting into the deep end at top speed. "Ow!" he shrieked as he hoisted himself out of the water. "That really hurt, Larry!"

Larry shrugged. "Still better than getting hit by Marty McLoughlin."

"That's for sure," he agreed.

Kylie was up next. "Truth," she said. "Ask me something hard."

Sebastian paused for a second before asking the most

generic Truth or Dare question ever. "Who was your first love?"

Kylie struggled to answer. Her face turned white like a sheet. "Uh—dare," she stammered. Per game rules, if you refused to do either a truth or dare, you *had* to do the other option, or you got eliminated from the game.

Sebastian then dared Kylie to cartwheel across the room. She stood on her hands and gracefully propelled herself from one end of the pool house to the other—and back. "Done and done!" she yelled in victory. Soccer, football, *and* cartwheeling—with a *sprained knee* to boot. What couldn't she do?

Then it was Hannah's turn. She chose "truth."

"What was the most embarrassing thing that has ever happened to you?" Kylie asked her.

Hannah grimaced. "Oh jeez. Well, when I was in fifth grade, I was cast as Dorothy in my school's production of *The Wizard of Oz*. During the premiere, I was singing 'Somewhere over the Rainbow,' and out of nowhere, my voice cut out. For literally half of the song, I was awkwardly mouthing the words with *no sound*."

We all laughed. That was a pretty embarrassing story—especially knowing how seriously Hannah took her acting roles.

I then realized I was sitting to Hannah's right, which meant that *she* was going to ask me "truth or dare." I tensed up. She might have already agreed to go out with me, but I still was nervous as I didn't want to say or do something that could make her back out.

"Okay, Charlie," she said, "you're up. Truth or dare."

"Dare!" I boldly chose.

"I'm gonna make you regret this," Hannah said, smiling at me.

Oh, God. What in the world is she going to make me do?

Hannah continued. "Since I told everyone about *my* singing debacle, I *have* to dare you to perform a live song—with the band."

For starters, I was a *terrible* singer. I was so bad I was even embarrassed to sing in the shower out of fear that Maddie would hear me. Now she had to witness me sing, as did all my friends—and Hannah.

The things I do for a pretty girl, I thought.

"Is there any particular song you want me to sing?" I asked her.

"No," Hannah replied, "just surprise us and wow us."

"Oh, he's gonna *wow* us, all right," Maddie sarcastically remarked.

I walked across the length of the pool to the grotto, where the band was wrapping up their cover of an eighties hair metal song. Krix had to come along with me to make sure they obeyed my request. After all, his dad was paying them handsomely.

The four-piece band was a motley collection of men, all in their early to mid- twenties. Their name, "Run of the Bulldogs," was etched in bold typeface on the outside head of the bass drum. The lead singer sported a spiky jet-black hairstyle with a goatee, and a single fake diamond stud in his left ear.

When he finished singing, I turned to him. "Hey, I just wanted to let you know that I—uh like your music!"

"Thanks, man," he said. He then pointed to the guitarist, a serious-looking man with heavy eye makeup and a presumably Jimi Hendrix-inspired afro, who masterfully strummed a five-second solo.

"Any requests?" the lead singer asked me.

This was my time. "Actually—uh, I was wondering if I could sing a song with you guys. It's for Truth or Dare and—uh, I was dared to do it."

Krix gave the band a thumbs-up. It was the cue they were looking for.

"I remember Truth or Dare," the singer reminisced. "Hell of a game. What song did they put you up to do?"

Hannah told me she wanted to be *surprised*. I thought of all the songs I knew the words to and ultimately settled on an oldie—but a goodie.

"Let's do 'I'm Henery the Eighth, I am'!" I declared. I had learned the song from watching *Ghost*, one of my mom's favorite movies. I figured it was very fitting since I was playing an English king in the school play. Hannah would appreciate it.

The drummer turned to the band's front man in flat-out confusion. His hair was in a skin-fade faux-hawk, and his neck was enrobed in a sea of colorful tattoos. Judging from his face, he was clearly the youngest member of the band, probably no more than three or four years older than I was. "What the hell is that?" he asked. "Never heard of that song."

The lead singer scoffed at him. "Just take a smoke, Jared. I'll play the drums on this one." He then took his place behind the drum set as a still confounded Jared exited the stage equipping himself with a cigarette.

The bass player, a tall, scary-looking fellow with greasy, long brown hair and a studded snakeskin leather biker jacket, stared motionlessly at me. He was giving me the creeps.

I sidled toward the mic. I noticed a giant crowd had formed between the pool and the grotto. My friends who had all come out from the pool house to watch me perform my "dare" formed the front row. I usually would have been consumed with stage fright, but with several beers inside of me, I had let my guard down a little.

"Let's go, Charlie!" Hannah cheered as the band began playing the first few bars of the song.

I moved the mic closer to my face. "I'm En-er-ry the Eighth, I am!" I belted in my best Cockney British accent. "En-er-ry the Eighth, I am!"

I was a little—well, a lot—off-key, but my friends and the rest of the audience seemed to love it. They clapped along as I continued the song.

Both Hannah and Kylie were wildly dancing. Even Maddie was getting into the groove.

"En-er-ry," the partygoers howled in reply. I might not have been Tom MacDonald, but I was putting on quite the show.

I continued, "En-er-ry the Eighth, I am!"

I thought I was done for a second, but I quickly remembered that I still had half of the song to go.

I repeated the chorus one more time. The crowd was even rowdier than before. *This is probably how Justin Bieber feels.*

"En-er-ry the Eighth, I am!" I finished with a bit of a vocal flourish and threw the mic in the air, catching it with my hands.

The audience thunderously applauded. I boastfully bowed and jumped off of the stage.

"And *that's* how you do a dare!" I declared to Hannah, slapping her a high-five.

"Well done," she replied, impressed. "If only *Richard III* was a musical."

Maddie ran up to me, smiling, with Leo at her side. "Oh my God! That was hysterical!"

I thanked my sister as the crowd dispersed. Then we all trekked back to the pool house to finish the game. On our way back, Larry turned to me.

"Awesome job, bro," he said, "but you know, it was a bit weird you sang *that* song considering Henry the Eighth's father *killed* Richard the Third."

I looked at him, surprised. Yes, I happened to know that already, having taken European History in addition to reading up on the historical character I was portraying. But I was shocked that *Larry* knew.

"I had no idea you were a history guy." I had thought of him as only a jock.

"Yep, there's *a lot* about me you don't know."

I instantly thought about his brief disappearance in the morning. It was just best to leave it alone, I figured.

My friends and I finished playing Truth or Dare. When we all had one turn, Maddie and Leo ran off by themselves to who-knows-where. *Young love*, I thought, which was what my mom would often sardonically remark in their presence. Neither of them had any idea what "love" actually was. For the record, I didn't either.

The rest of us decided to take a long soak in one of the Krikorians' hot tubs. As Larry turned the jet to the max, I climbed into the comfortably hot, effervescent water. I wedged myself between Kylie and Hannah, who both looked simply stunning in their bikinis—the two of them could have been on the cover of *Sports Illustrated's* Swimsuit Edition in a few years. I didn't want the party to end.

The next few hours went by in a blink of an eye. After being in the hot tub for at least twenty minutes, Larry, Jeremy, Sebastian, Alang, and I had the *genius* idea to take a swim. As I jumped into the deep end, my entire body became limp and overwhelmed by the biting temperature drop from the hot tub. I briefly froze in place. For a second, it was like I had hurled myself into a vat of liquid nitrogen.

"Brrrrr! That's c—cold!" I protested while shivering.

Alang chuckled. "That ain't cold. The San Francisco Polar Bear Plunge, now *that's* cold."

I dried off, changed back into my shorts, and went back inside the house to down a couple more glasses of beer. Krix showed me his massive state-of-the-art game room, where

Kylie and I played a ping pong match. She smoked me—scoring eleven points to my measly two. *Ouch.*

I returned to the yard to partake in the lavish dessert buffet, complete with a gigantic chocolate fondue station. I gleefully dunked a generous boatload of freshly baked Bavarian pretzels, Czech pirouette cookies, and skewers stacked with marshmallows, apples, peaches, and mangos into the oozingly rich, chocolatey cascade. It was decadently delightful.

Before long, I had found myself lazily lounging underneath the crown of an olive tree, with Larry a few feet from me. It was deep into the night, yet most students were in no rush to leave the party. The next day was Saturday, after all. It was pitch black. The only light I saw was emanating from the numerous stars that sprinkled the night sky. I was not wearing a watch, nor did I bother to look at my phone, so I had not an inkling of what the time was. But, if I had to guess, I would say it was 11:30 p.m., at the very earliest.

All of a sudden, I saw Maddie run up to me at breakneck speed.

"Charlie!" she shouted as she sprinted toward me. There was an urgent, uneasy tone in her voice. "Charlie!"

She *never* sought my attention like that. Usually, she couldn't care less about me. Something had to be up.

"What is it, Maddie?" I answered, half out of it.

She looked at me as tears streamed down her face. "It's awful. Leo and I had a fight. He's breaking up with me."

11

THE WALK

"He's what?" I asked in disbelief. It seemed that there was no way *this* could have been happening. They were all lovey-dovey just an hour before.

"It's over!" Maddie sobbed feverishly as she threw her arms around my body.

Wow, if she was actually hugging me, it must have been bad.

"Calm down," I said, trying to be the *adult* in the situation. "So, take me through what happened."

"He was like saying that I didn't spend enough time with him or something! Like all I do is go on TikTok and Insta and Snap!"

That is a true statement, but I don't think it would be a good idea to say that.

Maddie put her face on my shoulder and cried even harder than before. "I *loved* him!" she wept. "He was my first boyfriend! Now he's gone."

Having not even been on my first date, I was literally the *worst* person to help my sister through this situation. I anxiously looked to Larry for help. "Larry!" I loudly whispered. "You know more about this stuff than me."

"Come on. Let's take a walk," he suggested. "The three of us. We can talk it out."

Maddie, Larry, and I got up from the shelter of the tree and walked back toward Krix's giant house.

Larry turned to Maddie. "I remember my first girlfriend," he calmly stated—though he was beginning to tear up a little himself. "Her name was Mollie. Mollie Flannery. She had the most beautiful blue eyes and soft, delicate cheekbones. And the prettiest, most melodic laugh too. Man, I loved that laugh."

"And?" Maddie asked, still crying uncontrollably. "Get to your point."

"Well, early one afternoon, I was walking home from scout camp. I just received my basket-weaving merit badge, and I spent hours making this intricately woven reed basket. I was going to surprise her with a romantic picnic—either that or just give it to her for her to put her makeup in. When I was about halfway back to town, I heard her sweet, innocent laugh, coming from behind a boysenberry bush. I could pick that laugh out from a mile away."

Maddie cut him off. "And?"

"Well, I—uh. I—uh looked behind the bush, and would you know, there was Mollie passionately making out with Gary Finkelhouser. So, I took that basket, and I threw it into the nearby stream—along with any future the two of us had."

I could tell Larry was getting heated just by recalling the scene. He took a second to cool down before resuming.

"Anyway," Larry continued, "my point is heartbreak is just a fact of life. The first one always hits the hardest, but you learn to live and deal with it over time. You compartmentalize. You will find someone who will love and accept you for *who* you are. I know I will too. I have faith in the man upstairs." As he said that, he pointed up toward the starry sky.

"Look, thanks for talking to me," Maddie stated, "but I want *my* Leo back! He's the one!"

Although Larry was helping, it still wasn't enough to get my sister out of her funk. What she really needed was a female perspective.

As we re-entered the mansion, we approached Hannah and Kylie, talking to each other by the end of the Krikorians' great room. Maybe one of them could help Maddie.

Hannah caught sight of Maddie's teary eyes. "What's wrong, Maddie?" she asked compassionately.

"Maddie and Leo broke up," I bluntly answered out of turn.

"That's rough," replied Kylie, who also looked at my sister with concern.

Instead of responding, Maddie just continued to bawl her eyes out.

"We were going to take a walk to clear our heads," I said. "It would be cool if you girls came. Maddie could *really* use your advice."

"Maybe we can leave the party a bit earlier as well," Larry added. "I'm starting to get tired."

"Me too," I agreed, yawning. My first time actually drinking was starting to get to me.

"It's funny you say that," Kylie replied. "I was just about to get going myself. I have Saturday soccer practice tomorrow morning."

"And me too," said Hannah. "I was actually asking Kylie to drive me home."

The five of us decided that it was best to get going before it got too late. All of us were exhausted, and Maddie seemed like she wanted to get as far away as possible from her new ex-boyfriend. We made tracks toward the road where Larry and Kylie parked.

On our way out, Maddie was explaining the details of her breakup to the girls. "And he was like, 'Maddie-Moo, you are not ready to have a boyfriend,' and I was like, 'What do you mean, of course I am.'"

"One step at a time," Kylie counseled her. "What made him think you were not *ready*?"

"I don't know," Maddie replied, lost for words. My sister was always the confident, self-assured one of us two. I had never seen her as broken down as she was.

"Well, why do you think he said that?" Hannah asked her.

"I don't know!" Maddie was getting frustrated. "He kept saying that I go on TikTok too much. And I was like, duh, of course, I do. I'm gonna be a TikTok star!"

"Commitment is an important part of any successful

relationship," Hannah remarked. "Maybe Leo just didn't think you were committed to *him*."

"But I *was too* committed to him! I know I might not be perfect, but he needs to give me a second chance! He was my first boyfriend!"

"Look," Kylie jumped in, "just because he was your first, that absolutely doesn't mean he has to be your last. You're only fifteen. Your entire life is in front of you. There's plenty of fish in the sea."

The girls spoke back and forth, trying to console Maddie, but it didn't seem like anything was getting through to her. Our group checked out with the guards and exited the Krikorian estate for the last time. The party was an amazing experience while it lasted, but we didn't want to overstay our welcome.

As we walked down the road, silence filled the air. Although the party was quite loud when we left, we couldn't hear a thing, even from a few hundred feet away. It was clear that the congressman had soundproofed his entire estate. That, and the fact that his closest neighbor was a reasonable distance away, showed how he could get away with serving alcohol to minors every time.

We were about halfway to our cars when we spotted a dozen little lights in the distance. They seemed to be getting closer as every second went by. I quickly realized that they were bicycle reflectors.

These kids are late to the party. It started like five hours ago.

A MATTER OF TIME

As we got closer to the bikes, they kept picking up speed. We were on a collision course toward them.

These bikers weren't headed toward the party.

They were headed toward *us*.

12

THUGS ON BIKES

It was too late to turn around. The gang had already closed in on us.

There were at least ten of them—perhaps as many as fifteen. They ranged from Maddie's age to their mid- to late twenties. What they all shared in common were their threatening appearances and ripped physiques—I would have been dead if I had to fight any of those guys one-on-one. As they came closer, I could see that each of them was wearing a matching snakeskin leather jacket brandishing an image of a green serpent next to the letter "K." It looked familiar—I'd seen that logo before. I just couldn't remember where.

In no time, the gang members caught up to the five of us. Some stopped their bikes right in front of where we were. Others immediately flocked to the sides and the back of my group. They had us encircled.

One of the older men, who also happened to be the

largest, placed his kickstand down, hopped off his bike, and inched toward Larry. I was petrified.

He placed a bony finger in Larry's face. "Did you bring my weed?" he growled.

"Sir, you must be mistaken," Larry said, holding up his hands. "I don't smoke weed. *None* of us here do."

"Well, I do sometimes," Kylie blurted before realizing her mistake. "But I don't think that's gonna help the situation."

The man completely ignored Kylie, and his eyes remained fixed on Larry. "Let me repeat myself! Where is it?"

"Sir, we're not here to cause any trouble. We're just a bunch of high schoolers on our way home from a party. That's all."

"We can do this the easy way or the hard way!" The man's grumbly voice was akin to a hacksaw. "Give me the weed, and I'll let you go. It's as easy as that."

"But you don't understand. You have the wrong people. We don't have any weed."

"Okay, so the hard way it is." The man waved his left arm, and a dozen or so *more* bicycles sped down the road at record speed. We were doomed.

How was it that all these gang members were allowed into the high-security gated community? This neighborhood was the safest in the city. Something just wasn't adding up.

Yelling for help didn't do us any good. We were already too far from the Krikorians' soundproofed house or any other house for that matter. Hannah immediately reached for her phone in a desperate attempt to text someone for help.

"I'll be taking that," another gang member barked as he snatched the phone right from her hand. Similarly, other men came around to all of us and grabbed our phones. The man personally harassing Larry gathered all five of them and roughly threw them into a burlap sack.

"You ain't going nowhere." The grumbly-voiced man eerily smirked.

Two gang members also went down the line, searching us for car keys. Since only Larry and Kylie had licenses, the gang confiscated their key sets, adding them to the sack. Now we really had no way of getting out.

With the second wave of gang members joining the first, there were now at least five of them for every one of us.

I was praying that *someone* would notice the commotion and call the police to help us. I then saw a single motorcycle ride up to the scene. *Could this be the police?* My hopes were quickly dashed when I saw that piloting it was none other than the scary-looking bass player from the party band. When I glimpsed at his jacket, I saw the same snake logo the other gang members were wearing. *So, that's where I've seen it before.*

He had been keeping tabs on us all this time and likely *planned* this attack. But why? What did *we* have that *they* wanted?

The motorcycle weaved through the bikes until it was almost an arm's length in front of me. The bass player then braked and idled his ride. He leaped off and thrust his face in front of mine.

"Hello, hello," he said, flipping his long hair out of his face so he could see us better. "I see you failed to bring my associate his weed. Not good—not good at all. Allow me to introduce myself. People call me Skull and Bones, and this is my posse, the K Street Kobras—that's Kobras with a K!" He contorted his arms to resemble a cobra in attack position with his right hand on top as its mouth. The rest of the members copied the gang sign at once.

Honestly, I was all but prepared to die at that moment. This "Skull" reminded me more of Freddy Kreuger than a petty street gang boss.

"These ain't the Jets or the Sharks," Hannah whispered to me, referring to the relatively harmless gangs in *West Side Story.*

Larry stammered. "Look—look, Mr. Bones. I was telling your friend before, we don't have any weed here." He emptied all his pockets to show him. I did the same. The girls also started removing some of the contents of their purses, showing that we weren't hiding anything. "See?" Larry said.

The gang leader wasn't impressed. "Mr. Bones was my father! I'm *Skull* and Bones."

Sweat began pooling on Larry's forehead.

I panicked. "Look, *Skull*—"

He cut me off. "*Skull and Bones!*"

"Look, Skull *and* Bones," I continued, frantically placing my hands on my chin, "we can—uh, make it up to you." Feeling that I was hanging on for dear life by a thread, I dug into my wallet and fanned a few bills at him. It was seventeen dollars, the only cash I had on me.

Larry, Maddie, Hannah, and Kylie followed my lead. As we held the money for the Kobras to see, one of the younger members quickly counted all of it. It came out to a total of ninety-six dollars and nineteen cents between all five of us.

After the kid conveyed the total amount to him, Skull and Bones cackled. His "laugh" sounded like a duck choking on a fish. "You think that's enough for us to let you go?!" he yelled.

They didn't want our money. They wanted our *lives*.

When it became clear that the gang had no interest in taking our wallets, Larry and I shoved them back in our pockets, and the girls placed theirs snugly in their purses.

"This is what's gonna happen," Skull and Bones continued. "I'm gonna take you to my boss, and he's gonna decide what happens to you."

Skull and Bones has a boss? I thought he was supposed to be the boss.

Just when it seemed like it couldn't get any worse, two red Ferraris zoomed up to the crowd. The bikers, expecting their arrival, made way for them. Two *more* Kobras from each car poured out. They popped open their trunk, pulling out rope and body bags. As I gazed at the empty trunk, it became clear that *we* were going to go in *there*.

"They can't be doing this all because of weed," Kylie cried out, stating the obvious.

The Kobras who were in the Ferraris threw the bags and ropes to their fellow members closest to where we were standing. The man blocking me from the front was nearly *double* my size. He effortlessly raised the bag and dangled it over my head. However, when he was about to pull it down over my helpless body, Kylie came to the rescue from my left side, roundhouse kicking the man squarely in the nuts.

The large man shrieked and winced in pain.

This event set off Skull and Bones, who reached for his belt, pulling out a Glock pistol. He cocked the gun at Kylie's forehead.

"You didn't need to do that, honey," he snarled. He slowly pointed it at each of us before placing it back in its holster. "All of you are gonna get in those bags. If not, *that's* gonna be the last thing you ever see. Did you hear me?"

None of us spoke.

What happened next was unclear. The last thing I remembered was Larry reaching for his jacket pocket like he was going to grab something. I then heard a loud hissing sound.

And in an instant, my entire world faded to black.

PART TWO

13

THE MORNING AFTER

I opened my eyes. The morning sky was bright blue and clear, apart from the occasional cirrus cloud. The sun was shining on me at full force.

I was lying on a seemingly endless grassy plain. Deerbrush and goldenrod sparsely dotted the ground. I could make out a few trees up ahead in the distance, but otherwise, the landscape was brazenly empty.

I pondered for a moment. *Have I died and gone to heaven?* If so, I was surprised by how bare it was.

I stretched my arms and legs and catapulted myself up onto my feet. I got a better view of the field. Kylie and Hannah were lying right next to me with Larry and Maddie a few feet away. In the next few seconds, the others also woke up, one by one. I was just happy everyone was still alive.

Hannah was the first to speak. "What happened? Did they capture us?"

"It looks like they did and dumped us here," Larry replied,

rubbing his eyes.

"But where is *here*?" questioned Maddie. She reached into her purse and poked around, searching for her beloved phone—to no avail. Seeing that reminded me that the Kobras had taken all of our phones and placed them in that burlap sack. We had no way to call for help, let alone look up where we were.

"There's only one way to find out." Kylie set out toward the trees. We followed her lead, hastily walking side by side.

As we came to the trees, we noticed that they were a fig grove. Toward the end of it, we saw a man picking the ripe figs and placing them into a bucket. He looked like one of those old-school farmers you would see on TV. He wore dirt-stained overalls, and on top of his head sat a wide-brimmed straw hat, probably to block the sunlight. A bushy salt-and-pepper mustache tickled his upper lip.

I politely walked over to the man. "Excuse me, sir," I said, "we're lost. We're trying—"

The farmer abruptly cut me off. "*What* the hell do you hippie punks think you're doing trespassing on *my* farm?" He pronounced the word "what" almost like "hwat"—similar to how I've heard some older people from the South or England say it.

I was slightly taken aback by his outright refusal to help us. "But—um we're actually—"

He didn't want to hear it. "Listen, son. This here farm is private property. You and your friends are gonna leave now or I'm calling the cops!" The farmer glanced over at Kylie,

Hannah, and then Maddie, and his anger partially turned into confusion. "I've never seen anyone dress like *that* before," he remarked. "You definitely ain't from around here."

Defeated, we continued walking into the distance. *Where are we?* I thought. *For all I know, we could be hundreds of miles away from home.*

After we left the farm, we soon found ourselves amidst a dense forest of ash and sycamore. Bluebirds and robins loudly chirped in the canopies. We pushed on through, following a narrow dirt path. A few yards away from us, a red fox frolicked, dragging the lifeless carcass of a squirrel.

"I'm scared," cried Maddie. "I've never been in the woods like this before."

"*This* scares you?" Larry responded. "Imagine if there were bears and mountain lions."

"I don't want to!" My little sister was frightened by the mere mention of dangerous wild animals.

Larry sighed. "It's a shame the younger generation doesn't appreciate the outdoors. I'm an Eagle Scout, and back in Alabama, my troop and I would go camping practically every other week. You learn so much about yourself when you're in the elements. And you also realize how much you take nature for granted."

I instantly thought of what my dad might have been like. According to my mom, he practically *lived* for the outdoors.

"Who needs nature?" snarked Maddie. "Plus, Mr. Grandpa Larry, I'm only like two years younger than you."

"Three," Larry corrected her. "I'm *eighteen*. So technically,

I'm an adult, and you're a *child*."

Maddie scowled at him. I ignored her the best I could.

After about twenty minutes of walking, we came to the edge of a slow-moving river.

"Wait, I know where we are," Kylie declared optimistically. "This has to be Woodward Park. I've been to this spot before—I think."

I shook my head. My mom used to take me to Woodward Park *religiously* when I was a kid. It was one of my favorite places to go. I had never been to an area that was so underdeveloped, like where we were standing.

I asked Larry—an Eagle Scout, after all—for advice on what to do next. He said that we should follow the river downstream in hopes of finding civilization—or at least one human being who would not threaten to call the cops on us. Having no other choice, we listened to him and set forth along the riverbank.

A half hour later, I spotted a road. Actually, it was better than a road. It was a freeway.

"Well done," I said to Larry.

"Thanks. Troop 363 didn't nickname me Larry the Navigator for no reason."

We made a left onto the freeway and began to follow it.

"Hey! It's Freeway 41!" Hannah noticed as she saw a sign on the roadside. "We can't be too far away from home!"

The sign might have *said* Freeway 41, but it did not remind me of the road that lay only ten minutes from my house. There were not as many cars as usual. Instead, there were more pickup trucks and eighteen-wheelers. Also, the few cars I did see didn't look like any of the modern, primarily foreign automobiles that usually graced Fresno's city streets. It must have meant that we were in the countryside.

"This isn't Fresno, though," I concluded. "This is somewhere farther down on Freeway 41."

"Google Maps would come in handy right now," Kylie stated.

"I hope I get my phone back when we're home," Maddie butted in, now sounding more annoyed and inconvenienced than scared.

In a short amount of time, we stumbled upon a diner adjacent to a humongous gas station. The rest area loomed large in front of us on the right side of the freeway. The restaurant's name, Freedom Café, was displayed in a giant neon sign, eye-catching even during daylight. A long convoy of eighteen-wheelers queued in its parking lot.

"Look at that, a truck stop diner!" shouted Larry. "Our prayers are answered!"

"We can kill two birds with one stone!" exclaimed Hannah. "A delicious breakfast *and* directions home!"

"I can go for a Western omelet right now," I added, rubbing my stomach.

"That's like animal cruelty three times over," remarked Kylie. "And don't get me started on that talk of killing birds." She glared at Hannah. It didn't seem like Kylie cared that it was only a figure of speech.

"Let's just agree to disagree," I responded. "I, for one,

happen to love animals—I just can't help that I also think they're *delicious.*"

We all checked our wallets to make sure we could even pay for breakfast. Oddly enough, all of us had the same amount of money we had the night before. The gang didn't even bother to steal a single dollar.

"That's strange," said Hannah. "Why would those Kobras—or whatever they called themselves—capture us if it wasn't for money?"

We all briefly checked our possessions to see what we had left. It appeared that we had everything we had when we left the party aside from our phones and car keys.

Kylie shrugged. "Probably to steal our cars and phones. Or perhaps it was just mainly a power trip. Sometimes street gangs just pull crap like that in their 'territory,' so more people suck up to them."

We entered the restaurant. We were greeted by an attractive hostess with a voluminous platinum blonde haircut and a red headband. She was wearing a long blue button-down shirt with a name tag that read "Shelley."

"Welcome to the Freedom Café! How many today?"

"Uh—five," I told her, "and—uh—by the way, we were wandering around here and are kinda lost right now. Where are we?"

"Why you're in Fresno, of course!" Shelley answered quite exuberantly.

So, Kylie was right. We weren't far from home after all. Still, something seemed a bit off.

"May I please borrow your cell phone?" I asked Shelley. I wanted to call my mom to make sure she knew Maddie and I were okay. Since we hadn't come home the last night, she had to be worried sick about us.

Shelley looked at me like a lost ball in the high weeds. "I beg your pardon? My *what*?" She said "what" in a similar manner to the farmer, albeit less pronounced.

"Your cell phone," I repeated, making sure I didn't slur my words.

"A *cell* phone? By golly, the *prison* is a mile away!"

Also, like the farmer, Shelley only made things worse when we asked her for help. "Forget it. Let's just get seated," I said.

She led us to an empty booth in the corner from the restaurant. It had been a while since I had set foot in a traditional Americana diner. A broken miniature jukebox was mounted on the wall next to our booth. On the opposite side of the restaurant, a tiny TV set dangled from the ceiling, complete with bunny ears antennae. We crammed our five bodies into the minuscule space.

Maddie spoke first. "That headband lady was nuts! How could she not have a cell phone! Like, I had an iPhone when I was six."

"It's not just the fact that she didn't have a cell phone," Kylie clarified. "It was like she didn't even know what a cell phone *is*."

I looked around the dining room, and oddly enough, I didn't see *any* customers on their phones—not one. Some were reading newspapers. Others were smoking—yes, *inside* the building. "I know she said this is Fresno, but I've never been to a part like *this*," I said. "This ain't the Fresno I know. It's Hicktown, USA."

"Since you guys feel uncomfortable here, do you just want to leave and go somewhere else?" asked Hannah.

"It's okay," said Kylie, twirling her hair. "I mean, we're all starving, and this is the only place with food we've seen the entire morning. Who knows, there might not be another place to eat for at least another few miles."

"She's right," agreed Larry. "And not to mention, these prices are *insanely* cheap." He pointed to his open menu. "A dollar fifty for a Western omelet? You can't even get that deal at Taco Bell."

"Don't tell Alang that," I joked. "He thinks Taco Bell is the answer to all of the world's problems."

The waitress came by to take our order. Larry and I each got a Western omelet with home fries, toast (I got rye, and he got wheat), and four strips of bacon on the side. Hannah got pancakes, Maddie got French toast, and Kylie had to settle for oatmeal and fruit—it was the only vegan thing she could find on the breakfast menu. We all got coffees to drink, except for Maddie, who ordered a chocolate milk.

While we waited for the food, we took in some more of our surroundings. Classic country music, sung by the likes of Hank Williams and Patsy Cline, loudly played, filling the room.

"Can't they put some top forty hits on?" asked Kylie, not digging the diner's music selections. Larry and I weren't either.

"Country and pop music both suck," Larry chimed in. "I

want something with soul, like Otis Redding, '(Sittin' on) The Dock of the Bay.'" He tried to get the jukebox to work, but it was busted.

"Hey, I love country!" Hannah exclaimed.

"Me too!" screamed Maddie. "I hope they play Taylor Swift next!"

When the waitress brought us our food, we gobbled it down like it was our first meal in days. *It really could have been.* The gang very well could have held us hostage for more than one night—we just didn't remember it.

I turned my attention to the TV screen where the *Today Show* was on. However, the hosts I knew weren't there—instead, there were these two people I'd never seen before—I think their names were Barbara and Jim. They were there droning on and on, talking about things I had only learned about in American History class—the Soviet Union, the Vietnam War, and Watergate. They also mentioned Elvis but talked about him in the *present* tense, like if he was still *alive.*

Then it all clicked for me. I put two and two together—the farmer calling us "hippies," the underdeveloped park and freeway, the fact that the hostess didn't know what a cell phone was, and the bizarrely low prices on the menu.

No. It can't be. That's—that's—impossible. I had to see it to believe it.

I excused myself from the table. Not wasting a second, I ran to the front of the diner, where I grabbed the first morning newspaper I could get my hands on.

And there it was, in plain sight, on the top right-hand corner of the front page—the day's date.

September 9, 1974.

14

BACK TO THE PAST

I was floored. Somehow when the gang attacked us, my friends, my sister, and I were transported forty-eight years into the past. My entire life, I had heard that time travel was nothing but fiction. Now, it was my new reality.

I returned to the table with the newspaper in my hands. I didn't say a word. I just passed it around for everyone to take a look. Once the paper had made the rounds, there was deafening silence amongst my friends. It persisted for nearly a minute. None of us could believe that all of this was actually happening.

"So, now what?" Maddie finally said.

"We're gonna have to go back to the future," Kylie answered honestly.

"Now's not the time for jokes or references to eighties movies," Larry sternly reprimanded her.

"I wish we were in the eighties," replied Hannah. "At least it's closer to 2022 than where we are *now.*"

"And also," added Larry, "how the hell are we gonna pay for this meal?" He scratched his head. "We have money from *2022*. No wonder the Kobras didn't take it. We might as well have Monopoly money."

"We're gonna have to come clean," I answered. "Well, at least somewhat. We tell the waitress that a gang robbed us, and they replaced all our real money with 'funny money' with the wrong dates."

It wasn't the best idea, but it was the only one we had. The waitress soon came by our table asking if we wanted our check. I told her that we were robbed—which wasn't a lie after all—and handed her the modern money.

As she palmed through the bills and felt the coins, she burst out laughing. "This is the worst counterfeit I've ever seen in the twenty-plus years I've been working here. And believe me, I've seen a lot."

"What's so bad about it?" I asked, making an effort not to blow my cover.

"The pennies aren't even made out of copper!" the waitress said. "And come on, we all know that by *2022* we'll be using computerized money!"

All of us except Maddie forced a laugh.

The smile then faded from the waitress's face. "Unfortunately, though, you guys still have to pay your bill, all eleven dollars and forty-four cents of it!"

I was scared. I didn't want all of us to get arrested over *eleven bucks*. "But—but what if we can't?" I asked.

When the waitress was about to answer, a silver-haired

man dining alone at the adjacent table stood up and walked over to us. He was wearing a gray suit and a cream-colored fedora. The man looked like he was in his early sixties, although he could have been older. "I'll pay for them." He slid the waitress a twenty-dollar bill. "Keep the change. The rest is for your tip."

The mystery man had not only paid our entire bill, but he had also left a seventy-five percent tip. My mom, who used to waitress herself, was known for being a generous tipper, and she would only give twenty-five, *maybe* thirty percent.

"Thank you so much, sir!" I said to him. "You bailed us out—literally."

He smiled at me and shook my hand. "It's Al," he replied. "You can call me Al. And the pleasure's all mine. I live for moments like these where I can perform random acts of kindness for strangers."

Well, his gesture sure went a long way for us. After Al paid our bill, we left the Freedom Café in a rush and continued walking south on Freeway 41.

"What are we doing?" Maddie asked.

I tried to answer, but I was drawing a blank, as was everybody else. How to travel home from the past wasn't anything you could ask on Quora, after all.

"Maybe we can find a DeLorean," Kylie suggested.

Larry was not having it. "Are you out of your mind, Ky? First of all, that movie was one hundred percent fiction. And second of all, the DeLorean didn't come out until 1975, one full year from *now*."

I had to jump in to calm the squabble. "So, I was thinking about all of our choices, and there are only two things we can do," I said. "Option A is to accept that we are in 1974 for good and try our best to start new lives here. We might never see our families again—hell, they might never even be *born*."

"And what's Option B?" Hannah asked.

"Option B is that we actually find out *how* we got stuck here in 1974. Whatever it is—a time machine, magic car, or something else—we use that same method to get us *back to the future,* for lack of better terms. What got us here is bound to get us back."

"Okay, Marty McFly," Kylie replied.

"Hey, I'd still rather be him than Marty McLoughlin."

"But how are we going to find out what that gang actually did to get us here?" Larry asked. "Or why they sent us here, to begin with?"

"Well, I think we can all agree that the reason we're here has nothing to do with weed," said Kylie.

"Whatever the case is, it's gonna take us some time to work everything out," Larry stated. "We need to find shelter because we'll probably be in 1974 for quite a while."

"One thing about that," interjected Maddie. "We have no money."

"No money, no shelter," Hannah said. "We're pretty much homeless now."

"All we have are the clothes on our backs." Kylie rephrased it.

"Wait," said Larry. "You just said 'the clothes on our

backs.' That gave me an idea. Remember how the farmer was fascinated by our outfits? Especially you ladies." He looked at Hannah, Kylie, and Maddie, who were all wearing designer brands. It just so happened we all had on the same outfits we wore to Krix's party.

"I see where you're going, Larry," I said. "Please continue."

"Well, we're wearing stuff from 2022. In 1974, this kind of fashion has *never* been seen by anyone before. We're a half century ahead of trends. Imagine how much money we could get if we sold *all* our clothes to a pawn shop."

"But I don't want to sell my dress!" Maddie protested.

"We have no choice," said Hannah. "Do you think I want to part ways with mine either? I *love* Vineyard Vines. But it's that or go with Charlie's Option A."

Kylie, Larry, and I nodded in approval.

"Fine!" Maddie groaned. "If wearing lame hippie clothes is gonna help us get home, so be it."

I turned to Kylie. "I wonder if the pawn shop guy is gonna think my name is Levi because it's on my jeans."

"Well, once we get home and I see a Levi from 1974 in my history textbook, I will know it's you," she said.

With that in mind, we set out for downtown.

15

FILTHY PHIL'S

We trekked farther into the heart of Fresno and came across a tiny storefront at the bottom of a large apartment building. The shop was wedged right between a firearms dealer and a record store. A large wooden sign hung above the door: *Filthy Phil's Goodies: We buy your old stuff!* Without hesitation, we barged in.

The five of us were welcomed by a stout man, probably in his mid- to late thirties, wearing a tie-dyed Creedence Clearwater Revival shirt, Birkenstocks, and a necklace with a giant peace sign. He had not shaved in weeks, and his thin, wispy red hair was tied into a ponytail. *This must be Filthy Phil.*

"Greetings, travelers!" he warmly exclaimed. "What brings you to my emporium?"

I immediately turned to Kylie. She was the closest to a hippie out of the five of us. If *anyone* could speak this Phil guy's language, it was her.

"We're—uh from the commune down in the valley," she said. "A gang attacked us, and they stole all of our money."

"Man, that's a bummer," Phil responded. Yes, he called Kylie *man*. "So, what can I do for you dudes and dude-ettes?"

"Well," Kylie continued, making her story up as she went along, "we have these handmade clothes we're wearing right now, and we wanna see how much you can give us for them, and the other stuff we have—you know, to make up for the money the gang jacked from us."

Phil then analyzed each of our clothes. "Far out! I've never seen hippie clothes as beautifully detailed as the ones you all got on! I can definitely give you a haul for these. I'll tell you what." He pointed to a rack where cheap seventies shirts, shorts, and shoes were lying about—they were likely secondhand. "I'll include these in the price because you're obviously gonna have to wear *something*. Don't be like my old pal Streakin' Stu."

None of us asked Phil about this Stu character. Some things were better left unsaid.

As we were about to grab the clothes to change, Phil stopped us. "Wait," he said, "what commune did you say you came from? Maybe I know someone from there."

"Uh—I'm sure you don't," I replied, trying to divert the conversation.

Kylie jumped to my rescue. "Coachella," she replied, thinking on her feet.

"Coa—what?" questioned Phil. "I don't think I've heard of it before."

"Well, you're missing out," replied Kylie. "They have a huge music festival there every year."

Phil's eyes lit up with joy. "Like Woodstock?"

"Just like Woodstock—if not better."

"Groovy!"

We grabbed the clothes and made a dash to the back of the store. Since there was only one changing room, we had to take turns using it. Once we had finished, we regrouped with Phil, carrying all our clothing and possessions from 2022. We placed everything down on a folding table for him to take a look.

"Let's see what we got here." Phil sifted through the pile of clothes. He grabbed Larry's hoodie first. As he thoroughly inspected the logo on the front, his face displayed a baffled look. Under Armour," he said, reading the brand name. "So, you're telling me you wear this *under* something else?"

Larry slightly chuckled. "No sir. That's just what it's called."

"Interesting," Phil replied, placing the hoodie on a pile to his left. "I dig it."

He then held my checked American Eagle shirt up to the light. "Looks a little preppy," he stated. "Like something you'd wear to a Nixon rally."

I got a little anxious when he said that. I remembered from American History that hippies weren't particularly fans of Nixon, to say the least.

"But I see what this shirt is getting at," he continued, now smiling. "This is clearly a parody of those fuzz-loving yuppies and their lame fashion sense." He pointed at the small eagle logo on the pocket. "Yep, definitely one of *our* shirts." He stacked the shirt on top of Larry's hoodie.

Phil was even more impressed with the girls' dresses—particularly Hannah's Margo shirt dress. He closely examined its fabric, holding it up to his lamp. "Wow. This is a beauty. How long did it take you to sew this?"

Hannah tried to play along. "Uh—a week."

"That's unreal!" Phil replied. "My ex-girl couldn't make a dress half as good as this one in a *year*."

Phil then lifted Maddie's beloved Gucci watch. It was her second favorite thing in the entire world, after her phone, of course. When he viewed it, his face reeked of utter disgust. "Gucci!" he shrieked. "Those *fascist* Italians are good for nothing. Not even that cheese bread thing they eat."

Maddie was livid. He had insulted both Gucci *and* pizza.

"Gucci is the work of the Man!" Phil continued. "Be gone, watch!" He threw the diamond-studded watch into the trash can underneath the table, disposing of it like it was infested with the plague. "I don't know why you bother being friends with *her*," he said to the rest of us. "She's just one of them *sheeple*."

Maddie's face said it all—she was devastated. That watch meant a lot to her. It cost my mom at least two grand, at a minimum. She had splurged on it, spending almost all of her past year's bonus.

Once he had finished going through our clothes and jewelry, Phil turned to the girls' handbags. Hannah and Maddie both had Louis Vuitton bags. Phil felt the surface of the purses only to rapidly pull his hand away in disgust. He also proceeded to throw them in the trash.

"Leather?" he replied. "Who do you think I am? That's animal murder."

Kylie smiled in agreement. "I will assure you, Phil, my bag is one hundred percent vegan."

Phil touched the relatively cheap bag, which Kylie had probably gotten from a craft fair, and nodded. "Yep. This is what all them pocket-bags should be made out of." He placed the purse on top of his "good" pile.

Phil finished gathering all of the emptied contents from the girls' bags—their wallets (except Maddie's leather one, of course), makeup, lipstick, lotion. He had us cleaned of almost everything. Following suit, Larry and I also placed the items that were in our pockets on the table. We needed all the money we could get.

I happened to have a Lego figurine of Darth Vader buried in the lining of my front left jeans pocket. Pasta had lent it to me during my last sleepover at his house because I had misplaced the one from my own Lego Star Wars set. I meant to give it back to him on the first day of senior year—but we had our falling out.

Phil picked up the tiny, plastic Sith lord, complete with an inch-long red lightsaber, and carefully studied it. "What is this?" he asked. I remembered that *Star Wars* didn't come out until three years after 1974.

Trying to appease Phil, I responded, "The Man, of course."

He nodded. "Far out," he said, as he placed it on his

windowsill, next to a dreamcatcher.

I quickly wondered if he would sue George Lucas for "plagiarizing" him once the first *Star Wars* movie actually came out.

Once we had no more stuff to give Phil, he pulled out his clunky printing calculator and speedily punched a series of numbers. When he was finished, he ripped out the receipt and presented it to us. "Your total reimbursement comes out to one thousand twenty-six dollars and eighty-five cents!"

All of us were smiling ear to ear—except for Maddie, who was still heartbroken about losing her watch *and* purse. *Over a thousand bucks? And in 1974 money!* I thought we'd get a few hundred at the very most. I was pleasantly surprised—no, more like thrilled.

Phil handed us the money, and we evenly split it among the five of us. We thanked him and walked out of the shop.

"Well, that went better than expected," I said to the rest of the group.

"Are you kidding me!" cried an enraged Maddie. "That watch was *everything* to me, and the hippy-dippy guy just threw it out like a piece of trash! First, I lost my boyfriend, then my phone, then my Gucci watch." I found it very interesting how she put Leo in the same category as two inanimate objects.

"You know you could've just told him to take it out of the trash, right?" I said. "He seemed like a very nice guy—I'm sure he wouldn't have cared."

Maddie's face turned white as a sheet. Her eyes darted

back at Filthy Phil's, which was now a couple of blocks behind us. She began to cry. "He would never have listened to me. He *hated* that watch, and my Louis Vuitton bag, and me!"

I quickly realized that I was partly to blame. *If only I didn't just stand there and do nothing while Phil threw Maddie's watch away.* I was a crappy big brother sometimes.

Larry glanced at Maddie with concern before turning to me and then the rest of us. "Look," he said, "I'm the oldest, so I gotta be the adult here. We have bigger fish to fry than a dumb watch. Remember, we're in *1974*."

"And we do have a thousand bucks," said Hannah.

"A thousand bucks is *nothing*," replied Larry. "Even in 1974's money. We need a place to stay, a car to get us around, food and gas." He then asked if anyone had something to write on, and Hannah passed him a small notebook and a pen from her pocket—the only things she didn't give Phil. Larry flipped to an open page and began to jot down some numbers. "Okay," he continued. "Let's see. So, the cheapest hotel we can probably find around here would be something like a Motel 6."

"They leave the light on for you," I noted, referencing their commercials.

"Now's not the time for this," he replied. "Anyway, I remember learning from the last time I stayed there that they used to charge six dollars a room a night in the sixties and seventies. Hence the name. So, two rooms means we're paying at least twelve bucks a night for lodging."

"Two rooms?" Maddie interjected. "But there's five of us."

"We're getting two rooms. Deal with it. It's either that or we sleep on the street."

Maddie quieted down once she realized just how dire the situation was.

"As for food," Larry went on, "based on the prices at the diner, I say we can get by spending *at most* three bucks, per meal, per person. So that's forty-five bucks a day. Car rental, I'm not quite sure, but if we're going with the cheapest clunker we can find, I'd guesstimate five bucks a day at a minimum. And gas, using the prices I saw at the truck stop, would be at least twenty dollars a week."

Larry took a minute to do some math. "So, if we do the bare minimum to keep us alive, we're spending $454 a week. And that's without *any* incidentals. So pretty much, we're looking at running out of the entire $1,026.85 in two weeks."

"Two weeks!" shouted Kylie. "That's not nearly enough time for us to find the gang and figure out how to get back home."

"Maybe we should get jobs," Hannah suggested.

Larry shook his head profusely. "That sounds like a great idea until you realize that none of us *exist* right now. We're not born yet. So that means if we got jobs, they would have to be off the books, and if our covers get blown, we'd be in *big* trouble."

"But wait," I said, "since we don't exist and have no valid ID, how would we even be able to rent a car?"

"It's funny you say that," said Larry as he formed a partial smile. He reached into his wallet and pulled out a faded

Alabama driver's license. As he showed it to me, I saw that the person pictured looked very similar to Larry, except for his hairstyle. Its expiration date was in 1975. Once I saw the name, I knew exactly who it belonged to—William Travers.

"Your uncle Bill's license from the seventies!" I exclaimed. "That's genius—random but genius."

"That's awesome you have it now, Larry, but why?" Kylie asked.

"Well, when I was running errands the other day, my uncle asked me to give it to Geico for some veterans' promotion or something. I honestly don't really remember what it was. Then I had that thing for my friend I had to do, and I completely forgot it was still on me."

"That's weird," commented Maddie. "Why did he still have it after all this time? Couldn't he have just thrown it out—like my watch?" She *still* wasn't over it.

Larry shrugged. "Uncle Bill is a—well, let's just call him a *pack rat*. That guy literally has one room filled with nothing but the *thousands* of model airplanes he has collected since he was a kid. He also has tons of vinyl records—most of them broken—books of postage stamps, even random stuff like those creepy Russian dolls. Throwing stuff away is just not something he does—ever."

"I guess it's just our luck," I replied. "We could use a break for once."

We continued walking downtown and soon found a garage, where Larry, pretending to be his uncle Bill, picked up our rental car—a faded green 1968 Datsun Sunny four-door sedan.

It might not have been as good-looking as Larry's Stingray, but it could fit all of us and get us from point A to point B.

After the transaction was finalized, we hopped in the car, and Larry drove us to the closest Motel 6, which had to suffice as our new home for the time being.

Once we had settled in, Larry and I called Maddie, Hannah, and Kylie over to our room to game plan the next few days. Though before we could get started, the girls began to voice their grievances.

"For the record, Maddie was right about getting two rooms. There's three of us and only two beds," Kylie complained.

"And she snores," Hannah said, pointing at Kylie.

"No, I don't," Kylie defended herself.

"Yeah, you do," Maddie agreed.

"Girls! Girls!" Larry shouted. "Complaining ain't gonna get us anywhere but 1975!"

I got the conversation back on track. "So, let's start with what we know about this gang." I paused and racked my brain before continuing. Little came to mind as the gang's capture of us was a blur to me. "They were called the Kobras—with a K. That is as much as I remember."

"The *K Street* Kobras," Hannah added.

"And they were all decked out in that creepy leather that resembled snakeskin," replied Kylie.

"Their leader's name was Skull and Bones or something," remarked Maddie.

Larry looked at Hannah. "You just said K Street, didn't you?"

"Yeah, that's what I remember that Skull guy saying."

Larry shot her a thumbs-up. "That might be the lead we need to start our investigation." He pulled out a large map of Fresno we had taken from the hotel lobby because we didn't have phones to help us get around.

I put my finger to the map and began to furiously look for K Street. *Duh, that's where we'll find them*, I thought. However, I couldn't find it—anywhere.

"That's strange," I said. "There's no K Street in downtown Fresno."

"There's no I or J Street either," noted Larry. "It goes H Street, Broadway Street, Fulton Street, Van Ness Avenue, then L Street. What genius came up with that idea?"

I saw a lightbulb go off in Kylie's head. "I figured out where they're based," she said. "It's Van Ness, without a doubt."

"What makes you say that?" I asked.

"You may not know this about me, but I grew up in one of the poorest sections of downtown Fresno. I lived there until I was twelve—until my parents saved up enough money to move us to the nicer part of town. Street gangs constantly ravaged my old neighborhood. I had many friends who lost family members to gang violence. So, I do know a little more than I should about how these local gangs operate."

"Please do go on."

"Well, many of the gangs I have encountered use a code for where their hideout is to throw off the cops and rival gangs."

"How clever," I said. "So, since Van Ness Avenue is actually where K Street is *supposed* to be, it makes sense that's where the Kobras are based."

"Bingo." Kylie smiled at me. I was thankful to have someone with street smarts with us.

"This sounds great and all, but why 1974?" Hannah questioned. "And why *us*?"

Larry yawned. "I think we had enough for today. Let's get some sleep. We all sure need it."

Larry and I said good night to the girls, and as soon as they left, we turned off the lights and went right to bed. Tomorrow was a new day.

16

A TRIP TO THE LIBRARY

Early the following day, we all headed over to the Fresno County Public Library. We came to dig up as much dirt on the Kobras that we could possibly find. As I walked inside the large brick building, I could see that it was teeming with visitors of all ages. Everyone seemed to be with a book in hand—either reading one, looking for one, or checking one out. Across from us, a man in a suit sat in an armchair. He was engrossed in his copy of *Adventures of Huckleberry Finn.* I had been to the library plenty of times before, but I had never seen it as packed as it was in 1974. It sure was a simpler time before technology ruled the world.

I was born in 2005, so the Internet had been around the entire time I'd been alive. If you asked me to research something, I'd simply Google it and click on the first result I found—usually Wikipedia. I had *never* conducted research the old-fashioned way before—at a library with books and monstrous, clunky encyclopedias.

As we made our way to the reference area, I gazed upon the vast assortment of books housed in the library. There had to have been *thousands*. We were hoping that out of all of them, one could help us get back to the present day.

As a starting point for our sleuthing, we asked the librarian for a general reference book on Fresno's history. She handed us a gargantuan, dusty encyclopedia—aptly named the *Encyclopedia of Fresno*. I placed the book on the table and flipped to the index in the back, where I searched for the word "gang." I soon found it and noticed that five page numbers were written underneath it: 169, 288, 353, 367, and 590. Working as a team, we flipped to each indicated page and carefully read their contents. Although the first four pages contained extensive material on some of the gangs in Fresno, no pieces of information popped out to any of us as being particularly useful.

Finally, I turned to page 590. I immediately focused my eyes on a black-and-white photograph of a young, long-haired Latino man wearing a snakeskin jacket. Each of us silently read the caption underneath: *Arturo Bonilla, founder and first leader of the Nessies, a downtown Fresno gang. Bonilla was captured by the police in 1968 and committed suicide in prison just a few months later, marking the end of one of the most notorious crime organizations in the city's century-long history.*

Once I finished, I had a eureka moment. Bonilla—Bones, as in *Skull* and Bones. The Nessies—Van Ness Avenue. This *had* to be the Kobras. But didn't the encyclopedia say the gang disbanded after Bonilla died?

"That looks just like him," Hannah said. "Spitting image."

"You think Bones time traveled?" I asked.

Larry shook his head. "It's more likely that he's his grandson or something. I mean, sure, there's a resemblance, but you can see that they're clearly two different people."

Hannah pointed at Bonilla's jacket. There was an image of an elongated serpent-like creature on its side. "You can barely make it out," she said, "but doesn't that look a lot like the logo the Kobras were wearing—apart from the letter K?"

I remembered my European History class again. "That's a Nessie," I replied, "hence the gang's name."

"A who?" Maddie asked. "Never heard of her."

"A Nessie. Short for Loch Ness Monster. It's a mythical lake creature from Scotland." I paused. My dad was of Scottish descent, and sometimes I got teary eyes just thinking about him.

"Which is interesting because it's also a reptile like a cobra," Larry said.

Kylie piped up. "It seems to me that they are the same gang, or at the very least an affiliate. It was likely that the Nessies changed their name to something similar—but not too similar—when their leader was captured by the authorities. This is something a lot of gangs would do to be considered more reputable."

"This is a good start," I responded. "But we need more information on this *particular* gang—especially this Bonilla guy. He might be the connection to the past we are looking for."

Having narrowed our focus, I asked the librarian for any book she could find dealing explicitly with the Nessies or Arturo Bonilla. She went to the back of the library and returned a few minutes later, handing us three small books, all dwarfed by the giant encyclopedia we last used.

The first book was a burgundy hardcovered edition entitled *An Anonymous Account of the Fresno Police in the 1960s.* I palmed through it, skimming it for any mention of the Nessies or Bonilla. The author was an unnamed retired cop who detailed some of the city's notable crimes during his tenure in law enforcement: serial killers, kidnapping cults, and drug cartels, to name a few. When I came to the middle of the book, I saw not a page but a whole *chapter* devoted to Bonilla. "This guy must have been a pretty big deal," I said to the group.

I started to read the chapter aloud. "Bonilla had to have been the most well-rounded, meticulous criminal I had faced in my thirty-plus years on the Department's Major Crimes Task Force. His impeccable work ethic was not rivaled by any of his contemporaries. Although his motives still remain a mystery to myself and the rest of the Force, one thing is clear—he was far more vicious and dangerous than your standard, garden-variety gang boss."

"Wow," Hannah interrupted me. "That's not very good news for *us*, to put it lightly."

"At least the other book said he's dead," Larry pointed out.

"I wouldn't count on that," replied Kylie. "After all, we just learned that time travel is real."

"Guys," I said, "let me finish—there's more."

I continued reading. "He had to have been part of something greater than the Fresno street crime scene. Unlike leaders of the opposing gangs, crime was not just the way of life Bonilla chose—it was the only way. It was personal to him."

The author described some of Bonilla's savage tactics, some of which he witnessed firsthand. For example, Bonilla would often decapitate his victims and mount their heads on stakes—which he would then place on public city streets for the world to see. And then, there was also a time when the Nessies kidnapped a cop and brutally tortured and beat him to death. Bonilla even had a gang member record the entire ordeal and ordered a messenger to deliver the tape to the Force. The author thought it was a regular police recording and watched his partner meet his brutal end on video.

"What a classy dude," Hannah sarcastically stated once I had finished reading the chapter.

"You said he could have been part of something *greater*?" Larry asked. "Could that potentially be referring to time travel?"

"I don't know," I replied, "but we have two books left."

The second book the librarian gave us, *Brought to Justice* by Leland Wise, was half again as large as the first. It talked about the captures of various well-known American criminals, from Al Capone to Charles Manson. As I skimmed through its yellowish off-white pages, I came across a section about street gangs, where I found a half-page blurb on Bonilla. I read it to myself and placed the book back down, stunned into silence.

"Hey, get this," I finally said. "I think this is what the other author was referring to."

I read out loud from the page. "Bonilla was alleged by the Fresno Police, albeit without any substantial proof, to have been heavily involved with the Greenies, the infamous Chicago-based white-collar mob, led by none other than Aidan 'The Green Dragon' Brown." After uttering his name, I slammed the book shut on the table. I couldn't believe it.

The rest of the group looked unconvinced, though. "Aidan Brown?" Kylie mumbled. "I think I've heard that name before. Wasn't he like one of Whitey Bulger's buddies?"

"Not really," I responded. "He made Bulger look like a cat burglar."

I had written a paper on Brown for my junior year Criminal Justice class (and had received an A- on it), so I was very familiar with the work of the ruthless crime lord who effectively ruled over Chicago during the late sixties and the majority of the seventies. It was not enough to merely call him a criminal mastermind. His tactics had the city police and the FBI totally befuddled. For all I knew, if rival gangsters had not captured him, his reign of terror would have continued for many more years, if not decades. Brown had quietly built himself an empire to the point where *he* was effectively the one managing much of the affairs of the third-largest American city, much like Al Capone had a half century earlier.

At first, I was skeptical that Brown was responsible for our mysterious arrival in the past. We even doubted that he worked with Bonilla in the first place. After all, his organization and the Nessies, while both despicable, seemed to occupy completely different spheres of crime. Brown's group, the Mount Greenwood Boys, or "The Greenies," as everyone called them, mostly stuck to white-collar jobs. They engaged in racketeering, loan sharking, money laundering, illegal betting, and pretty much any fraud you can think of—similar to Bulger's Winter Hill Gang and the Mafia. They weren't too keen on drug trafficking, unlike the Nessies and other Fresno street gangs. Why would the most powerful white-collar criminal of his era waste his time associating with a street gang based *two thousand* miles away? It just didn't make sense. I needed more proof.

Our final book, *The Unconventional Gangs of Fresno* by Betty Mae Lang, was the smallest of the three, clocking in at only 144 pages. Larry suggested that we use the index in the back to see if the author mentioned Brown in conjunction with Bonilla and the Nessies. Sure enough, we found that the mention of "Brown, Aidan" appeared once in the book—on page 81.

I eagerly flipped to the page and read it out loud from the top. "The Nessies were not your run-of-the-mill street gang. Unlike their scrappier rivals, they had developed a level of criminal sophistication unforeseen on the streets of the San Joaquin Valley. It was one that could've been learned from the Mafia, but a far more likely source was Aidan Brown's

Greenies, who were purported to have made regular contact with Bonilla's inner circle."

We stood corrected. The last book had essentially confirmed the second's hypothesis that the two gangs worked together.

"So, I guess Brown *was* involved with them," noted Hannah.

"But why?" Larry asked.

"Who knows," I said, "could be for a number of reasons." I shrugged. "Maybe Brown was bored with running Chicago's business scene and wanted to take his 'talents,' for lack of a better word, elsewhere, and the Nessies were his vehicle to do so. Pretty much, they were his pawns in his chess game against law enforcement."

"I could see it," Kylie responded.

Maddie had a puzzled look in her eyes. "Hold on, slow down, guys. My head is spinning. There's this lady named Nessie and some guy named Brown—and I don't know, I'm lost. *What* is happening now?"

I sighed before summarizing our last hour of research to my sister. "So, the gang that captured us in 2022 is the modern reincarnation of this brutal sixties gang called the Nessies."

"Reincar-what?" Maddie was genuinely confused.

Larry butted in. He was better at explaining things than I was. "Arturo Bonilla, the leader of the Nessies—the guy who put people's head on stakes, is most likely Skull and Bones's granddad. These last two books showed that he was also a friend or at least an associate of Aidan Brown. *The* Aidan Brown—the notorious Chicago mobster."

Maddie was starting to catch on, but she was still confused. She turned to face me again. "So, wait. Aidan Brown, isn't that the guy you wrote that stupid school paper on?"

"Yes," I replied, "and based on all the evidence we have found thus far, *he* had something to do with us being brought back to the 1970s."

"Think about it," Larry continued. "He knew Grandpa Bonilla, so he would likely know his descendants—such as Skull and Bones. Just like he used the Nessies to expand his reach, he used the Kobras—the modern-day Nessies—to trap us modern-day people in the past."

It made perfect sense to all of us—even Maddie—once we thought about it. Time travel was something everyone thought was impossible. Whoever transported us back must've been someone with a vast network of resources—someone who knew that time travel was real while most reputable scientists doubted its existence. The Kobras-slash-Nessies didn't fit the bill. Brown, on the other hand, certainly did.

"I know what this was," Maddie stated with a newfound sense of confidence. She pointed at me. "It was all because of that paper, Charlie. He read it and was pissed off."

"I wouldn't put it *past* him, no pun intended," said Larry. "It's something he would do. In 1974, Brown was at his peak. Maybe his present self sends everyone who pisses him off back in time so, you know, his past self can 'take care of them.'"

"Yeah," agreed Kylie. "This all could be just an elaborate scheme to kill Charlie or hold him hostage for writing a paper. Sounds sick, but it's something a psychopathic gangster would do."

"There's just one problem with this theory," I interjected. "Brown died in 1981."

17

IN-N-OUT OF TROUBLE

After our morning of research generated more questions than answers, we decided to take a much-needed break to refuel and ponder over what we just learned. So, we headed down to my favorite place in the whole entire world—In-N-Out Burger. At least those existed in 1974.

After waiting for nearly twenty minutes, the five of us placed our orders. I got my usual—a Double Double Animal Style, no lettuce, no tomato, Animal Style fries, and a 7-Up. Kylie, the only person who voted *against* going to In-N-Out (she opted for "Flower Child Salad Bar" instead), reluctantly got fries, but only after the cook told her he fried them in nothing but vegetable oil—*five* times.

As we patiently waited for our food to arrive, I caught a glimpse of a man wearing a fedora, standing kitty-corner from us. He wasn't waiting in line, nor was he eating. He was just standing there, *watching* us. He looked like somebody I'd seen before—and then I remembered. He was the same silver-haired man who had paid for our meal at the Freedom Café the day before—Al.

I whispered to the rest of the group, "That's him." I subtly pointed at the man. "Al from the diner. I think he's following us."

Larry brushed it off. "Don't be ridiculous," he said. "It's probably just a coincidence. He was nice to us, after all. I don't think he's one of the bad guys."

"I don't know," said Hannah. "What are the odds we just *bump* into him in both places?"

Despite Hannah's and my suspicions, we decided to ignore Al. Our food soon arrived, hot off the grill, and we made our way over to an empty table. I couldn't wait to savor all of the deliciousness.

As I wolfed down my burger, I glanced over at the corner of the restaurant and saw that Al was still standing in the same spot. He hadn't moved, although I could have sworn that I saw him turn his head as soon as I looked at him—it was like he didn't want us to notice that he was watching. "Guys," I said, trying to get everyone's attention, "he's still there."

"The more I think about him, the more he creeps me out," Maddie said. "I mean, look at that hat! He looks like a gangster! For all we know, he's one of Brown's friends!"

"I honestly think we should talk to him," Larry responded, changing his tune from before. "Like this way, based on how he responds, we'll know if this is *really* a coincidence."

"Yeah," Hannah agreed. "It's worth a shot."

"*You* can talk to him," Kylie replied, not wanting anything to do with the situation. "I'll just sit here, eat my fries, and pray we get home in one piece."

Larry, Hannah, and I slowly walked over to Al. Kylie and Maddie remained at the table, making a point to look away from us.

When we approached the man, Hannah lightly tapped his shoulder. "Oh, hi Al!" she said in a forced, friendly voice, trying to suppress any ounce of insecurity she might have had. "That's right! We remember you!"

"Fancy seeing you here," I jumped in.

"Can we help you?" Hannah asked, being polite while still coming off as self-assured.

Al looked at us, paused, and laughed for a second. He then responded. "Miss, shouldn't you be asking how *I* can help *you*?"

The way he said it just irked me. Maybe Maddie and Kylie were right.

"Uh—thank you for paying for our meal," Hannah nervously mumbled to him.

"Please, it was nothing," he replied as he adjusted his hat. "As I said before, I *thrive* on random acts of kindness."

I heard a voice from the back. "So, we would like to know. Are you following us?" It was Kylie. She had decided to get up and join us. Maddie remained at the table with her head down, shaking in her boots.

"More or less," Al replied. "I'm just doing my job."

"Your job?" I assertively asked. "And what exactly would your *job* be?"

"Look," Al continued. "I know what's up. I know that none of you belong *here*."

"Well, I definitely don't belong *here*," Kylie replied, thinking Al was referring to In-N-Out. "Vegans and fast food do not necessarily get along."

Al completely ignored Kylie's attempt to lighten the mood. "You know what I mean," he said. "I'm not gonna elaborate here because this is a public place, and it's broad daylight right now."

"So, Al, cut to the chase," I told him. "What do you want from us?"

He looked at us with a dash of compassion. I started to trust him a little, or should I say not *completely* distrust him. "Look. I know the unique situation you're in right now, and I'm the only one who can help you. The other day when I first saw you kids, I was half hoping you'd follow me. So, I kept following you with hopes that you'd finally notice, and look at that, you did."

"So, you're telling me that you followed us to the hotel and the library too?"

"Yes, I did. It was my first time in a while staying at a Motel 6. I usually go for more *exclusive* hotels, but sometimes all you need is a bed and a color TV. And as for the library, I was the guy in the corner reading *Huck Finn*."

"You haven't answered his question," Larry said. "What do you want from us?"

Al stroked his chin. "As I said before, I can't get into much detail here, but if you kiddos want to know how to get back to where you *belong*, meet me at O'Malley's in Tulare at nine tonight." He reached into his pocket and handed Larry a crumpled piece of paper. "These are the directions," he said.

"Oh—okay," I stumbled to say. "See you there tonight, Al." I didn't necessarily want to go. At that moment, I just wanted to get Al away from us.

Al said goodbye and exited through the door. Larry, Hannah, Kylie, and I sat back down to join Maddie and finish our meal. We filled her in on what happened.

"Oh my God!" she gasped. "It's obviously a trap! He's gonna kill us!"

"I think we should go," Hannah said. "We have nothing to lose."

"Except our lives!" Maddie exclaimed.

"Hannah's got a point," said Larry. "Right now, it's our only way home."

"I'm with Maddie on this one," Kylie uttered. "I didn't get good vibes from that dude. Like, seriously, what grown man has the nerve to follow a group of teenagers around everywhere for two days? We gotta blow him off and get the hell out of here, so he loses track of us."

It was two votes for, two votes against. The decision of whether or not to meet Al at the bar came down to me. It wasn't an easy choice, but it was the one I had to make.

"Sorry, girls. Majority rules," I said. "We're going."

18

A BAR CALLED
O'MALLEY'S

The bar was a forty-five-minute ride from Downtown Fresno. I'd been to Tulare several times before. Maddie's paternal grandparents lived there, and I used to visit them all the time when our mom was married to Maddie's dad. So, I was familiar with the drive. However, it was a completely different experience going there in *1974*. There were more trees and wildlife (Larry got a few feet away from running over an antelope that was unsuspectedly grazing on the side of the freeway), but much fewer people and buildings. The landscape simply looked more pristine—like it was barely touched by man.

The five of us arrived at O'Malley's ten minutes early. It was a dark, garishly decorated hole-in-the-wall dive bar. As we looked for Al, we saw a group of men off to the side playing pool. It looked like fun—but we were not there to have *fun*.

We finally spotted Al, who was seated in a quiet corner of

the bar, of course, where no one could hear our conversation. He was wearing an expensive Italian suit, marked with a shiny silver tie, which seemed to mesh well with his fedora. Seated next to him was an identically dressed huge man, whom I had never seen before. *Maybe he is Al's bodyguard.* He had to have been at least six-and-a-half feet tall and weighed 350 pounds—at a minimum. He sported a scraggly, unkempt beard and a chestnut man bun, which starkly contrasted with his nice clothes. Al's friend looked like a third NFL offensive lineman, a third *Duck Dynasty* cast member, and a third sumo wrestler.

"I think we're underdressed," Hannah whispered to me. I didn't know if she was being serious or sarcastic.

"I don't think this is the kind of place you have to dress up for," I whispered back.

We carefully sat down at the table next to Al and the other man.

"Glad you kids could join us," Al said. He then pointed to the large man. "I would like to introduce you to my colleague Manny Santos. He's not a man of many words."

Manny didn't speak. Instead, he slightly bobbed his head up and down.

"Manny Santos!" Hannah exclaimed, forgetting where she was for a second. "That's a character from *Degrassi*! But isn't she a girl?"

Manny, visibly infuriated by Hannah's comment, pounded the table and scowled at her with a heavily lisped Spanish accent. "Nektht time thomeone mentionth that *Degrathi* theeng whatever that eeth, I thwear they gonna looth their head!"

"I guess you can see who the good cop and the bad cop are here," Al replied, making light of Manny's threat.

"So, wait, you're cops?" I asked.

Al smiled. "Just *cops*? Are you trying to insult us?"

At once, Al and Manny each pulled out, from their pockets, a gold badge with an eagle on top. The letters "FBI" were written on both of them. *Oh, God. Now the government wants us.*

"Allow me to *formally* introduce myself," Al continued. "My name is Special Agent Alphonse Cannella, but as I always say, you can call me Al."

"I believe Paul Simon said that too," Hannah noted.

"He has?" Al replied, confused. "I am a huge Simon and Garfunkel fan, and I don't recall a song where he says that."

Hannah forgot that song came out in the *eighties*. She was making us stand out even more with all these future pop culture references.

Al continued. "And this is Special Agent Manuel Enrique Fernando Alejandro Esteban de Santos y Fernandez," he said, pointing at Manny.

"Damn, you make me jealous," Kylie responded. "I only have *three* middle names."

Al and Manny proceeded to shake everyone's hand. When Manny shook my hand, he looked at me sternly and squeezed it very tightly as if he had it in a death grip. Hannah downright refused to look Manny in the eye. His reaction to her comment still shook her.

"So, let's get down to business," Al said. "The other day, I was in the diner, just having my normal pre-work breakfast, and I saw you kids. I couldn't help but notice those clothes you were wearing. It doesn't take a genius to know that there's no way in hell *those* clothes came from 1974. You're not gonna convince me by telling me that was some handmade hippie crap. I know brand names when I see them. Those are just brands that don't exist *now*."

There was a long pause. Finally, after nearly half a minute, I broke the silence. "So, you mean to tell us you think we're time travelers."

My friends sputtered in nervous laughter. Al and Manny weren't humored in the slightest.

"Not exactly," Al replied. "'Time traveler' implies that you came here of your own volition. Instead, we have a hunch that *someone* dragged all of you unwitting punks here from your time."

"Since you're so certain we're not from the seventies, what year do you think we came from?" Kylie questioned.

Al placed his right hand on the brim of his fedora. He thought for a few seconds. "If I had to guess, I'd say between forty and fifty years from now? Am I right?" He was on the money.

"You better not tell a soul if we tell you," I said. "We don't want the government to do science experiments on a bunch of teenagers just because we *supposedly* come from the future."

Al removed his hand from his hat and took a sip of his beer. He then raised his eyebrows at me. "Why would we tell the *government*? If we told them, no one would believe us. They'd think we're a bunch of loons. We'd both lose our jobs. Plus, we're the FBI. *Classified* is our middle name."

"Okay, fine," Maddie relented. "We come from 2022."

Al smirked. "I knew it. You're too different from seventies teens to be from any time less than four decades from now. Yet you are too similar to be from a time more than five."

Larry wasn't having it with the two agents. "So, do you know *why* we're here? And more importantly, how can you help us get home?"

"Well, to answer your first question. We don't *know* why you're here—but we can make an educated guess. Manny and I aren't from the local Central California FBI. Actually, we're both organized crime experts and are on a trip here from the Field Office in Chicago."

I gulped when he mentioned Chicago—Brown's city. Our fears were confirmed.

"Anyway," Al continued. "For the last few years, we have been assigned to investigate the infamous Mount Greenwood Boys Gang—the Greenies. You might have heard of them or their leader, Aidan Brown."

"Yeah," I replied, "I wrote a school paper on him."

None of us told Al about our research earlier in the day. We figured he probably already knew since he was watching us the whole time.

"So, I see Brown made his way into the history books," Al

went on. "Not surprising. Not surprising at all. After spending all this time analyzing his methods, it became obvious that he was eluding the Chicago PD by using what we could only describe as completely unorthodox tactics and technology—nothing like we've ever seen before. Many cops have even gone as far as to suggest that he is in communication with extraterrestrials. However, this is extremely unlikely as there's no actual evidence that backs that possibility. The far, far *likelier* explanation is that he somehow has gained access to some kind of *future* technologies—including the ability to time travel." He pointed to all of us. "And by the *future*, I mean *your* time."

"So, what are some of these tactics?" I asked. "Please expound."

"Well, we have figured out that Brown is always able to avoid law enforcement because he seems to know where and when everyone and everything is—at all times. So, in some uncanny way, he's always two steps ahead of the good guys."

"Sounds like he has the Internet!" Maddie emphatically blurted.

"Precisely," Al resumed, "he's a twenty-first-century criminal in a 1970s world."

"He must be having a field day then," Larry said. "Brown against the cops is like the 2017 Golden State Warriors playing a pee-wee basketball team."

"And unlike the Warriors, I don't think Brown would ever blow a 3-1 lead," I added.

Al glared at me. "For the last few years, Manny and I have

been searching non-stop for the place from where Brown gets his intel, but we've been coming up empty. Then a few weeks ago, we finally got a lead here in Fresno. The Central California Field Office was investigating murders by local gangs when they found that the late Arturo 'Bones' Bonilla had been in regular communication with Brown and the Greenies regarding so-called 'secret gang practices.' So, we came here a few days ago to talk to some people who knew Bonilla—to see if we could find anything. And then we came across you."

"It's funny you mentioned Bonilla," I stated. "When we were in the library this morning, we pretty much confirmed that Brown used *his* gang to transport us back in time."

A grin appeared on Al's face. "So, my hunch was right after all. Well, I guess District Chief Marshall isn't gonna give us any more crap about our 'wild goose chase' in Fresno."

Although we were getting a lot of helpful information from him, Al still wasn't answering the one question burning in all of our minds.

"So, why did Brown bring *us* here?" I asked. "What do we have that he doesn't have already?"

At that moment, Al briefly locked eyes with each one of us. His mood had shifted from being all business to conveying a sincere amount of empathy. He looked like he was gravely *worried* about our well-being.

Al placed his hand on his chin.

"My guess is he doesn't want any*thing* you have. He wants *one* of you."

19

BAD, BAD
AIDAN BROWN

We all frantically looked at one another. Which *one* or *ones* of us did Brown want? The more I learned about the present situation, the more I feared for my life.

"Do any of you happen to have family from Chicago?" Al asked.

Maddie and I raised our hands. Our mom, whose maiden name was Kazlowski, proudly hailed from the Windy City.

"It can't be us because of *that*," I said, hoping to rule my sister and me out of being Brown's primary target. "Our mom was born in 1983. She would have been *negative nine* right now."

Al narrowed his gaze. "Hmm, weren't her parents living in Chicago during this time?"

"Yes," I replied. My grandparents were first- and second-generation Americans. They and their parents—my great-grandparents—were the epitome of the American dream.

They had worked their way up from poverty, with each generation becoming more successful than the last. Grandpa Paul's parents, both Polish immigrants, came to Chicago to escape the rise of communism. They arrived with nothing except $750 and my great-great-grandmother's famed pierogi recipe. With perseverance and dedication, they used this to start Kazlowski's, which soon became the most famous deli and restaurant in all of northwestern Chicago. Grandma Vicky's family, of Irish and German descent, had similarly opened a laundromat. My grandma and grandpa had met when they were around my age, and both worked at Kazlowski's. In the mid-eighties, my great-grandma, by then a widow, sold the family restaurant for quite a fortune. My grandparents used their share of the money to start a successful construction business, and about a decade later, they had enough money saved in the bank to finally get out of Chicago. Being sick of the abominable winters, they wanted to relocate somewhere far warmer and drier. So, without any further delay, they moved my mom and her six siblings across the country to Fresno—and the rest is history.

Al motioned to Maddie and me. "It looks like you two are who Brown wants."

"But our grandparents are only teenagers now!" Maddie cried. "And they are model citizens! They would have *never* associated with Brown or his group of thugs."

"Neither of them has ever even gotten a speeding ticket in their life," I added. *My grandparents are two of the most moral people I know*, I thought. Hell, they made it a priority to return their shopping cart after they finished bringing their groceries to the car.

Al shook his head. "Let me explain. Based on the extensive research the Bureau has conducted on the Greenies, we have concluded that Brown is likely using his affiliate gangs, like the Nessies, to kidnap kids from the future and hold them hostage so their ancestors will obey him. Pretty much, he's using his knowledge of time travel for *blackmail*. First, he stole your 'Internet' thing, and now he's stealing people's future descendants. It's a stroke of evil genius."

"But why? As Maddie just said, they're *our* age *now*," I replied. "Plus, they're just restaurant employees. My grandma is a waitress, and my grandpa is a busboy. It's his parents' restaurant."

"Exactly my point," said Al. "Brown's main *modus operandi* is extortion. Yes, he does plenty of other crap too, but milking city businesses dry is how he makes most of his bank. You know, the whole 'nice restaurant you got there, it would be a shame if anything happened to it' schtick. While some places suck up to him, others won't go down without a fight. Your family's place is in that 'others' category. So when Brown doesn't get his way by threatening, he pulls one of his schemes. That, kids, is what we think he did by sending all of you here. He's not planning on returning you back to your time until your great-grandparents pay up. That is, of course, *if* he doesn't kill them first."

Larry, Hannah, and Kylie looked at Maddie and me with sympathy. The two of us froze in complete shock and terror.

Then, without saying a word, we fell into each other's arms with tears flooding our eyes. We might have had our differences over the years, but we were family at the end of the day. We were in this together.

After waiting a while to get my emotions in check, I sat up again. "So, what can we do about this?" I asked Al, trying to suppress everything I was feeling at that moment.

"When we were in In-N-Out, you specifically said you could get us home," Maddie recalled.

"That's right. I did. You're not going to like this. But there's only *one* way you can get out of here," Al dryly said.

We were all ears.

"You're gonna have to go right into the belly of the beast. It's the only option you have at this point. If he brought you kids here, he could bring you home."

"So, you're telling us we have to go to Chicago and meet this asshole *ourselves*?" Larry asked.

Al nodded. "I'm afraid so."

20

ADVENTURE OF A LIFETIME

"**A**re you serious!" I cried. "Brown *wants* us!" I pointed to myself and then to my sister. "If we come to *him,* we're just making it easier for him to capture, torture, and kill all of us!"

"That you are," Al agreed. "But it's a risk worth taking if you want to get home. If you wait around and do nothing, there's a good chance you're gonna be stuck forty-eight years behind schedule for the rest of your lives."

Manny, who had been silent the whole night since flipping out on Hannah, bobbed his head in agreement.

"So, what's the plan, Stan?" Hannah asked Al.

"It's Al," he responded, slightly annoyed.

"Guess that Paul Simon song didn't come out yet, either," she muttered under her breath.

"We're gonna give all of you kids new identities," Al instructed. "It's likely Brown knows his prey by their names

174

more than their faces, so this might be enough to throw him off-kilter for a while. Each of you will pretend that you are a Fresno high school student targeted by Brown's crime organization via the local gangs. You're going to look the part as well." He looked at our cheap clothes in repulsion. "May I ask where you got *those* rags?"

"From some good-for-nothing, long-haired, watch-stealing hippie!" Maddie interjected. She sounded more like a seventy-year-old man than a fifteen-year-old girl.

"This very nice secondhand store owner named Phil," I rephrased my sister's snide remark. "He was a little off-the-beam, but he gave us a great deal for our 2022 clothes and even threw in the ones we're wearing now for free."

"Well, once we're in Chicago, we're gonna buy you all *real* clothes."

Maddie perked up. "We're gonna go shopping?"

"No," Al scolded. "This ain't no time for 'shopping.' Once you're in the Field Office, we're gonna go right into your training. Think of it as an intensive one-week boot camp on how to infiltrate the most powerful crime organization in America."

"Wait, wait, wait," Kylie interrupted. "Did I hear that right? Like we're actually gonna pretend to be *part* of the gang?"

"Listen, kiddos. Do you want to go home or what?"

We stopped complaining. We all knew that Al had the answer.

He continued his spiel. "We're gonna teach you everything we know about Brown and his band of miscreants so you're prepared as much as you can be when you finally go toe-to-toe with him. If you even *get* to that point alive, that is. You're gonna have to learn how to blend in, so don't blow your covers—because if you do, Brown will figure out who you *really* are, especially you, *brother* and *sister*." He stared at Maddie and me. "And, of course, you'll need to learn hand-to-hand combat and basic improv skills."

Hannah's face morphed into a half smile at the sound of the word "improv." I knew she had that part down already, without any training. It at least felt somewhat assured that the best actress I knew was with me.

"So, when are we flying there?" Hannah asked. "Tonight? Tomorrow?"

"You ain't flying," Al replied as if we missed something obvious. "It's far too risky."

"But this is *1974*," Larry said. "Isn't it easy to fly now? Like you just hop on a plane? You don't have the TSA and all those metal detectors like in our time?"

"We still need to take the precaution," he explained. "Remember, technically, none of you have been born yet. So when you're asked for your IDs, you'll be flat out of luck."

"But can't you just make us new IDs with our covers?" asked Kylie. "Like, isn't that what the FBI does?"

Al stumbled to answer her for a second. He lightly stroked his tie. "Well—it's not that easy," he said in a calculated manner, "for reasons that I can't explain to you right now."

"Like what?" I pressed him.

Al adjusted his fedora. "All I'm going to say is that if we

did go that route, given the *present* situation, it would breach our security clearance with the Bureau."

He does have a point, I thought. The last thing we wanted was to *also* have the federal government against us. Brown and the Kobras were enough already.

"But if we're not flying, how are we going to get there?" Maddie questioned.

"You're gonna have to drive yourselves. You leave tomorrow morning. It's a three-day trip, but we're gonna be extra nice and give you four days to get there. Since today's Tuesday, that means Sunday morning at nine sharp is when your training begins."

"Really?" objected Larry. "Don't you have a van you can just take us in? Or better yet, a private jet?"

I knew that he was annoyed because *he* would end up getting stuck with most of the driving. I could've helped out if I hadn't failed my road test. *Maybe I should've actually paid attention during Driver's Ed—instead of playing video games in the corner with Pasta the whole time.*

Al was adamant. "No can do. Again, security clearance. Breach."

"Well, I guess we have ourselves a road trip," I stated, trying my hardest to look at the bright side of the situation. It wasn't easy, though. The more Al kept talking, the more I realized we were royally screwed.

Al removed his hat and placed it on the ear of his chair. He ran his fingers through his argent hair and inhaled deeply before speaking. "I know this might not be the news you kids wanted, but keep in mind that by infiltrating the Greenies, you're gonna get us some valuable intel on them that we never would've been able to acquire. You see, many officers and even some of our special agents have tried to go incognito on Brown before. They've all failed quite miserably. He is such an experienced gangster that picking up who is undercover or a 'rat' is his sixth sense. We're hoping that you being *kids* is enough to throw him off."

Maddie was getting restless. "Teens. We're teens. Stop calling us kids."

Al propped the hat back on his head. "Kids, teens, young'uns, suit yourselves. Also, we have an absolute dearth of information on his exact practices and whereabouts because Brown is just so damn secretive. One of his biggest assets is he trusts *no one*, not even his own men. He knows that in large crime syndicates, the leader's demise is almost *always* because one of their top lieutenants grows jealous and betrays them."

I thought back to the research I did on Brown for my Criminal Justice paper. Brown *was* eventually betrayed by one of his men and turned over to and fatally shot by a rival gang. But that didn't happen until 1981—seven years after 1974.

"So," Al resumed. "What I'm proposing is a win-win proposition. You gather some info on Brown for us, and we will do everything in our power to get you home. It's as simple as that. Is everyone in?"

"Show of hands," I uttered. All of us—even Maddie—

raised our hands high. Although each of us liked that we were doing a good deed in helping the FBI attempt to defeat the worst criminal of his generation, that wasn't why we were making the trip. We just wanted to go back to our old lives and families.

Al and Manny grinned. Al handed Larry a business card and two hundred dollars for gas and incidentals—not that we needed it, as we still had almost all of the money Phil gave us. The agents then doled out a series of maps we were to use—*paper* maps. I guess this was how everybody had to get around before cell phones or Garmin Nüvis were a thing.

"That card has the address for the Field Office. We'll rendezvous there Sunday morning." Al checked his watch. "It's getting late now, and I suggest you kids get to bed as early as you can tonight. You got a long way ahead of you."

The five of us thanked Al and Manny for their time and left the bar in stunned silence. Everything was happening much quicker than we could process it. I was glad we had a road trip to kind of look forward to, though.

After all, it could have been the last trip of all our lives.

21

BORN TO BE WILD

We set our wake-up call for 3:30 a.m. the next day. Larry and I showered and got ourselves ready in record time. We met the girls down in the lobby.

"Guess what," Kylie said. "Maddie, Hannah, and I spent the hour before we fell asleep last night looking over the maps Al gave us—and we planned out our trip!"

"We figured that since the FBI gave us a little more time than we need to get to Chicago, we can do some sightseeing on the way there!" Hannah added enthusiastically.

Maddie handed me the itinerary the three girls had compiled. "And you're welcome for the rodeo," she said. "That was totally my idea."

I read bits and pieces of the list out loud. "Grand Canyon mule ride. Concert in Vegas? This is awesome! All three of you should be hired to make tours for Rick Steves if we eventually end up getting home."

"Thanks a lot," Hannah replied. "We put some time into

it. After all, none of us have traveled across the country in the *seventies* before. We surely won't ever get to do this again!"

"Plus, we got all that money from Phil," said Kylie. "Since now we got the federal government taking care of us, we might as well put it to good use."

I passed the list to Larry for him to review. "Casino?" he noticed. "How exactly is that happening? You're forgetting that we're all under twenty-one."

"Don't you have Uncle Bill's ID? Can I see that for a sec?" Kylie asked him. He pulled it out and passed it to her. She read the birthday. "July 9, 1956. And last time I checked, eighteen was the legal age in 1974."

Larry smiled. "So, you want me to show off my blackjack skills. Challenge accepted."

We all situated ourselves inside the Sunny. As I climbed into the back passenger seat, I could see that the front bumper was dangling by a corner and could fall off at any second. We had to be super careful, as car trouble was without a doubt the *last* thing we needed on our way to confront Brown. Larry and Kylie agreed to split the driving, changing after every stop we made.

"Time to say goodbye to Fresno," Larry announced as we blazed down Freeway 99.

"If all goes according to plan, we'll be back before we know it," said Hannah.

"That's a big *if*," Maddie mumbled.

Kylie, who was sitting in the shotgun seat, studied the map. "First stop, Death Valley!"

Maddie groaned. "How fitting. We're probably driving to our *deaths* anyway."

Although my little sister had always been a huge complainer, her comment seemed fairly accurate to me. Following our discussion with Al at O'Malley's the night before, I found it suspicious he was adamant that our *best* way to get home was to face Brown head-on. "Do you think the FBI is using us?" I asked the rest of the group. "Like, it seems to me that they really don't care if we get back to 2022 at all. To them, it is just their desperate attempt to get to Brown."

"Yeah," Kylie agreed. "They were probably like, 'all else failed, so hey, let's just throw a bunch of high schoolers from the future at him!' We're not people to them. We're just their next 'secret weapon.'"

"Of course they're using us," Larry answered. "But as we established last night, this is not just our best shot; it's our *only* shot."

"He's right," stated Hannah. "And to be frank with you guys, we've had way too much negativity in the short time we've been in the car. The point of this road trip is to bond and have fun together as a *team*. We have no idea what the future has in store for us, so instead of bickering over events that have yet to happen, let's enjoy the time we have right now, in the *present*."

"But—but it's not the present!" Maddie cried. "It's 1974! There are no phones, no social media, no—"

Looking to shut Maddie up, Kylie turned the radio on and jacked up the volume to the maximum level. A familiar proto-heavy-metal guitar riff blared out of the stereo and filled the tiny vehicle. Maddie immediately slammed her hands over her ears—but the remaining four of us were *loving* it.

The vocalist blissfully roared in a borderline psychedelically gruff voice. I recognized the song—"Born to Be Wild" by Steppenwolf.

Hannah and I knew the words, so we joined in. Before we knew it, Kylie and Larry were singing along as well. The windows of the sedan were all rolled down, and the crisp, early-morning desert wind was blowing. My right arm was drooped out of my window, swaying at the mercy of the gust. We were having a grand old time—except for Maddie, of course. My childish sister was writhing with "pain" in the middle-backseat, sandwiched between Hannah and me. She was still trying to block out the sound without an ounce of success.

We finally got to the chorus. Seemingly attempting to break the sound barrier, Hannah, Kylie, Larry, and I belted out the words from the tippy top of our lungs. We all pointed at Maddie, who looked like she was in the fetal position. *"Born to be wild!"* we deafeningly repeated, as if we wanted people in Chicago—or even New York to hear us.

"Okay! Okay! You guys win!" Maddie admitted in defeat as she sat back up in her seat. "Ugh! I guess I'll at least *try* to have fun."

The rest of us burst out laughing at what a little curmudgeon she was being.

We arrived at the first pit stop on our list by ten o'clock:

Death Valley National Monument.

"Here she is," Larry said as he found a parking space. "The hottest place on earth." He passed us each a large bottle of water. It was a good thing we had stocked up on them the other day.

We exited the car, revealing a vast eggshell-white salt flat that appeared to be cracked like shattered glass. The site was desolate, except for the mountains that rose on the horizon. I had been to the Mojave and Sonoran Deserts before, but they were nothing like the wasteland in which I found myself. Besides the other visitors and us, there was no living thing to be seen—no scuttling lizards, no shrubs or palm trees, not even cacti. After spending all my life in the midst of the Information Age, being in such an empty place for a change was kind of strangely refreshing.

"Isn't this where they used to shoot those old Spaghetti Westerns?" I commented. "You never know. We might run into Clint Eastwood right now."

"That would just *make my day*," said Hannah.

We traversed the unhospitable yet beautiful landscape on a wooden boardwalk. Eventually, we came to a sign. I read its faded lettering, *Badwater Basin. 282 feet below sea level. Lowest point in the United States.*

"Bad *water*?" remarked Larry. "I don't see no water."

"It must have been so bad that it didn't want to show its face," Kylie replied.

Maybe this is the place where Brown takes people who cross him, I wondered. He literally couldn't stoop any lower than Death Valley.

For a little while, we continued along the boardwalk to the middle of the salt flat. Then, suddenly, Kylie skipped off and started walking on the basin's rugged terrain.

"Guys, come on!" She signaled to us as she bolted into the distance. "You better catch up before I leave you in the dust!"

Well, you only live once. Larry, Hannah, and I simultaneously followed after her. Having no choice, Maddie also left the boardwalk behind and ventured into the unknown.

The temperature was scorching hot. It was even more sweltering than a midsummer afternoon in Fresno. However, due to Death Valley being exceedingly arid, it was a drier, more enjoyable kind of heat than I had anticipated. As we hiked, aside from taking frequent breaks to douse my parched mouth with water, I was wholly absorbed in the serenity of the environment. I wished I had a camera to capture the moment.

Although this was my first time to Death Valley, it seemed like I had been here before. Just then, I remembered that my mom once told me that she had gone there with my dad when she was pregnant with me. In fact, it was the last trip they went on together before his illness took a turn for the worse. I looked up at the sky and spoke in a loud whisper. "Dad, if you can hear me, I want you to know that I love you. If I don't make it out of Chicago alive, I hope to see you soon." I didn't cry, but only because the hot desert air was drying all the moisture out of my eyes.

We spent at least an hour and a half in the desert. I wasn't keeping track of the exact time. A little while after hitting the road again, I spotted a small green sign reading, *Now Leaving California.* As far as I was concerned, our time in Death Valley could have been the last I ever set foot in my home state again.

22

WHAT HAPPENS
IN VEGAS. . .

We approached the famed Las Vegas strip at around three in the afternoon. Although it was by no means a ghost town, it was not as bustling and vibrant as the Vegas of the twenty-first century. It reminded me almost of Reno, a smaller Nevada city I had visited when my mom took me along to one of her Mayors of Medium-Sized Cities conferences.

There was a large building complex at the end of the strip, surrounded by an expansive but mostly empty parking lot. Behind it was nothing but a swath of barren desert stretching several dozen miles to the Spring Mountains. Aside from the giant casino that lay in front of my face, what I observed at that moment looked remarkably similar to what I saw at Death Valley just a couple of hours earlier. The casino itself was horseshoe-shaped—each of its sides resembling a mini U.S. Supreme Court building or the Greek Parthenon. Emanating from the building's center was a sequence of five spouting fountains that shot up to the sky like geysers.

"Caesars Palace," Kylie said in awe. "I always wanted to go here for my twenty-first birthday. Now I'm here four years earlier. I'll take it."

"You mean *fifty* years earlier," I jokingly corrected her.

"I stand corrected, Captain Literal Man," she mocked. Apparently, Kylie was in no mood for details.

Once we had parked, we made our way to the casino's entranceway. Even more fountains greeted us, each adorned with life-size Roman-style statues at the top.

"I have a random fact for you guys," Larry said. "You see these fountains here? Sometime in the sixties, Evel Knievel tried to motorcycle jump over them. Unfortunately, he failed big time and hurt himself real bad to the point he was in a coma for a month. Luckily, he made a full recovery and was able to watch his son succeed at the same thing twenty years later."

"Evil who?" replied a perplexed Maddie. "Like why was he *evil*? Was he like friends with Brown or something?"

Larry shook his head, albeit while smiling. "*Evel* Knievel. With an 'e.' He was only the greatest daredevil who had ever lived."

"Daredevil?" Maddie honestly had never heard the word before. "Isn't that like what the *Impractical Jokers* guys do?"

"If anyone's *daredevils*, it's *us* by going to Chicago," I said.

The Palace's interior was decorated as if an actual Roman Senate was going to hold a quorum there at a moment's notice. Marble columns outlined the circular reception room as circular glass chandeliers suspended by gold wire dangled from the ornately designed wood ceiling. Classical Roman artwork was everywhere—paintings, mosaics, pottery. To me, it looked more like a museum than a place where people gambled. A friendly receptionist stood behind a marble desk. She was a pretty young woman in her twenties with long coffee-colored hair.

"Excuse me, miss," I said. "We were just passing through and wanted to see if you had any concerts here tonight."

She pointed to a small sign attached to the front of her desk. "The Eagles are just finishing up their tour today. Their last show is at 4:30—" She paused to look at her watch. "Which is one hour and twenty-two minutes from now."

"The Eagles? As in the 'Hotel California' Eagles?" Hannah asked the receptionist.

Hannah was on a losing streak. She kept mentioning songs that didn't exist yet.

"No." The receptionist sighed. "The Eagles as in *the* hottest band in the West right now."

Larry piped up in an effort to save our reputation. "Uh— she meant to say 'Witchy Woman,' 'Desperado'—"

"Yep, that's them. We're pretty much sold out except for a few nosebleed seats. There's also some left in the front orchestra rows, but those are a bit pricey."

"I think we're all gonna do front row seats," Larry boldly declared. "How much are we talking?"

The receptionist looked at us like we were joking, like there was no way a group of teenagers would shell out that kind of money. "Fifty bucks a person."

Fifty dollars might not seem like a lot to you, but in seventies money, it was the rough equivalent of $300 in 2022. However, it turned out we had more than enough cash on us, thanks to Phil the Hippie, a.k.a. Maddie's nemesis. I didn't realize exactly how far a thousand bucks could get you in 1974.

Each of us handed the receptionist two twenties and a ten from our wallets. Then, amazed, she doled out each of our tickets in return. "Okay then. Enjoy the show, would you."

Before, I had only heard the Eagles' music on CDs at my grandparents' house. And now I was seeing them live, in concert, in their *prime*.

Since we had quite some time to kill, we decided to pay a visit to Caesars Palace's famous buffet. None of us had eaten anything the entire day, and all that walking in 120-degree weather made us hungry. The food was scrumptious—I could have literally eaten three full plates of those scalloped potatoes *au gratin*; they were *that* good. With that being said, the buffet still paled in comparison to the extravagant smorgasbord I enjoyed at the Krikorians' house party.

After we stuffed our bellies with food, Larry wandered over to the blackjack table. We waited for him in the lobby. After a few rounds, he returned with a wad of singles in his hand.

"Told you I'm a card shark. I just won us six dollars!"

Kylie laughed. "I'm sure I can whoop your ass in blackjack." Speaking as someone who once got crushed by her in ping pong, I did not doubt her claim one bit.

A MATTER OF TIME

As soon as it was time for the concert to begin, we filed into the Circus Maximus showroom and took our assigned seats. We weren't only in the very front row—we happened to be sitting right across from the Eagles' drum set.

The lights dimmed, and a mustachioed Caesars Palace employee walked up to the stage. *I guess he doesn't have to make a speech about silencing cell phones.*

"Ladies and gentlemen!" he announced. "Let's give a warm *Vegas* welcome to our opening act, performing his brand-new hit single 'Nothing from Nothing'—the one and only Billy Preston!"

"Oh my God!" Hannah said as the legendary musician and his band took the stage. "My dad's name is *Bill* Preston. A few of his friends still call him Billy too. That's such a coincidence."

The band's trumpeter and trombonist gleefully sounded the song's intro. Instantly, Preston began to bang away at his keyboard with meticulous precision. In seventeen years of listening to music, I had never seen anyone as skillfully adept on the keys as was Billy Preston. The intense passion and genuine love he had for music just tore through the showroom.

I whispered to Hannah, "I'm pretty sure your dad can't do *that.*"

"Not even in his dreams," she agreed. "My dad will have to settle for being a lawyer, but this guy is totally amazing."

At once, Hannah and I both got up from our seats. The two of us started to dance with each other in the space between our row and the stage. Yes, it was the first time I'd ever danced with a girl (if you don't count the time I danced with my mom at her cousin's wedding when I was twelve)—and I loved every second of it. In addition to being a great actress, Hannah was also an exceptionally talented dancer. Since I couldn't dance to save my life, I followed her lead the entire time I was up there. She twirled me around by my hand and sent me gliding across the replica Roman amphitheater. It felt like I was on the hang-glider ride at the Fresno County Fair, except this time, I was locked hand-in-hand with the prettiest girl in the room. It felt nothing short of magical. I just didn't want it to end.

At that moment, I realized that Hannah and I were supposed to go on a date the day after the fateful party. *I guess this could be our date*, I thought. I was just grateful to be able to share this moment with her. Neither of us knew if we would ever be able to get back to 2022 again.

When the song ended, Hannah caught me off guard, lifting me high and gently plopping me back into my seat. I turned to her in sheer ecstasy.

"Damn, Hannah, I can't believe we just did that," I said, still out of breath from all of the dancing.

"Well, we did." She beamed. "I'm having a wonderful time with you."

If I weren't already sitting, her gorgeous wide smile alone would've been enough to make me pass out.

"Me too." I smiled back at her. "How—how did you lift me?" I was surprised by how strong she was, given that she was shorter and lighter than I was.

Hannah laughed. "Well, I used to do ballet too, in addition to stage acting, of course. And come on, it's not like you're hard to pick up, *Skinny*." She rested her right arm on my left shoulder.

"So, when we get back home—if we get back home, that is—we're still on for dinner and a movie?"

She stroked my hair. "Of course we are, *handsome!*"

Overcome with euphoria. I completely forgot that it was time for the main event, as the Eagles came onto the stage to perform. The show was a mesmerizing experience. Listening to my grandpa's *The Very Best of* CD paled in comparison to watching the Eagles live in the *seventies.* If I thought I was starstruck seeing Tom MacDonald perform, words couldn't even describe the range of emotions I felt during this concert.

I noted some of the songs they performed, specifically "Take it Easy" and "Peaceful Easy Feeling." Could this possibly have been a message from God telling me that everything was going to be all right? Nevertheless, hearing those lyrics only made me worry more about what was to come. I thought back to my talk with my mom. Maybe this road trip, the concert, all this "fun" I was having now was just a *façade.* Was it the calm before the storm of our inevitable confrontation with Brown and the Greenies?

After the final encore, my group and the rest of the thousand-member audience erupted into a standing ovation, which lasted nearly two full minutes. We found our way out of the Casino and back to our car. While we were on our way, Hannah reached out her hand, and I gladly took it. *Another thing to check off on my list of firsts.*

Larry and Maddie were in high spirits as well. Maddie went as far to say she now even *liked* some "oldies" music. But the one person who seemed to be a little out of sorts was Kylie. She had a glum look on her face—and had not said a word since before the opening act. And she also was the only one who wasn't clapping along when Hannah and I were dancing to "Nothing from Nothing." It was almost like she wasn't happy that we were having fun together. Was it that she was *jealous* of Hannah?

I was not one to speculate about these things. We had bigger things to worry about—specifically how we, five clueless teenagers, were about to take on a cold-blooded criminal.

Kylie gladly took over driving—maybe because it was an excuse she could use not to talk to us. We headed deep into the desert, making a brief stop: to get gas and corn dogs for dinner—which Kylie skipped partly due to her foul mood, and partly due to the utter lack of vegan options where we were.

We arrived at our hotel near the edge of the Grand Canyon right before midnight. One day of adventure was down. Three more remained before the fight of our lives commenced.

23

PACK MULES AND BUCKING BRONCOS

We ate a quick breakfast of corn muffins and, making haste, set out for the Grand Canyon's south rim. When we got there, we found a sign bearing the words "Mule Trip Departure Area." We quickly paid at the ticket booth and walked up to a fenced-in area, where a man with a long gray beard and a cowboy hat was standing next to six variously colored mules. His tan shirt was mainly covered by a forest-green vest, decorated with his gold National Park Service badge.

"Howdy, fellas," he greeted us, as if we had walked into a scene of a Western film.

"Howdy, sir," Larry said.

"My name is Ranger Vic, and I'm gonna be your guide today for this here mule tour. Have y'all been on a mule before?"

We all shook our heads. I, for one, had not even *seen* a

mule in person before that day.

"Well, you're in for a treat," Vic continued.

He then assigned each of us a different mule, based on our "personalities," or whatever that was supposed to mean. I was given a chestnut and white spotted mule named Eeyore, like the *Winnie the Pooh* character. I stroked Eeyore on the muzzle, and he loudly snorted in my face.

"You're such an ass," I said to the mule.

"He's technically only half ass," Vic corrected me, "and half horse."

"Well, he better not do a *half-ass* job of carrying me." I pointed to the steep cliff in front of me. "'Cause if he does, it's a *long* way down."

I climbed onto Eeyore's saddle, grabbed the reins, and we were off. Vic led the expedition down a meandering, narrow path. Our team of mules steadily trotted in single file. As the trail progressed, it seemed to get closer and closer to the ledge. At one point, Eeyore was taking his steps so close to the edge of the cliff that I started to seriously wonder if he could see at all.

Don't look down. Whatever you do, Charlie, don't look down.

I kept my eyes fixed solely on what was in front of me. That just so happened to be the buttocks of Benjamin, Larry's mule. We pushed on ahead, keeping a slow but steady pace.

Maybe this isn't as scary as I thought. The scene was picturesque, with the canyon's red rocks magnificently blending with the crisp blue, cloudless sky. It looked just like the Grand Canyon postcard my grandparents sent me when they had visited there.

The ride lasted for nearly three hours, and disregarding my fears at the beginning, it was an amazingly breathtaking experience. After we had returned to the departure area, I dismounted Eeyore and scratched him between the ears. He definitely liked that spot better than his snout.

"Nay-aw!" Eeyore brayed in approval. I think he tried to say "neigh" and "hee-haw" at the same time.

"What a good mule," I replied.

We stayed at the Grand Canyon for another hour, exploring the enchanting place on foot, before grabbing some fry bread tacos for lunch. Then it was back on the road.

Our next stop was the Petrified Forest National Park. At first, it appeared to be quite similar to Death Valley, a vast, empty desert. That was until we saw the park's namesake, its endless deposit of fossilized logs.

Maddie reached out to touch the wood, and Kylie yanked her arm back at once.

"What was *that* for?" my sister barked.

"Did you read the sign?" Kylie chided. "Look, don't touch."

"Why? Is it gonna like turn me into a lizard if I do?" Maddie quipped.

"You guys wanna take a guess how old those logs are?" said Larry, trying to prevent an argument from brewing among the girls. "I learned it when I was in the Scouts."

"Five thousand years," I guessed.

"A million," guessed Hannah.

"Old enough to be *too important* for me to touch," Maddie snarked.

"All of you are *way* off," Larry said. "Try 225 million."

"So, you mean this wood was a tree when dinosaurs walked the earth?" Kylie asked.

"Yep," Larry replied. "In fact, odds are a dinosaur ate from the exact tree all of us are looking at right now."

"That's so cool," I said.

"And that even makes me more angry that I can't touch it!" Maddie whined.

She was really fifteen going on *five* sometimes.

"You don't wanna get bad luck," Kylie told her. "Do you?"

"Okay. *Whatever*. It's just wood." Maddie gave up. "The last thing we need to bring with us to Chicago is some curse from a dinosaur forest."

Maddie kept her mouth shut for the rest of the walk through the park—which I liked because I had some peace and quiet for a change. I pondered over my surroundings. The forest was basically a living time capsule—a place where past and present were indistinguishable, just like the reality I was living in. Now that I knew time travel was real, I wondered if it was actually possible to go back to the Triassic Period.

After our little excursion, we continued on our way, crossing the border from Arizona into New Mexico. Within a short time, we came to Santa Fe, where we were to stay for the night. We had our dinner at a quaint green chile spot called "Ricky's Hatch House." For all of us, it was our first time trying the staple dish of New Mexican cuisine. I had expected it to taste like the mild tomatoey chili con carne I was used to, but boy was I wrong. Instead, I was transported to a whole new world of flavor. I happily cleaned my entire bowl in just a few minutes and proceeded to order a second. I'd always enjoyed spicy foods, even though my mom—being Polish, Irish, and German—didn't use that many spices in her cooking.

We left Santa Fe early the next morning and continued through the Southwest, heading northeast on the scenic two-lane Route 66. I'd heard of the famous road through songs, TV, and movies, but I never thought I'd be riding down it.

"It's a shame Route 66 doesn't exist anymore," Larry commented from behind the wheel. "Back in its heyday, it was considered the 'Main Street of America.'"

"But it's neither that main nor a street," Maddie observed. I think it was her turn to be Captain Literal Woman now.

Kylie ignored her. "Yeah. It just goes to show you what life was like with fewer people and less technology. In 2022, you don't see any more charming roads like this. They're all busy interstates."

We finally got into Texas, which Kylie, who was on map duty, informed us was the halfway point of our journey. Hannah tried to make a Bon Jovi reference about us being "halfway there," but we all responded by telling her to save it for another ten years.

Soon everyone began to get hungry. "My stomach's growling," complained Maddie.

"Yeah, mine is too," I agreed.

"I could go for a steak right now," said Hannah.

"I could *not*," said Kylie. "But some tofu would be awesome."

"I don't think you'll find any tofu for a few hundred miles," Larry remarked as he exited the road to look for a place to eat.

After driving around for a little, we came across a place called the Big Texan Steak Ranch. A giant statue of a white and brown longhorn bull was outside.

"They say everything's bigger in Texas," Larry said as he pulled into the parking lot. "Let's see how big these steaks are."

Once we had sat down, our server informed us of the Big Texan's famous seventy-two-ounce steak challenge. It consisted of a steak, a baked potato, a shrimp cocktail, salad, and a buttered dinner roll. Whoever finished the *entire meal* in under an hour got it for free, plus their picture on the restaurant's wall and, most importantly, bragging rights.

Maddie, Hannah, Kylie, and I pointed at Larry in unison. If any of us was to take on this challenge, it was him. He was by far the largest of our group and, being athletic, had an enormous appetite.

"He's gonna be our tribute," Hannah said, somewhat appropriately quoting *The Hunger Games*.

"Guys, I would love to do it," Larry replied, "but I can't. There's shrimp—I'm allergic to shellfish."

We all looked like he let us down. Then Hannah turned to me.

"Charlie is gonna do the challenge," she declared to the waitress.

Damn it. She said my name—first the Henry VIII song and now this. Hannah is well worth it, though.

"Okay, I guess I am," I said. "Bring it on."

The waitress took the rest of our orders. Maddie, Hannah, and Larry all got (much) smaller steaks. Then it was Kylie's turn to order.

"I'll take what he's having." She pointed to me. "But hold the steak, the shrimp, *and* the butter."

The waitress looked confused. "So, ma'am, to clarify, you just want a potato, a salad, and a roll?"

"Yes, ma'am," Kylie replied.

Since I was doing the challenge alone, I was seated at a specially marked table, but close enough to the rest of the group where they could carefully watch my every move. The steak arrived looking even more foreboding than I had imagined. Doing the math in my head, I worked out that seventy-two ounces were almost five pounds, not factoring in all the sides. I breathed and focused. It was just a steak. It didn't make or break me. I remembered the first real conversation I ever had with Hannah when she spoke about risk-taking. *What's the worst thing that can happen? I fail? It's not like I can die.*

I sawed the steak into bite-sized pieces and forked them into my mouth. It was juicy, medium-rare, and cooked to perfection, which made eating it somewhat more manageable. After the first half hour, I was about seventy-five percent done with the steak and the sides.

"Let's go, Charlie!" Hannah shouted. "Do it for the state of California!"

"Yeah, Charlie!" Kylie cheered, despite not looking in my direction. She just couldn't handle watching me eat all that meat.

"Thanks!" I barely managed to get out to the girls. My speech was muffled as my mouth was stuffed with a mixture of steak, potato, lettuce, and shrimp.

Before I knew it, I was ninety percent done with my plate. And then, out of the blue, it felt like my stomach hit a brick wall. When I was still friends with him, Pasta told me that your brain only registers that you are full twenty minutes after eating. Well, that time, my brain was sending me the signal that I had *ten* times more than I should've.

I threw my fork down on my tray. "Guys, I can't finish," I said, defeated.

"Come on!" yelled Larry. "You only have a few bites left!"

"But you made it this far!" Hannah cried. "You can't give up *now*."

"You'll never hear the end of it from me if you don't finish!" Maddie exclaimed.

Well, I sure don't want that. I sharply inhaled, filling my lungs with air, and squeezed the inside of my wrist. I remembered hearing on a podcast that it was a pressure point to relieve nausea. Pretending that my life depended on it, I shoveled the remaining pieces of meat into my mouth and tried my best not to throw up. I swallowed my last bite with my body listlessly slumped over. Then once I was sure there was nothing left on my plate, I placed my utensils down—this time in victory. I had done it.

My friends—and Maddie—applauded. I showed the waitress my empty plate, and she confirmed that I had successfully completed the challenge in fifty-eight minutes and forty-seven seconds. She took my picture with a Polaroid and plastered it on the restaurant's Wall of Fame. When I rejoined the rest of the group at the table, Hannah pulled me in for a big hug.

"See!" she said. "I knew you would be able to do it!"

I buried my face in the warmth of her neck. I swear that when I hugged her, it felt like I was the king of the world. Standing back up, I replied, "Thanks for believing in me. I've learned more about myself in the last week of my life than I had in the previous seventeen *years*."

"Better late than never," she replied, smiling.

Stuffed to the point of bursting, I had no room for dessert, so I sat patiently as everyone else enjoyed a slice of Texas-sized cake. I thought about the strange fact that my picture was on the wall of a restaurant over thirty years before I was to be born. I wondered if it would still be there in 2022.

As we drove into the afternoon, Maddie randomly burst out into her screechy "rendition" of "Before He Cheats" to all of our chagrin. I guess this was her way of returning the favor for our blasting classic rock in the car the other day. She was surely savoring every minute of the drive through the rest of Texas and Oklahoma. My sister always had an affinity for country music and culture. Her favorite outfits always included cowgirl boots, and a giant Luke Bryan poster dominated almost an entire wall of her room. Finally, we stopped for the night in Tulsa, where appeasing Maddie, we looked for a rodeo (she had written it on the itinerary after all). Surely enough, we found one.

"Oh my God! I am *totes* excited!" Maddie shrieked in joy right after we had taken our seats. "I've always wanted to go to a rodeo!"

"You have been to a few already when you were a kid," I pointed out. "Remember?"

"Okay, sure, but still, this is an actual one! In Oklahoma!"

I didn't want to debate her. Maybe if she just got her way, she'd shut up for the rest of the trip.

The Sooner Spurs' Horse and Cattle Show began at 6:30 p.m. on the dot. It had drawn a much larger crowd than the rodeos I went to in Fresno, and I could see why. The performers were incredibly skilled and demonstrated an impeccable level of control. I assumed that most of them had been training in the sport for practically all their lives. I wondered what it was like to take *rodeo* lessons as a kid instead of football, baseball, basketball, soccer, or martial arts. Kylie and Hannah did not seem to enjoy the show one bit, as they spent its entire duration looking away, concerned about the welfare of the featured animals. Maddie, however, was the most ecstatic I had seen her since the time she got Jake Paul's autograph. She was on her feet enthusiastically cheering along to every minute of the action.

The final act of the rodeo was the one we had all waited for—the bucking bronco. Chet Carlisle, the show's veteran bronc rider, mounted a seemingly graceful bay stallion with a single white spot on his muzzle.

"This here is Chief," Chet announced to the audience. "When I count to three, Chief is gonna buck and try to throw me off of him. Y'all are gonna count to see how long I stay on the saddle."

Chet yanked his reins, and the horse kicked his hind legs off the ground, leaping upon his front hooves. After only three bucks, the surprisingly unprepared Chet lost his grip and was thrust backward onto Chief's saddle. Chief bucked once more, flipping his rider off his back and face-down into the dirt.

Chet rose to his feet, grabbing his fallen hat, as Chief freely bounded into the arena. "I'm okay! I'm okay!" he announced with his denim shirt and bushy gray mustache doused in mud. "I *misunderestimated* him!"

Kylie and Hannah applauded as Chief galloped in a victory lap around Chet.

"Yeah, horse!" Kylie cheered on. "You tell that man who's boss."

When the rodeo ended, we headed to our hotel to spend what would be our final night on the road. The next day we were to arrive in Chicago. Things were about to get real for us—big time.

24

THE REAL NATURE OF PIZZA

We didn't get to the Windy City until 6 p.m. the next day. We made pretty much a straight run from Tulsa to Chicago, stopping once for lunch in St. Louis, right next to the Gateway Arch.

Maddie turned to me after we reached the northeastern end of Route 66 and made a left turn onto Lake Shore Drive.

"Maybe we'll see young Grandma and Grandpa," she said. "That would be kind of cool."

"I hope to God that Brown doesn't hurt them," I replied. I thought about what Al told us in the dive bar about Brown likely using Maddie and me as bait to coerce our grandparents and great-grandparents. "Us being there is not going to make it any easier for them."

"If I were you guys, I'd try to avoid contact with them at all costs," said Kylie. "You know what happened in *Back to the*

Future when Marty met his young mom and dad. He almost *disappeared.*"

"This isn't a movie, Ky," Larry reasoned. "This is real life. We have no idea about the consequences of *anything* right now."

He spoke the truth. We were going into this situation as defenseless as a bunch of flies trapped in a spider's web.

"We just have to take it one day at a time," I said. "Which reminds me. It's only six right now, and we don't have to report to the FBI until tomorrow morning at nine. We have some time to explore the city. Out of the five of us, only Maddie and I have been here before, and that was eight years ago."

"Yeah, more than half my life ago," Maddie stated.

We found the hotel that the FBI had reserved for us. We were happy that they were generous enough to give us three rooms. The girls had a rock paper scissors tournament to see who would get their own room. Maddie won, which didn't surprise me at all, as I had taught her how to cheat at rock paper scissors. Pasta once told me that if you ask your opponent to name the capital of Florida (which is Tallahassee, *not* Miami, by the way) before you shoot, they will *almost always* pick scissors. It's not foolproof, but it has worked roughly ninety-five percent of the time in my experience. It worked like a charm on Hannah and Kylie. With little success, they both tried to hide that they were disappointed to have to share a room again. It was clear that they didn't care that much for each other, especially after what happened in Vegas.

After we had unpacked, we set back out for Lake Michigan.

Luckily, we still had the bathing suits we wore at the Krikorians' party. They were pretty much the only thing we had brought from 2022 that we didn't hand over to Filthy Phil. Well, now they came in handy.

We found a public beach and, after changing, hurled ourselves into the vast lake—which to me looked indistinguishable from the Pacific Ocean during low tide. Admittedly, it was a little cold for swimming as the air temperature was hovering around the low seventies. But, after adventuring through the desert, the invigorating, brisk water was a welcomed change.

When I was zoning out, Maddie hit me with a giant splash right in the face. *Bull's-eye.*

"Hey!" I splashed her back.

She giggled. It reminded me of when we were little kids, and our mom used to bring us to the beach in Monterey two or three times every summer.

Larry then cupped his hands and shot an enormous jet of water that somehow was enough to drench *both* Maddie and me.

"Haha! Take that!" he gloated. "Larry, one—Charlie *and* Maddie, *zero.*"

Hannah and Kylie joined in, and an all-out splash war ensued. Larry dominated the rest of us so much I wondered if they taught him how to splash in the Boy Scouts.

Once we had dried off and changed back into our street clothes, we headed to Uno Pizzeria on the Near North Side.

"Pizza!" Maddie shouted in great anticipation as we

entered the establishment. "Pizza, pizza, pizza!" I couldn't tell if she was more excited then or at the rodeo—it was a draw.

We soon placed our orders. Maddie, Hannah, Larry, and I ordered a Chicago Deep Dish pie, each with various toppings. Kylie got salad and bread—which, to be honest, was what she had been living on since we had been transported to 1974.

When the pizzas arrived, they were piping hot. The cheese was sizzling. A blissful aroma filled the air. I took a slice with the provided pizza server and quickly stuffed it into my mouth, saving the gooey cheese from dripping into oblivion. It was phenomenal. The chunky tomato sauce was fresh like it had just come from the vine, and the warm, thick crust tasted like freshly baked bread. The pepperoni, sausage, onions, and mushrooms melded well with the rest of the ingredients. There was a party in my mouth.

"So good!" I exclaimed, with the roof of my mouth still on fire from the cheese. Well, there was at least one thing that I was enjoying about 1974—the food.

"This is the bomb dot com!" Maddie declared.

"This is the best pizza I've had in my life, hands down," said Larry. "Well, there's really no good pizza places in Alabama besides the fast-food places."

"This tastes amazing," Hannah said. "But it's *not* pizza."

Maddie, Larry, and I looked at her like she was out of her mind.

"Let me explain," she offered. "This is *stuffed bread*." She pointed at her pie. "If you want *pizza*, then you're gonna have to go to New York."

If only my mom were there. She would've *schooled* Hannah in a New York versus Chicago pizza debate.

"At least they didn't put pineapple on this."

"Come on, Hannah, did you have to go there?" I teased. I'm a Californian, after all. Putting pineapple on pizza is what we do.

"Yes, I did," she said. "And just so you know, it's not pizza if you have to eat it with a *fork and knife.*"

"How's your salad?" I asked Kylie, trying to include her.

"It tastes like salad," she replied.

After we finished our pizzas—well, and salad—we walked across the Chicago River to the Willis Tower, which I learned was actually called the Sears Tower in 1974. It was at that point the tallest building in the world. The skyscraper looked brand-new because it was completed just a year before. We rode the elevator to the 103rd floor and walked out onto the Skydeck.

I looked around and observed a panoramic view of the illuminated Chicago skyline, as it twinkled in the night sky. We were so high up, and the Windy City was so windy (hence its name), I could feel the tower sway. I wondered what would happen if someone dropped a penny from where I was standing. I sure wouldn't want to be the person on the ground.

We enjoyed the early night breeze for a little while before making our descent to street level. *What a way to end a great road trip*, I thought. It marked our last day of freedom. From here on out, it was to be all work. No more playing around.

25

INFILTRATING THE MOB FOR DUMMIES

We arrived at the address on Al's business card at 8:50 a.m. on Sunday. We figured that being a full ten minutes early would make a good first impression on the FBI district chief. Given our situation, we certainly didn't want to risk getting on his bad side. And to refer to my mom's golden rule again, *there's never a second chance to make a first impression.*

When we walked into the District Office, we were greeted by Al and Manny. They were both standing by the doorway, likely in anticipation of our expected arrival.

"I see you made it here, right on schedule," Al said. "Well done, kids."

"Thanks, and we really enjoyed our trip here," Hannah said. "It was a much-needed bonding experience." She looked happily at me, and I smiled back at her.

Al was not in the mood to hear about mule rides or me

eating giant steaks. "Look, kids. Before we go on with our regularly scheduled program, I want to talk to all of you about something—outside."

Like an offensive lineman on my school's football team, Manny stood there stoically, ensuring we didn't venture into the office until Al had his word in with us.

We did as the agent had instructed and stepped back outside of the building. He joined us, shutting the door behind him.

"Look, kiddos." He spoke in the lowest possible voice that didn't yet qualify as a whisper. "We went out on a limb bringing you here. So you better not screw it up for us."

"We'll be well behaved," I replied. "Don't worry."

Al looked sternly at the five of us. "Well, that too. But the most important thing, and the reason I called you outside, is that you do not tell a soul about where you *really* come from. And that means the other agents *and* the chief."

"So, if they don't know that we're from the future, who do they think we are?" Larry asked.

"I told them that you're a bunch of students—which you are—but students from *1974* who Manny and I encountered on our trip to Fresno. All of you have been unsuccessfully recruited by Brown's syndicate via Bonilla's gang. The office buys this because we were there in part to interview unsuccessful recruits. You've all willingly agreed to come to Chicago to be part of our investigation."

"But why can't you just tell them the truth?" Kylie asked.

"Because of reasons we discussed in O'Malley's. Primarily

because they won't believe Manny and me, or they'll think we're out of our minds, or possibly, that we're deliberately trying to screw up the whole Brown investigation." Al coldly gazed at us. "It don't really matter what the reasons are. You ain't telling nobody because I *said* so. We are the *only* two people, well, good guys at least, who know the truth about who you are. Everybody else here doesn't, and you're gonna keep it that way under all circumstances. Understood?"

"Understood," we all replied.

Al grinned and led us back inside.

It then became clear to me why we couldn't fly or travel to Chicago with Al and Manny. The rest of the FBI had no idea who we were—Al had lied to them. I wondered what hidden agenda he had. Maybe he was gunning for a promotion. He must have wanted the accomplishment of defeating Brown so badly he was willing to cut corners to do so—including putting five unassuming teens in harm's way.

We walked into the office, past the reception area, where Manny was standing next to three men I had never met. Everyone was dressed to the nines—not just suits, ties, and dress shoes, but cuff links, handkerchiefs—the whole shebang.

He motioned to the three men to Manny's right. "This is Special Agent Tom Collins—not the drink—Detective Hank Gallagher, and District Chief Scott Marshall." They waved to us as Al said their names. "Us five are going to be training you five over the next week. Tom is our resident expert on undercover ops. Detective Gallagher is the Chicago PD's liaison to us on the Brown case. And Marshall, my boss, is the head honcho of the whole damn Greenie gang task force."

"We are all glad you have agreed to help us," said Chief Marshall. "The Greenies have been notoriously difficult for us law enforcers to get a hold of, so we need all the help we can get." The chief was a strapping man with well-kempt brown hair. He looked pretty young to have his job, probably forty at most. "Today, your first day of boot camp, you're gonna specifically focus on maintaining your covers in front of the gang. Tom and his girl will teach you how to act the part."

We nodded in agreement. *If only they knew who we actually were,* I thought.

With that, we followed Tom as he ushered us into a room deep inside of the headquarters. He was a small middle-aged man with a fully shaven bald head resembling a cue ball. He wore horn-rimmed glasses, much like the ones worn by Hannah's friend Franz, and was growing a sparse graying beard.

"This is my girlfriend, Misty," Tom said, pointing to the attractive auburn-haired woman standing next to him. She was about the same height as he was and looked like she was between fifteen to twenty years his junior. Well, something in that neighborhood.

"Hello all," Misty greeted us with a curtsy and a warm smile.

"Misty is an improv teacher by trade, so you kids are lucky to have her teach you," Tom continued. "Think of it as a master class on mob infiltration."

"You're selling yourself short, Tommy," Misty said playfully, nudging her agent boyfriend in the shoulder. "He's the real deal himself. He's too shy to mention it, but he was actually a semi-pro actor before joining the Feds."

"I was that guy on the side of the road in *Easy Rider*," Tom replied. "As Andy Warhol says, that was my fifteen minutes— well, *two and a half* seconds of fame."

We nervously chuckled.

"So, basically," Tom went on, "to get to Brown, you're gonna have to go through several recruiters." He refocused his glasses on the bridge of his nose. "Just to keep moving on to the next round in the Greenies' extensive and intensive vetting-slash-screening process, you *must* show them that you are fully dedicated to 'the cause,' as they call it. Remember, you kids came here all the way from Fresno to start a new life in organized crime. They're gonna ask about your families—your background. They're gonna ask about the Fresno gang that purportedly recruited you—and also why you chose to come to Chicago and not instead just stay put in your hometown and do petty crimes. We will teach you the right answers to these questions, but the rest is up to you. Brown and his confidants ain't easily fooled *at all*. One tiny, minuscule, microscopic misstep by any one of you, and *all* of your covers are blown."

Misty grabbed five bundles of clothes from a shelf mounted to the room's side wall. She passed them one by one to Tom, who threw them to each of us. I noticed that my bundle had a piece of masking tape attached to it, inscribed with the name "Donald Brian 'Donnie' Carpenter, Jr."

"This is what you will wear in the field," Tom stated. "There are five outfits in each of your bundles. And if you haven't already noticed the names on them, well, they're *your* names now."

"*Grandma* pants? Seriously?" Maddie said, holding up a pair of unusually baggy jeans from her bundle. She wasn't making it easy for us to blend in.

Tom flashed Maddie a dirty look. "Bell-bottoms are so *in* right now, Francine," he replied, calling Maddie by her "new name."

"This miniskirt better not be leather," Kylie said, inspecting her bundle as well.

"Here, Ky, trade with me!" Hannah threw her miniskirt into Kylie's hands.

"Thanks, Hannah," Kylie said, passing the leather skirt to her.

"*Sharon* and *Nancy*," Tom corrected them.

"Forgive me. Thank you, *Nancy*." Kylie snorted, not being able to hold back her laughter.

"So, let's roleplay," resumed Tom. "Misty and I are going to play the two recruiters. Each of you kids is gonna take a turn and try to convince us to let you join the infamous Mount Greenwood Boys Gang. First up is you, Donnie." He pointed at my face.

Of course I have to go first. It's just my luck.

I joined Tom and Misty in the corner of the room. Tom stood over me, as if he was one of Brown's henchmen.

"Whatcha doing here, kid?" he barked, almost like he was playing a mobster in a Martin Scorsese movie. "This ain't the candy shop."

"I—uh want to join the Grennies!" I stammered.

Misty laughed. "You don't just *join* the Greenies. It don't work like that."

"Yeah, you have to *earn* your stripes 'round here," Tom added. "Besides, you're just a random punk off the street. For all we know, you could be a rat."

"Who even are you?" asked Misty.

"Char—uh—Donnie," I mumbled, almost forgetting my cover.

"*Charuhdonnie*?" Tom replied, laughing. "Never heard of such a name. Did your parents name you after a brand of wine or something?"

"So, whatever-your-name-is, why do you want to *join* our cause so bad?" Misty's acting was so realistic I was legitimately terrified at that moment.

I hesitated. "Um—uh, I want to be a criminal!"

"Then go pick some pockets. You're just wasting our time here, kid." Tom wasn't letting up.

I was grasping at straws to save my performance. "But—but I came here from Fresno! That's in California. And—and I was recruited by the uh—Nessies. You might have heard of them!"

"I'm gonna give you to the count of three to get the hell out of here," Misty ordered bluntly. "One—two—"

Before she could say "three," Tom waved his hands

signaling that the drill was over.

"So, how did I do?" I asked. My grandpa taught me once, "Never ask a question that you already know the answer to." Well, at that moment, I didn't heed his advice as I *knew* I did terribly. Reading from a script was one thing. Improv was a whole nother ball game for me.

"I don't wanna sugarcoat things," Tom stated honestly, "but if those were *real* gangsters and you acted like that, I doubt you would've made it out of there with a head."

"Well, the good news is that it was only practice," Misty said. "You have an entire week to hone your improv skills before it's showtime."

A week didn't seem like enough at all.

Everyone else except Hannah, well, "Nancy," also failed miserably on their first attempt. Performing in high-pressure situations came easy to her. It was a gift.

We had a three-hour class with Tom and Misty every day for the rest of the boot camp. We also spent a lot of time with Manny perfecting our hand-to-hand combat skills. Despite our rocky start, he was starting to warm up to all of us—even Hannah. She was sure not to make any more *Degrassi* references. Plus, the guy was a black belt in just about everything, so I appreciated having the chance to learn from him. Since we were about to confront the very unpredictable Brown, it behooved us to have as many self-defense techniques as possible in our arsenal.

After teaching us a few moves, Manny gathered a few wooden boards from the corner of the room. "Eeth theemple," he said, showing them to us. "Preetend Brown eeth attackeeng you and thee board eeth heeth faith."

I think he meant to say his *face*, but I wasn't sure.

He held a single board up to my face, at eye-level. Then, using what I remembered from Taekwondo, I unleashed a roundhouse kick. "Hi-ya!" I yelled as the board split in two.

Larry, Kylie, and Hannah also broke their board on the first try. It took Maddie *six* tries.

When we finished, Manny motioned toward a stack of six or seven cement bricks, which I just realized was there. "Eef you thought that wath hard, watch me." He slammed his right fist down on the top of the stack. At once, the bricks crumbled as if a jackhammer hit them. I've never seen anyone nearly as strong. He could've taken Rick McCreery down with his pinky alone.

Toward the end of the training, Al called us into his office to go over the in-depth history of Brown and the Greenies.

"I just don't get it," Larry said to him. "I don't get why Brown is fascinated with being such a ruthless prick. I know that he sees organized crime as an art form that he's obsessed with perfecting. But what's his motive behind all of this?"

Al's eyes narrowed. "Well, to be honest. It's all about legacy to that creep. He wants to be remembered as the most fearsome gangster of all time. More than Bulger, more than Gambino, more than even Capone." Al then looked me square in the face. "So, you mentioned you wrote a paper on Brown," he said. "What specifically do you remember about him—his upbringing, his backstory?"

"I remember that he grew up dirt poor, and he was an orphan—and that's about it," I stated. "When I was researching him, there was a whole lot of information about his adult life. But there was next to nothing about his childhood."

"Well, luckily, you're in an FBI office, not a library," Al replied. "And here we have access to *classified* information about Brown." Al paused to adjust his fedora—we noticed he did that a lot. "So, I'll give you the skinny on the monster, from everything we know from our records. Aidan Séan Brown was born on July 29, 1945, in the basement of a drug house on Chicago's Southwest Side. His parents were unmarried, both first-generation Irish Americans and, by all records, in an abusive relationship. His father, Dermot Gahagan, was a petty criminal—what his son would call a 'wannabe.' Dermot was involved in a few local gangs and died in a shootout at the age of twenty when little Aidan was only two. His mother, Shannon Brown, gave birth to him when she was fifteen and died of dysentery less than three years later, a few days shy of her eighteenth birthday. Aidan was 'raised'—" Al used air quotes on the word "—by Shannon's parents, Patsy and Desmond Brown, who were both off the boat from Dublin. His grandparents spoke little English and had twelve other children and four additional grandchildren for whom they were responsible. They all grew up in abject poverty and did not have access to the many things we take for granted. Since he was as young as four, Aidan began stealing food to help feed his family—and crime soon became his way of life. As an adolescent, he was taken in by the local Mafia to be a 'gopher,' thus beginning his involvement in the Windy City's organized crime scene. He started with thefts, larcenies—small potatoes compared to what he's cooking up now—but he began to steadily up his game with each success. In 1964, Brown founded his organization, the Mount Greenwood Boys Gang, who soon, of course, became known simply as 'the Greenies.'"

I summarized what Al just said. "So, Brown entered organized crime because he saw it was his only way out of the slum he came from. And now he's terrorizing the entire city."

"Exactly. In order to beat a criminal mastermind, you first have to understand his psyche—what makes him tick." Al paused again, this time for nearly ten seconds. "At the end of the day, Brown is just a human being. He might be an awful, insanely disturbed, sociopathic one, but he is still, well, *human,* just like you and me. I've been dealing with gangsters for a while, and they love when the police constantly dehumanize them. They feed off of it. It makes them feel more powerful and dangerous. So, maybe your best way of getting to Brown is to level with him—easier said than done, of course."

"Exactly how are we going to do that?" I asked.

Al shrugged. "I wish I had an answer for you kids. But if I did, we wouldn't be in this predicament in the first place."

26

PLAN OF ATTACK

The day before infiltration was set to commence, Chief Marshall called Maddie, Hannah, Kylie, Larry, and me into his office to discuss what exactly was going to go down the following afternoon. We all took a seat near the end of a long table, with the chief sitting at the head and Al, Manny, Tom, and Detective Gallagher nestled in the middle.

"So, before we get into the thick of things, how was the boot camp? Any feedback?" Marshall asked plainly.

"Well, I definitely learned more about going undercover than I knew before," I replied optimistically.

"Turns out there's more to it than *21 Jump Street*," Kylie added, trying to be lighthearted but completely forgetting that no one except Al and Manny knew we were from the future. She quickly noticed her mistake when Al shot her a grimace.

The chief was not amused either. "I don't know what that is, and I don't care," he scoffed.

Gallagher spoke next. "The Chicago PD sent several plainclothes officers to sweep the city and find where Brown recruits. We received a few tips that point to one central location."

The detective pulled out a photograph from the Manila folder in front of him. It depicted the front of a restaurant, covered with a red awning marked by an image of a white eagle wearing a golden crown. I instantly recognized it as the famous deli owned by my mom's grandparents.

"Kazlowski's," Al said. "This high-traffic spot in Polish Downtown is apparently serving up more than Chicago's best pierogis. Several sources have verified that it is also a front for much of the Greenies' recruiting, transactions, and hob-knobbing."

Maddie and I were devastated. We were holding out hope that Al's hypothesis about our family being involved with the Greenies, and us being used as blackmail bait, was wrong— but that picture just confirmed it. A picture is surely worth a thousand words. Both of us were frozen in shock and terror.

"Why that deli?" Larry asked, trying to give Maddie and me a much-needed answer. "Why does Brown recruit there and not at any other downtown restaurant?"

"You don't understand how the mob business works, kid," Marshall explained. "It's a very *quid pro quo* affair. The Greenies strategically single out businesses that will help them expand their empire. Then, once Brown sets his targets, his mercenaries make their owners comply with his demands. If they do, they get to keep their business, *most* of their revenue, and their own families' lives."

"There are two options," Al elaborated. "Listen or die."

"Kazlowski's, as you might know, is a landmark restaurant," Marshall continued. "If Brown has it under his control, he essentially has the entire Polish Downtown."

All of this was hard to process. Though, one thing was for sure. The fact that Brown was singling out my family made me want to bring his ass down even more.

"So, we just go there tomorrow and look for the Greenies?" Hannah asked. "Are they like wearing something that makes them easy to identify?"

Tom shook his head. "Remember the code speak Misty and I taught you guys? That's when it comes in handy. You just say a random sentence and throw the words 'green' and 'brown' in there—something along those lines. If the guy looks at you like you have two heads, he's not a Greenie. Easy as that."

"This is what you're gonna do," Al interjected. "You arrive there between three and four tomorrow afternoon when business is relatively slow. That's the prime recruiting hour. First, you order some food, so things don't look suspicious. Then, using what Tom taught you, you locate a Greenie. And you take it from there. Any questions?" He asked that rhetorically—I didn't think the FBI was in the mood for questions.

Larry raised his hand. "What exactly do you mean by *take it from there*?"

Al glared at him. "Look, we don't have time to discuss

every possibility right now. Dealing with Brown is like playing Russian roulette. You never know what that bastard is gonna give you."

"How about this," Marshall offered. "You go there tomorrow, do what we said, and report back to us. Then, based on what you tell us, we'll decide what we want you to do next."

The chief dismissed us, and we headed back to our hotel in silence. No one wanted to talk about our grim reality. Maddie and I were especially terrified. It was definitely *us* who Brown wanted. Still, one simple question remained.

Why?

27

HOW I MET YOUR GRANDMOTHER

At 3:14 P.M. the next day, I opened the doors to Kazlowski's Deli and Restaurant. It didn't seem real that I was there, given that it went out of business before I was born, as its new owners couldn't keep up with the lofty quality standards my great-grandparents had set. Its spacious, two-story interior looked like a cross between a diner and a traditional deli. Red and white tablecloths—the colors of the Polish flag—covered many tables of varying shapes and sizes. At the end of the first floor stood a vast display case containing dozens of different varieties of meats, sausages, and cheeses. The walls were decorated with pictures of Kraków, my great-grandparents' hometown. Bouncy polka music was playing in the background.

Attached to the front inside the window was a laminated sign reading, *Proszę usiąść,* with the English translation underneath: *Please seat yourself.* We followed suit and sat down at the only table that could comfortably fit us all. Less than a minute later, a beautiful girl came to our table to welcome us and hand us all menus. She looked almost exactly like a younger version of my mother, except she was a brunette. *Wait a second.* I realized she was my grandma Vicky. She couldn't have been a day over sixteen.

"Holy crap, that's Grandma," I whispered to Maddie when she had left.

"She don't look like Grandma," Maddie replied. "She's like my age."

"Forty-eight years makes a difference," I said, stating the obvious.

A minute later, a genial young man with a rag in his hand came to the table and proceeded to wipe it down. He was fair-skinned with a healthy mop of blond hair and light blue eyes. When I looked at him, I had yet another *holy crap* moment: he was Grandpa Paul.

"Oh my gawd," Maddie muttered to Kylie and Hannah, oblivious to Paul and pointing to a young female customer in the corner wearing a long, bell-sleeved, patterned gown. "I don't know what she was thinking with *that* dress. It's more like a pillowcase if you ask me."

My grandpa noticed her heavy California accent. At once, he stopped what he was doing and turned to her with a wide, friendly smile. "Miss, I reckon you ain't from around here," he said. "Whereabouts did you travel from?"

Maddie struggled to answer, probably realizing at that moment that he was our grandfather. "Uh—California. We're on a—uh school trip."

"That's so cool," Grandpa Paul responded. "A trip this early in the year. I wish my school did that. Anyway, welcome to the Windy City, and welcome to Kazlowski's. The name's Paul. My folks own this place."

Paul resumed wiping the table, turning his head to look at Vicky, who was taking an order nearby. He definitely was eyeing her.

"Is she your girlfriend?" I playfully asked him.

He blushed. "I wish. That's Victoria Hanrahan. She's out of my league—as in *miles* out of my league. Plus, my dad would *kill* me if I dated another restaurant employee. He gives me that lecture about 'mixing work and pleasure' all the time." Paul sighed. "It's just never gonna happen."

"Never say *never*." Maddie winked at him.

"Thanks for the encouragement," Paul replied, "but I don't think she'll go for a guy like me." He lowered his voice to make sure no one beyond the table overheard him. "She'll probably end up with one of them no-good Greenie boys."

"Who?" Larry asked, playing dumb. I guess he didn't want Paul to think we had any connection with Brown and his gang whatsoever.

"You're really not from here," my grandpa Paul continued. "They're only the mob that practically runs the *entire* city's business community. They're here all the time and hang out at the bar upstairs." He lowered his voice even more. "My dad would love to kick them out of here or just call the cops on them, but they'd retaliate and set the place on fire—or worse."

"That's terrible!" reacted Hannah.

"It's not like they can just go away," Paul said, in an even *more* hushed tone. "The Greenies are like roaches. Just when you think you've gotten rid of one, *seven* come back."

"So, Paul. What do you recommend we order?" I asked, crudely changing the subject.

"Well, in my humble opinion, there's only one choice," he said with a big smile, picking up my menu and flipping to the special pages. "You can't go wrong with #7, the Polish sampler. You get a little bit of everything: kielbasa, *gołąbki, kotlety schabowy,* and of course a heaping portion of the best pierogis this side of the Vistula."

We all thanked Paul as he returned to the kitchen to speak to his parents.

Then, Vicky walked over to the table to take our orders, and all of us—except Kylie—got the #7, per my grandpa's recommendation.

Kylie asked the same question she asked every time we went out to eat. "What are your vegan options?"

Vicky looked very confused. "Pardon me?" I don't think she had ever heard the word "vegan" before.

"Never mind, then," Kylie replied. "I'm just sticking with water."

The food arrived in record time. Everything was absolutely delicious and tasted nearly identical to my mom's cooking. That wasn't a surprise, given that she used the same secret family recipes passed down through the generations. If Maddie and I were lucky, we would know them one day. The experience of being in the restaurant and seeing my young grandparents made me miss them and my mom even more. I longed to return home so much I was willing to do *anything*—even collide head-on with a vicious crime syndicate.

I tried to calm myself down by stuffing my face with the savory meats and pierogis. The golden-brown dumplings were generously filled with potato and farm-fresh cheese, coated in a rich, buttery sauce, and finished with caramelized onions and scallions. As I cut each pierogi in half with my fork, the crisp half-moon-shaped noodle exterior lightly crackled, and the soft, gooey filling oozed out like molten lava. It was a pure culinary masterpiece.

"These pierogis are phenomenal," Hannah observed.

"Too much butter. I don't do butter," Kylie remarked, clutching her glass of ice water.

She was, without a doubt, the odd woman out—as my mom would say, *different strokes for different folks.*

I gladly cleaned my plate, scooping up every last morsel. Hannah turned toward me. "I hope your grandpa doesn't chicken out and asks your grandma out already."

"He better—otherwise, Maddie and I will be in *big* trouble."

"If he doesn't ask her out for *any* reason, Charlie and Maddie will all of a sudden—*poof!*—vanish into thin air," Kylie said, gesturing like a magician.

"Another *Back to the Future* reference," Larry snarked. "How original of you, Ky."

"Yeah, that's certainly not helping," I noted. "First the

gang, now I have to worry about becoming part of the atmosphere."

"So, where exactly are we meeting this big bad gang?" asked Maddie.

"Grandpa said it," I answered her. "Upstairs is where we have to go to find them."

My grandparents had described the restaurant to Maddie and me plenty of times before, but they had never mentioned it had an upstairs. Now I knew why.

"We have to be discreet," said Larry. "We don't want to invoke any suspicion in granny and gramps."

After we had paid, we kept our eyes on Paul and Vicky. A few minutes passed, and Paul hurried back into the kitchen. Right after, Vicky, the young woman who one day would become his wife, went to bring a ticket to the counter. We had our opening.

The five of us quietly sneaked up the staircase. We found ourselves in a room that looked entirely out of place compared to the well-manicured main level. Empty Jameson bottles littered the tables. Paisley wallpaper was peeling off the dilapidated walls. It made O'Malley's, the dive bar where we had met Al and Manny, look like a Buffalo Wild Wings. Since it was still daytime, the bar itself was closed, as there were no restaurant employees to be seen. *What a perfect time and place to do shady stuff,* I thought.

Sitting at the far table was a ghoulish man in his mid-twenties, with a shaved head, dark circles under his eyes, and a dangling earring in his left ear. His sleeveless shirt showed off his large left bicep, covered with a tattoo of a green dragon.

Remembering my practice sessions with Tom and Misty, I approached the man. "Hey, sir. We were just looking for directions to Mount *Green*wood. We want to go to this Irish pub called *Brown's.*"

The large bald man perked up at my words, almost like a dog at the sound of the word "squirrel." "Who sent you punks here?" he barked.

I froze. Luckily, next to me was Hannah, the star actress, who jumped in to bail me out.

"The Nessies," she said. "Well, they're called the Kobras now—I think."

The man spit out his chewing tobacco. "Oh. You're just some of those wannabe thugs from California. No thanks," he scoffed. "We don't have room for any of you. You Californians ain't nothing but drama queens. I see why they put Hollywood there."

Another burly man with bright red hair began to escort us away.

In desperation, I yelled out. "But wait! We'll do anything to be a part of your group and help you."

"Do you mean *anything*?" the bald man questioned. "Or do you just wanna get paid so you can buy some booze and weed, because that's what it looks like you is trying to do."

"You *is*?!" Hannah corrected. "You can sure use a grammar lesson, Uncle Fester!"

Enraged, the man slammed his fist on the table. Hannah

was making every effort to get on his nerves—and it was working.

"We *are* not who you think we *are*," I added, stressing my plural verb form. "If we were just doing this to get drunk and high, we would get jobs in this restaurant. Instead, we want to join the Greenies because we *believe* in your mission. We admire Brown. We drove all the way out here—four days— just to learn from him. And you just want to turn us away like that."

Baldy looked at me. "I'm listening," he said in a calculated tone.

"Actually, we're doing this because we *love* Brown," Maddie gushed. "It's just amazing how he quickly took control of this city in such a short time. We would love to be a part of his wonderful—I mean terrible—I mean *terribly wonderful* organization."

"You see, we all come from nothing too. We're farmers' kids," Kylie lied. Her eyes attempted to form crocodile tears. "There was a big drought in Fresno this past summer. We called it the *Dust Bowl* 'cause there was no rain at all. We lost everything—and no one from the government or any local authorities came to help us and our families. Now we're going to *fight* to get it all back. We will do whatever it takes to get what we want, how we want it—no matter the crime."

"And when we say crime, we don't mean small jobs," Larry chimed in. "Oh, no, no. We've spent enough time hustling drugs on the street. We're ready for the big leagues now."

The man looked slightly impressed—key word, slightly.

"I'll see what I can do for you slugs," he uttered plainly. "I gots to talk to the boss to see if you can help us with anything. No promises."

"At the very least, can I have his autograph?" Maddie asked. "I'm Brown's number one fan. I literally have a poster of him in my room, right next to David Cassidy!"

The bald man cackled. "Brown only does autographs in blood." He spit more tobacco out on the floor. "Come back here tomorrow first thing in the morning, and we'll tell you his decision. His *final* decision."

The red-headed man guided us toward the stairs, and we quickly followed, making our way down and out of the restaurant. Once we were back out on the street, I turned to the rest of the group. "Well, that went a lot better than expected."

"Due to your awesome ad-libbing!" said Hannah.

"Yeah, Charlie," Kylie added. "You saved all our asses with that little emotional-ass speech of yours."

"Your sob story about the Dust Bowl helped too," I replied. "But honestly, didn't that happen a long time before the 1970s?"

"It's not like that Greenie paid attention during history class to even know what that was," Larry said.

"Guys," said Maddie, "what if we don't get into the gang? Then what? How the hell are we gonna get home?"

"Oh, we're gonna get in," Larry assured her. "This isn't like rushing a sorority. As Al was telling us during training, the Greenies see their new recruits as disposable pawns. They take anyone with a pulse who wants to submit to their will. Unless they picked up that we're undercover already—but believe me, I don't think we were *that* obvious."

"True," Kylie said. "I think it's just a mental game they play. They're probably trained to play hard to get, so the prospective recruits think positions are scarce, and they don't have second thoughts about joining up."

We soon regrouped with the FBI and filled them in on what had transpired in Kazlowski's. "So, they said they'll think about it," I stated to Al. "We were invited back tomorrow morning."

"Good work," Al replied, impressed. "The plan is working to a 'T.'"

"Thanks to Tom," I said. "His improv tips really helped us."

Tom nodded in acknowledgment. "See!" he said to Marshall. "When they assigned me to this office, I heard from the grapevine that you were complaining that you didn't need a failed actor in the Bureau. Well, who has the last laugh now, Chief?"

"Don't count your chickens before they hatch, kids," Marshall said to us, ignoring Tom. "What happens tomorrow is anybody's guess."

Per the bald man's instructions, we arrived at the upstairs lounge the next morning, right after the doors of Kazlowski's had opened. Greeting us was the same red-haired burly man who was with him the day before and four equally large men, none of whom I had seen before. The four men behind the redhead were all holding revolvers. Were they about to use them on us? I was scared crapless.

I looked around for the bald man, but I couldn't find him—anywhere. *Maybe he is late*, I figured.

Suddenly, one of the armed men opened his mouth. "You kids looking for Brennan? The guy you was with yesterday?"

We all nodded.

The mobster glared at us with his evil gray eyes, for what had to be ten seconds. "He's dead."

28

THE CREAM
OF THE CROP

None of us could believe it. I guess that's how life in organized crime works. One day you're fine—and the next, you're gone.

"It happened right after he was talking to *you*," the armed man continued, with his harsh, gravelly voice tinged by a slight Irish brogue.

"I swear, we had absolutely nothing to do with it!" I anxiously blurted out.

"We're just kids," Maddie pleaded.

The burly red-haired man was incensed. He finally spoke up. "You think we think *you* punks killed Brennan?" When he spoke, a droplet of his saliva grazed my face. "I bet none of you even know how to fire a gun."

The man who had spoken before continued, "Brennan told Cormac over there that he did not think you have what it takes to be Greenies. Cormac left his side to piss for one second, and the next thing he heard was gunfire—and *bam!* Brennan was on the ground, dead."

"It was a coincidence!" Hannah cried. "It had to have been."

"No," the man continued. "There ain't no coincidences where I come from—somebody really wants you to join."

Uh-oh, this is not good. Was it possible that Brown already knew who we were, and he killed Brennan so we could be brought to him more quickly? It appeared that Brown was such a madman he used Brennan as a literal human sacrifice to scare the rest of his gang into submission. He was a genius indeed—an insane, evil genius.

"So, we have no other course of action but to accept you," the man with the revolver said reluctantly. "Welcome to the family. I guess."

"So, we're Greenies now?" Maddie asked, pretending to be excited, keeping consistent with our covers.

"No," stated another armed man. "You don't just *become* Greenies on the spot, you idiot kids. You have to pay your dues and work your way up. Now, you're just recruits."

"You're gonna start out doing the grunt work," said the man who was doing most of the talking. "Pretty much you do what we say. If one of us says hop like a bunny rabbit, you sure as hell gonna hop like a bunny rabbit. The life you had before is over."

"If you want to be badasses, you gotta eat, breathe, and sleep whatever we tell you," uttered a third armed man.

"When do we get to meet Brown?" Maddie asked. She

was playing the "fangirl" persona as Tom had taught her.

The five men in front of us all laughed.

"You seriously think Brown would want to meet *you*?" Cormac scoffed, almost spitting in my face *again*.

"Yeah, we do," Larry confidently piped up. "Unless you want to die like your friend, Brennan."

"Is that a threat?" barked one of the Greenies in the corner, who was silent up until this point.

"You bet it is," Larry stated confidently. "Y'all told us yourselves that what happened to dear ol' Brennan *wasn't* a coincidence. So what's it gonna be?"

The five Greenies were speechless.

Larry continued. "You better think long and hard about this. The same reason Brennan got killed will be the reason at least one of *you* also gets killed if you don't take us to see Brown. So who wants to be the next Brennan? Any volunteers?"

Though they tried not to let on, the Greenies seemed somewhat unsettled by Larry's bluff—even though they were twice the size of us and armed. Boy, they must have been terrified of Brown.

The lead man with the revolver resumed speaking. "Well, I guess we'll have to introduce you to him now. Let's go. We're getting this over with."

The men exited the bar and motioned for us to follow them down the narrow stairs. Instead of making a left and leading us out of the restaurant through the front door, they took us through the fire exit in the back. Opening it, they revealed a back alley.

The tallest of the men stood over us, with his gun pointed. "Get in your car and wait until you see a black Impala," he ordered. "We will give you a signal so you know it's us. You're gonna follow that Impala—Cormac will be following you. One wrong turn and consider your careers *and* your lives over. Then you can say hi to Brennan for me."

We turned down another alley and were back onto the street where Larry parked the Sunny. Sheepishly, we hopped into the vehicle and waited until we saw the gang's car. A minute or two later, a jet-black 1967 Chevy Impala slowly passed by us. The driver, who we recognized as the Irish-accented Revolver Guy, stuck his arm out of the window, curving his fingers to the point where his hand resembled a claw you would see in one of those arcade machines. *The dragon hand.* I remembered my school paper—that was the Greenies' gang sign.

Larry immediately took off, following the Impala. The Greenies led us on a winding route with frequent turns. I assumed that they were taking us a roundabout way to our destination on purpose so there was no chance we could memorize the directions. Brown's men had sure mastered the art of being sneaky and clever.

"You think Brown killed Brennan because he didn't want to take us?" Hannah whispered to me in the backseat.

"I don't know," I replied. "But one thing's for sure. The real Brown seems just like the Aidan Brown I researched and wrote about. He's not afraid to get rid of *anybody* who stands in the way of his plans, even his own men."

We drove for fifty minutes to an hour. Finally, the Impala stopped in front of an abandoned building in what appeared to be an industrial park located in a highly impoverished area. Larry parked behind it, and we quickly got out of our car. The Greenies rounded us up like cattle at the rodeo, making sure that none of us left their sight.

"Follow us," commanded Revolver Guy as we marched forward, pushing open the mysterious building's metal doors.

My group was led down a half-dozen poorly lit flights of stairs into a dark, humid, and empty cellar. *Forget six feet under.* My mind raced. *If I die here, I'd be sixty feet under the ground, at least.*

We walked across the long chamber, with the top of my hair grazing against the asbestos popcorn ceiling. Larry had to duck the entire way through. He was too tall to stand.

At the end of the cellar, we heard one of the men remove an object and punch in a passcode. In doing this, he opened a hidden door to an extremely narrow corridor with an even lower ceiling. It was, at most, four feet wide and five feet high. We had no choice but to crawl in single file. The cement floor was not kind to my bell-bottom jeans, which ripped at the in-seams as I dragged my shins and knees to dodge hanging cobwebs and scurrying rats. Once we had just about reached the end of the corridor, Revolver Guy stopped to type another passcode into the wall. This caused the ground in front of us to open, revealing a circular compartment. We followed the men into the narrow opening and down a ladder.

No wonder Brown hasn't been caught yet, I realized. *He sets up shop in the bowels of the earth.*

I carefully descended the twenty-foot metal ladder. When I reached the ground, I found that I was in another dark, cobweb-infested corridor eerily similar to the one I had just left. For how much longer did this labyrinth continue?

We crawled some more until the ceiling suddenly got higher. Finally, I could stand again. I also could see. A sole lightbulb lit our way. We were soon at a doorway guarded by a menacing, bull-faced man. His shaved head, face, and neck were completely covered in tattoos of snakes, dragons, and what seemed like a bevy of occult symbols. He had at least twenty piercings on his ears, nose, lips, and chin. "*A théann an?*" he asked in Irish.

Revolver Guy answered the tattooed guard, "*Ta roinnt francaigh againn don cheannaire!*"

The guard punched yet another passcode into the wall, opening the door and allowing us to proceed. We walked into what appeared to resemble a high school hallway. There were numbered lockers on the wall, complete with combination locks, and numbered "classrooms" as well—though I highly doubt there was any homework being done there. Each room had a different scary-looking guard in front of it.

At the end of the hallway was *another* large door, blocked by *another* large guard. "Password!" he barked to the Greenies who accompanied us.

"*Is maith bhean í ach níor bhain sí a broga di go foill,*" Revolver Guy replied.

"Access approved!" the guard growled.

The room in front of us looked like a carbon copy of a stereotypical corporate boardroom. There were blackboards with chalk. A heavily marked eight-by-ten-foot street map of Chicago, and its surrounding suburbs, covered the wall. However, my eyes fixated on the giant table, where twelve or so physically imposing men were seated and engaged in intense conversation. The man doing ninety percent of the talking was a youthful figure seated at the table's end. He was of medium height and build—looking like a "nerd" compared to all the burly mobsters he was with. His face was clean-shaven, and his strawberry-blond hair was cut in a skin fade. He wore a single gold chain around his neck and a cut shirt that displayed his two full sleeves of tattoos. But what gave him away were his eerie, soulless grayish-brown eyes. They were creeping me out even though I was quite a distance away from him. I immediately recognized who he was.

I was standing twenty feet away from Aidan Brown himself.

The Greenies who had led us into the headquarters ordered us to wait until Brown finished up with his current order of business. As we waited in the back corner of the room, I couldn't help but listen in on what was going on in front of me.

"Don't you speak-a-da English, Vinny!" Brown taunted the tan-skinned, middle-aged man seated next to him. "I made-a myself a-clear. If I don't have the money you owe me by tomorrow morning, you guys are *finito*. *Capeesh?*"

"You better watch yourself, young man," Vinny replied.

"I'm Vincenzo di Carlo of the Scungilli Crime Family, and you're just some *Mick* who steals from mom-and-pop shops."

"And I do a pretty damn good job of what I do, unlike you, you filthy *wop*." Brown scowled. "I'm practically the mayor of Chicago as far as your *Guinea* ass is concerned—and I strongly suggest you watch *yourself*, Vinny. Come on, call me a *Mick* one more time. I swear you ain't gonna have a pot to piss in or anything to piss *with,* for that matter."

"Are *you* threatening *me*?" responded Vinny, not doing a very convincing job of hiding the terror and horror in his voice.

"Why, yes, I am," Brown stated matter-of-factly. "This ain't the twenties no more." He spat in the direction of Vinny's men. "The Mafia is such a joke now, that bearded hippie, Frank Cappicola, or whatever the hell his name is, made a movie about you. Get it through your olive oil brain. You guys only still exist here because *we* fund you."

"I think you meant Francis Ford Coppola," said Vinny. "*The Godfather* is a great movie. You should watch it."

Brown placed his left hand in Vinny's face. "Please. I'm too busy controlling the city to watch a damn movie. Now, remember what I said, *Goombah.* You're giving me the money tomorrow, or you can kiss the Mafia in Chicago goodbye. Capone would be spinning in his grave if he saw what it had become. So you pay me, or you can sleep with the fishes in Lake Michigan. *Capeesh*?"

"Us Italians don't really say that, but whatever floats your boat, Brown. See you tomorrow with the money."

"Wow," Kylie whispered to us. "Brown was talking to that Mafia guy the way Principal Jenkins talks to students in detention!"

"He's even worse than I thought he was," Maddie whispered. "We're toast."

Vinny and the rest of the Mafiosos got up and left the table, walking past us and exiting the way we had come in. Revolver Guy, Cormac, and three other Greenies we had come with escorted us forward.

"And what do we have here?" Brown asked Revolver Guy.

"A bunch of teenagers from Cali," he answered. "They know the Bonilla gang and claim to be big fans of yours."

Brown stroked his chin with two fingers before replying. "I see. Well, take a seat. We have a lot to discuss. I'm Aidan Brown, the reason why you are all here."

29

THE JOB

The five of us took seats at the opposite end of the table from Brown.

"Here's how this is gonna work," he said. "This ain't the Bonilla gang—the *Vipers* or whatever the hell his brother calls it now."

"Kobras with a 'K,'" Kylie corrected him. She was visibly shaking and trying the best she possibly could to avoid locking eyes with Brown.

"I didn't ask you for your opinion, sweetheart," Brown remarked. He stopped for two long seconds before continuing to speak. "Arturo Bonilla, I loved that guy—taken from the world way too soon. As he could tell ya, this ain't bush league. You may be young but I ain't gonna treat you like children. If you can get the job done here, I don't give two craps if you're nine, nineteen, or ninety."

Larry interrupted Brown. "How old do you think we are?"

"Irrelevant," Brown scoffed. "Consider this pow-wow your

first official meeting as Mount Greenwood Gang recruits. Please start with your names."

"Ken Jackson," Larry answered.

"Nancy Smith," said Hannah.

"Sharon Reilly," Kylie replied.

"Francine Myers," Maddie said.

Brown looked at me. I tried not to make eye contact with him, afraid that just one glance into those eyes would be enough to suck my entire humanity into a vortex, for it never to return again. Without wasting a second, I replied, "Donnie Carpenter."

"Well, hello, hello," Brown creepily said to all of us. "Welcome—I'm gonna get right to the punch." He paused to stroke his chin again for a good ten seconds. "Your first order of business. I need you to kill Janusz Kazlowski."

My great-grandfather.

30

THE GRANDFATHER PARADOX

Brown's words were a gut punch to the core of my very being. I harkened back to a conversation I once had with Pasta about the so-called "grandfather paradox"—traveling back in time only to kill your own grandfather. Pasta convinced me that this phenomenon had rendered time travel impossible. If only he knew I was *living* it.

Since we still weren't sure if Brown knew our true identities, Maddie and I tried our best to hide every emotion we felt. I gulped as I forced myself to keep a straight poker face. "The owner of Kazlowski's?" I asked.

"Precisely," Brown coolly said. "You are obviously familiar with the place. Go in there tonight toward the end of business hours. Strike up a conversation about his stupid dumplings or something. Then when he's not looking, slip a few drops of *this* in his drink." Brown handed me a one-ounce vial of a clear, translucent liquid poison. "He's always drinking a glass of vodka at night. And he's a pretty big guy. No one will suspect any foul play. They'll think his poor Polish heart or liver or something just gave out."

"Yan-ush?" Maddie confusedly pronounced our ancestor's name. "That's Paul's father. Right?"

"You mean that annoying blond busboy?" Brown jeered. "Yep. That's Janusz's son. I heard that bumbling idiot thinks he can nail that foxy waitress who works there. What a pathetic loser."

I was utterly disgusted and appalled at Brown's characterization of Vicky—not only because she was my dear grandmother, but because she was, without a doubt, underage in 1974. Brown was almost thirty. Not only was he a murderous creep, but he was also a pedophile. *Now that's what I would call a real pathetic loser,* I thought.

"Any more questions?" Brown barked at us. "Or did I make myself clear?"

We all stared away from him, refusing to look him in the eye. Then, fearing that we would all get killed if we objected to his demands, we timidly nodded.

"I take that as a yes?" Brown roared like he was a killer from an eighties horror movie.

"Yes, sir," we answered in unison.

"Delightful." Brown smirked, making a toothy, evil grin. He had some of the worst oral hygiene I had ever seen— and smelled. The few teeth he did have were butter-yellow, thoroughly chipped, and decaying. His breath reeked of hard liquor mixed with a severe case of sewer breath. If I weren't so terrified for my life, I would have asked him when was the last time he saw a dentist.

"Anything else you need from us?" Hannah asked. Like the rest of us, she wanted to get the heck out of there as soon as humanly possible.

"Just do your *job*," Brown reinforced, emphasizing each and every word. "Show me that you are loyal to the *cause*, and I will consider taking you kids seriously. But for now, I am finished with you. Be on your merry way, *gabhair*."

The burly men escorted us out of the room. They marched us back up the long way we had come down—through the rusty ladders and grisly corridors. Midway on our trek, we ran into a nest of screeching bats. Once we were about to exit the building, Cormac's giant frame loomed over my body. He scowled at me in his heavy brogue. "If you tell a soul about *anything* that was said in there, consider you and all your families dead."

"Be at the restaurant at ten sharp tonight and get the job done," Revolver Guy added. I called him that because I never learned his real name. "A few of us will be there just in case there are any *unexpected* occurrences."

God help us, I prayed. Of course the Greenies were sending reinforcements. They probably had already assumed that there was something suspicious about us.

The men said "goodbye" to us by throwing our hapless bodies in our own rental car.

As soon as we had shut the doors and Kylie began driving, we all felt our minds swirling in panic mode.

"We're soooo screwed!" Maddie shrieked.

"We need to go back to the FBI office and tell them what's up ASAP," Hannah said. "If anyone can get us out of this pickle, it's Al and Marshall."

"I don't think that would be a good idea," Kylie objected. "I'm sure that Brown's men would somehow find out who we are, and that would only expedite our demise."

"Yeah, I'm with Ky on this one," Larry replied. "We can't risk showing our face to *anyone* right now."

"You're right. But maybe there's a way we can talk to them. Like on the phone," I offered.

"Okay, fine," Larry agreed. "We can do that, but let's see if we can lose the green bastards first."

We followed the Impala back downtown, to the vicinity of the restaurant, before the gangsters finally let us go on our own. Well, at least that's how it looked. We were all nearly certain that they were still keeping a close eye on us.

Once we found our bearings, we drove around aimlessly for nearly an hour, trying desperately to get the Greenies off our tail. It was the early evening, and we still had a good while before the sun set. Once we were somewhat confident that no one was following us, we came across a payphone. Kylie idled the car, and I hopped out and went into the phone booth. Since I grew up in the era of cell phones, this was my first time seeing such a contraption, aside from in superhero movies—let alone the first time I ever *used* one. I dug into my pocket and grabbed a dime and the business card Al had given me. I inserted the coin and furiously dialed the

FBI District Office. *Please pick up, please pick up,* I silently begged.

After three rings, the secretary picked up.

"I need Special Agent Cannella!" I cried to her. Sensing the urgency in my voice, she didn't hesitate and immediately put Al on the phone.

"Al, it's an emergency! Something has gone terribly wrong. I met Brown. He wants to uh—" It was hard for me to say it. "Uh—he wants me to kill my great-grandpa tonight. At the restaurant! Tonight at ten! And he's sending his men there to make sure we do it! Please send help!"

Al seemed pretty composed on the line. I guess that was his job. "Calm down, Donnie," he said to me, using my alias, even though he knew my actual name. "I knew this was going to happen. I told you this is all a blackmail plot. I highly doubt he expects you to follow through with it, for well, you know, obvious reasons."

"It's not like his death would prevent me from existing, though," I said. "My grandpa is already born so—"

I cut myself off mid-sentence. When I was on the phone with Al, I recalled something Brown said to me about Janusz. "He's a pretty big guy. No one will suspect any foul play. They'll think his poor Polish heart or liver or something just gave out."

The situation I was in made me think more about my grandparents. Grandpa Paul was my primary father figure growing up, since my dad died before I was born, and Maddie's dad showed little interest in me. I remembered one time when I was about seven or eight. I felt extremely sad that, unlike my peers, I didn't have a father with whom to play catch or go fishing. In an attempt to relate with me, my grandpa sat me down and told me that his father—my great-grandfather—died of a heart attack when he was a teenager. It was sudden and happened when he was working in the restaurant at night, right before it closed. One second, he was in good spirits chatting with a customer—and the next, he was dead.

When he was a teenager. I thought of my young, naïve grandfather, who I saw with my own eyes bussing the tables at Kazlowski's and pining for my grandmother. And I thought back to what Brown ordered me to do. I didn't think it was a coincidence that out of my entire group, he gave the vial of poison to *me*.

Janusz Kazlowski. All this time, was *I* really the one who killed him?

"No!" I screamed. "Noooooo!"

"No, what?" Al asked, confused.

I was so lost in the moment I forgot that I was even on the phone with him. "This is awful. I'm going to pay the price for what I did! I'm going to die!" I panicked.

"Listen, Donnie," Al said. "We can't guarantee any outcome, but we, the FBI, are going to do everything we can to help you and your friends through this difficult time."

I wanted to scream at him, but I was so horrified, I couldn't even move my mouth.

"This is the plan," Al continued. "You go to the restaurant

at ten and initially pretend like you're going to obey Brown. Detective Gallagher will call the Chicago PD, and they'll fill the restaurant to the brim with undercover cops. When the time is right, the police will reveal themselves and quote-unquote 'arrest you.' They'll make it look so real those damn Greenies won't suspect a thing."

"Oh—okay," I mumbled. I was surprised I could even get those words out.

"Look, kid," Al consoled me. "I know you didn't ask to be in this situation you're in. Brown is relentless. He ain't like any other criminal we've seen. He operates by destroying people—breaking down their character and their morality, and he's trying to do that to you right now. And we, the FBI, *and* the police won't let him get away with that tonight. We want to bring that son-of-a-gun to justice as much as you do."

"Thanks for the help," I uttered. "We'll do what you said." I hung up the phone wanting to explode.

I slowly re-entered the car.

"So, what happened?" Kylie asked.

I summarized my conversation with Al and the plan he had come up with. Not once did I mention my realization about Janusz.

Was I, Charlie Henderson, a murderer?

"Brown is gonna pay for what he's doing," I vented to the others. "He's gonna learn to *never* mess with my family."

There were still a few hours left before ten. Since we all

agreed that it was too risky to go to the FBI office, we spent the time driving around in circles while trying to brainstorm how the night would go. But all of us were drawing blanks.

It was time to panic. And we did.

31

TEN O'CLOCK

When the time came, we parked and entered Kazlowski's, not making a sound. The kitchen was closed since it was late, and the establishment only remained open for its patrons in the upstairs bar. We ascended the rickety stairs, and all took seats on the tall, wooden stools. Vicky was not working that night, but Paul was—we saw him wiping down the tables behind us.

Sitting at the bar a few stools away from us were two of the same burly men who had escorted us to Brown's hideout. *The reinforcements are already here.* I knew that there were plenty more of them hiding among us.

Larry ordered a beer using his uncle Bill's ID to blend in with the rest of the bargoers. He technically didn't need it, though, as he was eighteen, and that just so happened to be the drinking age in 1974. He took a few sips of his drink as our eyes scanned the room for Janusz.

As Paul came up to the bar to wipe it down, he noticed us.

"Glad to see you're back so soon," he said innocently.

"Well, this place is amazing!" I replied, forcing myself to sound as natural as possible. Well, I wasn't lying. "So, you— uh said this is your dad's restaurant."

"Yep," he answered. "He is Mr. Kazlowski. *The* Mr. Kazlowski."

"Is he by any chance here right now? I would like to tell him personally how much I love his restaurant."

"Sure, he is. He's out on the patio right now. He went to take a smoke real quick, but I'll grab him for you." Paul placed his rag down on top of the bar and raced out to the attached deck to get Janusz.

Once Paul had disappeared from view, the Greenie to my left gave us a big smile. We were following Brown's plan to a "T" so far.

After a minute, Paul had returned with Janusz, a tall man in his early forties with wavy blond hair. He looked just like I had remembered him from family photographs. I couldn't look at him for more than a second. I was beyond remorseful and heartbroken for what I might have done, but mainly I was still in shock and denial. *How could I have actually killed my own great-grandfather?* I mean, I didn't do it yet, but it had to have been my doing for everything to make sense—it was the most logical explanation. I prayed to God to please spare Janusz and all of our lives.

Maddie and my friends began a conversation with Janusz. I didn't participate—I just sat frozen in shame and disgust. They talked about numerous topics: the food, Chicago, and

Poland, to name a few. Then out of nowhere, I saw Janusz freeze in the middle of a sentence. He glanced intently at Larry and then pointed at his face. "I've seen you before," he confidently stated, wagging his finger at him.

"Yes, you have," Larry replied. "We were here yesterday."

"No." Janusz continued staring my friend down. "I've seen *you* before. Before yesterday."

"You must be mistaken," Larry adamantly retorted.

"Dad, what does Mom always tell you about drinking while on the clock?" Paul obliviously joked.

Janusz ignored his son and took a sip from his cocktail glass.

The burly man flashed me a thumbs-up sign. The moment had arrived.

I tried my hardest to stall my act so as many undercover cops as possible could notice us. Intentionally moving at a snail's pace, I slowly reached my hand into the right side pocket. I carefully lifted the small glass vial out, hiding it between my thumb and the side of my palm, like I would if I actually was going to poison someone. I inched closer to Janusz, praying that everything would turn out okay. It seemed like an impossible proposition. Just then, I felt a hand on my shoulder. I jerked my neck to see that it was a large, muscular, bald man wearing a checked shirt.

"Whatcha got there, kid!" he shouted at me, pointing to my right hand.

Before I could respond, the Greenie who had given me the thumbs-up jumped off his stool and raced over to the bald man. "None of your damn business," he barked, proceeding to place the man in a chokehold.

Another man dived to the scene from the other side of the bar. He angled a gun at the Greenie. "Let him go, or I will shoot!" the man ordered, holding up a badge.

Thank God, I thought, my mind racing a mile a second. *At least the cops are here.*

My smidgen of hope was dashed when several other Greenies took out their guns and pointed them at the two cops. Plainclothes officers from throughout the lounge sprinted toward the scene, pulling out their pistols as well. It looked like a shootout was imminent.

The few patrons who were neither cops nor Greenies started screaming and frantically poured down the single flight of stairs.

Soon, it was evident that the undercover cops outnumbered the gangsters.

"These kids are rats!" a Greenie shouted. "We should have known! Brown is gonna kill us!"

"Not if we kill them first!" his long-haired compatriot growled, pointing his gun right at Maddie. But, as he was about to pull the trigger, another plainclothes cop came up from behind. He whacked the back of the unassuming Greenie's head with his gun's barrel. The long-haired goon keeled over, unconscious.

One of Brown's men fired his gun. Luckily, no one was anywhere near his line of sight, and the bullet struck the restaurant's window, shattering it to pieces.

The cops tackled and handcuffed the majority of the gangsters, but a few were able to elude them. Maddie, Hannah, and Kylie were all ushered to safety by a group of officers. All of the girls loudly cried for Larry and me to come with them, but we couldn't—there were still a few Greenies at large, and it was too dangerous for us to move. They had cornered us.

All of a sudden, a red-faced Greenie barreled toward me, trying to knock me out. He looked almost exactly like McCreery—the resemblance was scary. When the man was just inches away, Larry's fist struck his cheek at full force.

I owed Larry big time for saving my ass. I didn't know how skilled he was in hand-to-hand. *Where did he learn that move?* It certainly wasn't something Manny taught him in the FBI office, or something he learned in the Boy Scouts for that matter.

However, even Larry was no match for Brown's henchmen. Before he could lift another finger, another Greenie came up from behind and started to strangle him.

Larry had saved me, so it was time for me to return the favor. I spotted a stray pistol on the ground that belonged to either a Greenie or a cop. It didn't matter. I grabbed the gun, and I slammed its barrel on the side of Larry's attacker's head, knocking him—and Larry—down. *I'm sure he didn't expect that blow from a scrawny teen like me.*

I pulled the stunned Greenie off of Larry, wresting him free. An officer arrived on the scene and hauled Larry away to safety. Another one came for me, similarly lifting me into his arms.

Then I heard a stirring noise emanating from the ground. It was the long-haired Greenie the plainclothes cop had knocked out during the beginning of the fight. He was awake.

"Rats," he growled as he got up on his feet.

When the cop carrying me went to join the others, Mr. Long Hair and the Greenie who had tried to choke Larry ganged up on him. I couldn't see exactly how it happened, but the two men tripped the officer, causing him to lose his precarious grip on my torso.

I hit the wooden floor with a thud.

The pair of Greenies hoisted me up, with each one firmly taking a different arm. Fear consumed me as my bruised, limp body was carried away to the opposite side of the building. They brought me into what I thought was a closet, but it instead turned out to be a door leading to a wooden staircase. Since the stairwell was extremely narrow—and the men weren't particularly concerned about my well-being—my head repeatedly hit the wall and the banister during the descent.

We exited through another concealed door into the alley behind the restaurant.

"I got the one he wanted," I heard one of the men say to the other.

"Mission accomplished," replied his comrade. "Let's get him to the Dragon and then celebrate."

They walked me to a corner in the alley where they tied my limbs together and placed duct tape on my mouth and over my eyes. My world was now pitch black.

I heard and felt my helpless body being chucked into a tiny area. It was probably a car trunk, but it could have been a box for all I knew.

I gasped for air. Soon without warning, I felt my body being jerked and slammed against the walls of the small enclosure it now occupied—continuously thrust back and forth, like a ping pong ball.

That was it. All I could do was hope and pray that Maddie and my friends were safe. Especially Maddie, as she was now the only hope of continuing my family line and legacy.

There was no saving myself.

The cops had tried to save me, but they failed.

My life was over.

PART THREE

32

THE CASUALTY

The four teenagers were strapped inside of a blue-striped Chicago Police van, cruising down Halsted Street. Maddie and Hannah sat behind the two officers manning the front of the vehicle. It had been nearly fifteen minutes since they were rescued from the Greenies' ambush. Traumatized, everyone remained quiet.

Hannah finally broke the silence. "I still don't know how we're gonna get home, but all that matters is that we're all safe, alive, and together."

"That was terrifying," added Maddie. "But if we could survive *that*, I guess we could survive anything."

"We owe it to Larry," Kylie said from the back row. "I thought I was a good fighter, but he kicked the crap out of those goons."

"Thanks," replied Larry sitting next to her. "But Charlie was the real hero. I would've been dead if he didn't rescue me from that guy's death grip."

"Yeah, Charlie!" Kylie yelled.

The friends waited for Charlie to respond—but heard nothing.

"Come on, Charlie! Say something!" Maddie called out.

Again, nothing.

"Charlie!" she screamed again.

"I thought he was sitting in your row this whole time," said Larry.

"And I thought he was with *you* guys," Hannah added.

And then it dawned on the teens. They were not *all* together.

"Charlie!" Maddie yelled in a last-ditch attempt. Her only response was a faint echo.

"Oh no," Kylie said. "They *got* him."

"Maybe he's in another car?" Maddie suggested, still refusing to accept the truth.

"There wasn't another car. This was the only one they put us in," Larry recalled.

"We have to turn around!" Hannah yelled to the cops driving the van. "Go back to the restaurant! Our friend is still there!"

"It's too late," the officer responded. "There's no way in hell he's still there. Knowing those Greenies, they've taken him someplace far away by now. That's *if* he's still alive."

Maddie began to cry hysterically. It was the most grief she had ever felt in her fifteen years. Charlie was her only brother. They had grown up together and shared so many memories— and since Charlie was older, Maddie had literally never known a day without him. Yes, like in any healthy brother-sister relationship, they had their dose of disagreements—well, fights—but when all was said and done, both siblings deeply cared for each other. Maddie blamed herself, in part, for letting the gang capture her brother. She felt like she *failed* him.

"Please!" Maddie frantically begged the cop. "Please! For the love of God, we need to save him!"

"Look," the officer frankly stated. "There is nothing more we can do right now, kid. I'm taking you back to the FBI. They're gonna handle this."

Maddie wailed violently for the entire remainder of the drive. The others did not make a single peep.

———————— ◆ ————————

When the teens returned to the office, they were immediately walked to the same room where they had game-planned their strategy just two nights earlier. However, this time, in addition to Marshall, Al, Manny, Tom, and Gallagher, a dozen more agents, detectives, and officers were present—and of course, there was no Charlie.

"We need to send someone to get him!" Maddie howled with tears streaming out of her eyes.

"I know it *sucks* to lose your brother this way, but it's far too dangerous to send a rescue mission of any kind," Al answered emotionlessly. "Brown's been on the lam for eight years. We're not sending Chicago's finest to go after him for one person who *knew* the risks of infiltrating a major crime syndicate."

Tom nodded in affirmation. "I would have said it a bit differently than Special Agent Cannella here, but he's right. If Brown's actual behavior matches our FBI profile of him, Charlie is most likely dead by now."

Larry surprisingly agreed. "I mean, I don't want to say it, but this is Aidan Brown we're talking about."

"Brown kills his prisoners fast," Chief Marshall added, "especially the ones he can't use for his benefit. And let's be real. What use does he have for some random California teenager? Donnie, Charlie, whatever his name is—he is toast. His goose is cooked."

Maddie was inconsolable. Was her brother really gone forever? She knew she had to do something—and there was only one thing she could do.

"So," she mumbled still in tears, "if Brown has no use for Charlie, then why did he bring him here in the first place?"

The district chief was visibly confused. "But Brown didn't bring you kids here," he replied. "A gang in your hometown recruited you. Then being the good, upstanding citizens you are, you decided to work with us, the good guys, instead."

Al shot Maddie a dirty look.

She ignored him. "All of that's a lie," she bravely told the chief. "We made it up because we didn't think you would believe us if we told you who we *really* are."

The chief was bewildered, even more so than before.

Al, Manny, and even Larry were all fuming at Maddie.

She didn't care. Her brother was more important to her than a stupid confidentiality agreement.

Maddie spit it out. "We're from the future, 2022 to be exact. We were actually trying to *escape* a gang—our time's version of Bonilla's gang, run by his grandson. And somehow, when we were fighting him, we suddenly ended up fifty years back in the past. We did research and learned it was definitely Brown's doing. *How* he did it is anybody's guess. But by chance, we met Al and Manny, and they told us to come here so—"

Marshall, stunned beyond belief, interrupted her. "And how exactly do I know you're not just making this crap up because you want us to rescue your brother?"

"I can prove it," Maddie eagerly said.

"Fine," the chief replied. "Well, for starters, who's the President of the United States in 2022?"

"Joe Biden," Maddie answered.

Marshall laughed. "That bumbling young senator from Delaware?"

"Well, he's not young anymore *at all*—but he's definitely still bumbling."

"And who came before him?" Tom added, not being able to keep a straight face.

"Donald Trump."

Marshall laughed even harder. "Is this some kind of joke to you? You mean Donald Trump, the rich guy in New York City who owns all those damn apartment buildings?"

"Yep. That's him."

"You know," Kylie butted in, "this whole question about presidents reminds me of a movie that will come out in about ten years. It's called *Back to the Future*. It's pretty popular, even in 2022."

"I don't care who the president is," Tom remarked. "What I want to know is if there are flying cars in the future."

"I wish," responded Hannah. "But there are these things called Teslas that are almost as cool."

"And this thing called the Internet," Kylie said. "It connects the whole world, and it allows you to access information instantly."

The chief froze. "What did you say?" he asked, intrigued. His skepticism vanished.

"The Internet," Kylie repeated. "We have computers that can access it—small ones too—some that can fit in your hands. It allows you to find answers to things in the blink of an eye—and directions. No more thumbing through clunky books, paper maps, and encycla—whatever you call those things."

Marshall had an epiphany. "Holy smokes. This is it. *This* is what Brown uses. It's why we've been unable to catch him. He probably has the whole city on a digital map and can track where we are. Well—" He turned to Kylie. "Can the Internet do *that*?"

"Yes, it sure can. Well, it uses another technology called a Global Positioning System or GPS. We use it all the time to get places."

Marshall's jaw dropped even further. All the other adults were equally as shocked—except for Al and Manny, of course. They were beyond angry that Maddie spilled the beans—as was *Larry*.

"The GPS." Marshall couldn't believe he was saying it. "The Department of Defense just launched that project a year ago. It's top secret. We don't expect to even put the first satellite in orbit until another few years or so. For a kid like you to know what it is—" He cut himself off. "Good God, you kids are *actually* from the future. This all makes a lot more sense now."

Al, Manny, and Larry were furious. Al, in particular, couldn't contain himself. His face was red as an apple, to the point where steam was almost coming out of his ears.

"No wonder you called bell-bottoms *grandma pants*," Tom said to Maddie. "I got a little worried about your fashion sense there, Francine."

"My real name is Madeleine, by the way," she replied. The fact that she'd rather be called *Madeleine* showed just how much Maddie hated the name Francine.

"And that reference you made when we were in the war room the first time." Marshall looked at Kylie. "Man, if only you kids told us the truth earlier, we would've planned this differently. This revelation changes the whole damn dynamic."

"Well, now you know," Maddie continued. "And that's why we need to stop Brown. If he got my brother, he can and will get *us* too."

Al spoke for the first time since Maddie gave the group's secret away. He was trying his hardest to hide his wrath. "The best solution here is not to do anything yet and just hope Charlie finds the 'portal,' or whatever you call the thing Brown uses to communicate with the future. It's not worth it to put any boots on the ground just yet."

Larry looked at Marshall. "What do you say are the odds that happens?"

"Not likely at all," he answered honestly. "As I said before, Charlie is probably dead. And if Brown hasn't gotten around to killing him yet, he's gonna keep him as far away as possible from the portal."

Maddie pleaded with the chief. "Come on. We need to at least *try* to rescue Charlie. Think about it. We willingly went to Brown so we could get home. If we don't try, we'll never get home, and we will never see Charlie again."

"I agree," Hannah said, "but why not take it a step further? This finally gives you, the FBI, and the Chicago Police the chance to storm into Brown's lair and finally put an end to his gruesome operation once and for all."

"Exactly," responded Kylie. "This is the moment you have craved for nearly a decade. You have more than probable cause to warrant a full-on invasion. Your dreams of bringing him down are finally possible."

Marshall turned to the teens. "Do you remember where Brown's hideout was?"

"I don't." Unlike Al and Manny, Larry seemed to have somewhat gotten over Maddie disclosing the big secret. "I drove there, but I followed one of the mob cars the whole way. The Greenies made so many twists and turns, I don't even remember a quarter of the way to the place."

"It was like in the middle of nowhere," Hannah added. "Some industrial park."

"We haven't found those bastards in eight years," Al said. "It would be nothing but a lost cause."

Just as Al finished his sentence, the war room door opened. In walked an attractive woman ushered by a police officer. She looked like she was in her early twenties, with long reddish-brown hair and light blue eyes—the same shade as Charlie and Maddie's mother's. As Maddie looked at her face, she noticed a prominent dark scar underneath her left eye that she tried to cover up with makeup.

"Chief, this informant insisted on seeing you. She says she can help us get Brown," explained the officer.

"Ma'am, can I help you?" Tom said. "It's almost midnight. The office is closed."

The mysterious woman spoke with an accent similar to Hannah's. "When I was driving by and saw that there were people inside the office, I knew I had to come in. I know more about Brown than anyone else."

"Believe me," Marshall replied skeptically. "*No one* knows that son of a bitch."

The woman continued. "*I* do, and I heard you were talking about finally bringing him to justice. I can lead you to his hideout so you can put an end to that monster's reign of terror—but let me warn you, that place is more secure than the vault in the Federal Reserve Bank of Chicago. I know that because I've been down there more than a few times." She rolled up her blouse's right sleeve, revealing a tattoo of the Greenies' dragon on her shoulder.

"I didn't know the Greenies let women become full

members," Marshall remarked.

"There's a few of us. We work mostly behind the scenes."

"And what if this is some kind of trap?" Al questioned. "And you're the bait he's using to lure us? Typical Brown move."

"I'm not proud of most of the decisions I've made in the last few years, but I'm finally finished with him after what happened last night." She pointed at her black eye.

"Still, why would we trust one of *them*?" Al scoffed.

"Well, I don't believe I've introduced myself yet. My name is Kathryn Brown. Aidan Brown is my husband."

33

DRAGONETTE

"**A**fter leading his case for eight damned years, this is the first time I'm hearing of Brown having a wife," Marshall replied.

"I knew he was married." Maddie looked at Kathryn. "My brother, Charlie, who your *husband* is holding captive, wrote a paper on him for school. It was all he talked about for like a week. You're from New York—Long Island, right?"

Kathryn glanced at Maddie with somewhat of an angry look—but mostly, she was perplexed. "How do you know that? The public is not supposed to know *anything* about me. Brown hides me on purpose."

"The public from 1974 doesn't know," Al chimed in. "They're not from 1974."

Kathryn thought she had misheard him. "What? How is that possible?"

"They're from 2022," the chief responded. "Well, at least they claim they are. We have reason to believe that your husband has access to time travel, in some form or another, and he brought these kids back almost fifty years in time. Why? That beats all of us—but what's for sure is that he wants them."

"Holy crap," Kathryn mouthed. She took a few seconds to get her emotions in check. "It makes sense now. He—he kept a lot of secrets from me. I knew some of the techniques he used did not make sense with current technology." Brown's estranged wife paused again. "He was always gone too. I was lucky to get a half hour of attention a *week* from him."

"Let's cut to the chase," Marshall stated. "Where is Brown stationed?"

"Gary," she answered.

"Who's Gary?" asked Maddie.

"Not who—*where*," Kathryn clarified. "Gary, Indiana. His hideout is six stories underneath the basement of a defunct paint thinner factory on the corner of Sixth and Forest."

Larry looked at her earnestly. "So, you're telling me that all this time, the Mount Greenwood Boys were actually Indiana boys? *Hoosiers?*"

Kathryn nodded. "Exactly. In fact, they don't have any connection to Mount Greenwood or even Chicago at *all*. Aidan chose that name on purpose to throw off law enforcement."

"What a sly fox," Detective Gallagher noted. "No wonder we couldn't find him—we've had virtually the entire department combing the city from left to right."

Kathryn continued to stare at Larry. "You look very familiar. I could swear I've seen you before. It's your face. I remember your *handsome* face from somewhere."

Larry eked out a faint grin and slightly blushed.

The chief banged the table. "I don't know what the purpose of this chatter is, but it's irrelevant. Let's get back to business."

Kathryn continued. "Aidan's hideout is set up kind of like a high school hallway, which he did on purpose because he never went to high school—he literally has a third-grade education. My husband never wastes an opportunity to be ironic."

"Brown in high school? Now that image is gonna be stuck in my head for the rest of my life," Kylie interjected.

No one answered her.

Kathryn asked for a sheet of paper, and Gallagher tore off a page from his spiral notebook. She grabbed a pen innocently lying on the table and began to draw a rough sketch of the hallway, with the "classrooms" off to the side and Brown's massive boardroom or "lair" at the end. When she finished, she circled the rectangle representing the lair, which took up roughly half of the page. "This where most of the action happens."

"So, if that floor plan is, say, the central nervous system of Brown's whole operation, that room at the end is the brain," deduced Al.

"Exactly," Kathryn agreed. "Most of the Greenies call it the 'Dragon's Den.' Think of it as a cross between a boardroom and an interrogation room—but it's *much* larger than both and, well, loaded with bloodthirsty criminals."

"We were all in it," stated Hannah, pointing to herself and the other three teens. "It was huge—like half the size of our school's gym, just without the high ceiling."

"It's funny you're saying that," replied Kathryn. "Aidan named most of the rooms after school subjects. The English Room is painstakingly filled with nearly a decade worth of every newspaper article mentioning the gang. The History Room has a few more articles—the ones that couldn't fit in the English Room. But most of its space is taken up by these mysterious boxes I was never allowed to open—now that I know what you told me, it's probably the future technology Aidan has collected throughout his time travels."

"Wouldn't you know it," Marshall commented. "Brown's home base doubles as his armory."

"Exactly. His Math Room is the same thing—a bunch of boxes upon boxes. Then there's the Science Room, where he's never even let me in." Kathryn paused. "And finally, the lair or *gym*, if you want to call it that, is the very place where my husband navigates his ship from hell. Once you take control of that room, his entire network collapses."

"But before we actually do that, we have to figure out how to get law enforcement personnel down there," said Gallagher.

Kathryn took a deep breath. It was clear that she was consumed with anxiety. "I know the passwords and all—so that's not a problem. My Irish is a bit rusty, but Aidan taught me enough to get by. The thing is, there are guards in *every* nook and cranny of the cellar—especially now. Aidan is expecting someone to come for Charlie, so they're gonna be more fortified than usual. Knowing my husband, he already has that place crawling with *hundreds* of his men—his own, personal *army*. What I'm saying is, even with an entire squad of the PD behind us, it won't be enough." She turned to Marshall. "Chief, we're gonna need more manpower. A *lot* more manpower."

"Like what?" Chief asked skeptically.

Kathryn displayed a serious expression. "To be honest, to have any chance at all, we need the military to help us."

"That's ridiculous," Al replied. "There's no way in hell we're calling the armed forces to take down a white-collar mob boss in the middle of the night."

Marshall's eyes were filled with contempt. It was clear he had his disagreements with Al in the decade they had worked together. But that night, the chief was not going to let his *subordinate* boss him around.

Marshall immediately looked at Gallagher. "Tell Commissioner O'Leary right now we're doing it," he ordered. "Operation Green Dragon is a go."

34

JUDAS

I was jolted awake. The duct tape was ripped off of my eyes, almost taking my eyelids with it. I tried to rub them to ease the pain, but my arms and legs were twisted and tied behind my torso. I was a human pretzel.

Then the tape over my lips came off as well. I could finally speak. "Wh—where am I?" My words could hardly come out. My throat was dry as sand. I could barely breathe after being trapped in an inhumanely small space for an indeterminate amount of time. No one answered me—but no one had to. I knew where I was. It was the same place I had been, with my sister and friends, only a few hours earlier—the dungeon that Aidan Brown and his Greenies called home.

The two men who had seized me at the restaurant were still holding my roped body. They stood with me at the entrance to the boardroom. The door was open.

"Fellas. Bring him in!" I heard Brown zealously roar.

The men carried me through the doorway and to the

long table where the Greenies' diabolical leader awaited me. Brown motioned for them to sit me down on a chair across from him. The men holding me did just that, tying yet another rope around me, securely fastening my body to the back of the metal chair. They remained standing close by, with one on each side of me.

"Well, well, well," Brown proclaimed. "Look at who happened to join us. Why, isn't it the twenty-first-century boy himself. Your Snap Cham messages ain't gonna work here, kid. Welcome to the olden days."

I tried to squirm, but the way those thugs had tied me made it impossible for me to move a muscle below my shoulders. "It's Snap*chat*," I bravely corrected him. "And what do you want from me?"

Brown's mouth formed another evil smile. "I know who you are, Charles Paul Henderson, born on April 30, 2005, to Sarah Elizabeth Henderson, formerly Kazlowski, and the late Craig Andrew Henderson."

I was irked that he knew that much information about my parents and me. Yet, I wasn't surprised one bit.

"I've been doing quite the research on you," he went on. "I read your paper, by the way. It was surprisingly very well written. I have to say—you got my motivations down pat. What a solid A-minus job you did. I would've given you an A-plus if your grammar wasn't so *atrocious*. Go figure...you were always more of a math and science nerd."

I thought Brown was barely literate—who was he to understand a high school-level academic paper, let alone critique its grammar? Maybe he was way smarter than he appeared.

"Why—why do you travel into the future?" I asked. "Is it so that you can always have the upper hand against the law?"

"I don't, you *moron*. My future self travels to the past. Everything I know about your time, he tells me. Or should I say, *I* tell me."

"But that's—that's impossible. You're d—d—dead."

Brown widened his smile, showing off his bad case of gingivitis. "That's the one thing your paper got wrong, kid. I'm alive and kicking in 2022."

My head jolted back. "What? You—"

Brown laughed, scratching the whiskers on his chin. "If only you knew the truth about what happened to me. Well, what *will* happen to me. All you gullible and lazy *sheep* believe whatever garbage comes out of the media." He resumed stroking his chin before continuing. "Toward the late seventies, my gang took a hit in membership. We had quite a few setbacks, and things were looking bleak. My wife also left me and kept threatening to leak all my intel to the cops. So, I did the only thing I could. I had her killed."

"I remember writing about her. Kathryn, right? She was a very beautiful and smart woman. She wanted to be a veterinarian, right? It was such a shame her life had to end the way it did because she had a murderous prick for a husband."

Brown's malicious smile didn't go away despite my attempts to rankle him. "Yep, kid. That's me. Awful, rotten Aidan Brown. Good for nothing, except wreaking havoc on the very city that spawned me into a life of chaos and poverty."

He swept his arm across the table, hitting a cassette tape. It rocketed off, missing my face by a few inches—I flinched.

Brown continued. "And *so* sweet Katie she was. Don't get me wrong. I didn't *want* to kill her. She *had* to die. It was her or the cause. Anyway, when the police were investigating her death, they immediately suspected I was behind it. They worked even harder than ever to find me and even located this hideout. But we outsmarted them—we moved at the last second, so all they found was an empty paint factory. That whole ordeal took a lot out of me. I was already in my mid-thirties by then, and crime was simply boring me. It was all I'd ever known since I was in the womb. I wanted a change in scenery. I wanted to be the hero—the 'good guy' for once."

He narrowed his eyes to mine. I tried to move my head, but the heavy ropes around my shoulders and neck made it impossible to look away fast enough. This time, I couldn't evade his ice-cold glance. My stomach churned. If there was actually such a feeling of one's soul crumbling, I think I was experiencing it.

Brown continued. "I mean, good and evil, think about it, kid. All it really is—as my friend Immanuel Kant once said—is a social construct. So, about a year after Katie's death, I disbanded the Greenies and staged my own assassination. I left Chicago for good, moved to the East Coast, and essentially became a new person. I got a new name. I got a new wife. I got a new life. I had kids. I even got my GED, went to college and law school. But all this crap shouldn't matter to *you*."

I was utterly aghast at what Brown had told me. *How dare he say there's no difference between good and evil*, I thought. I've heard that line before in films and TV shows. It was always what the evil guy said to justify the warped notion that what he was doing was somehow good. I sure wasn't falling into that trap.

"So enough about me. Here's what's going to go down with *you*. Seamus over there is gonna give you a taste of some chloroform." Brown pointed to one of the burly guards who had brought me to him. "It's my signature drink on the house. We're gonna do some experimentin' on your body—see what twenty-first-century humans are like and all. But don't worry, we're not gonna just kill you then and there. That's no *fun*. Instead, we're gonna pump some juice into your vein." His stone-cold finger touched the joint opposite my right elbow. "No, not the apple juice you drink in boxes at your school. This is special juice my friend cooked up. It causes your blood to boil, so you die a slow and painful death. Then, since I'm in such a good mood today, I'll spare your corpse some misery. We were gonna cut you up and feed you to the dogs, but instead, we'll just burn you and throw your ashes into the sewer with the rest of the rats. You'll finally be with your own kind. Am I clear, *son*?"

"I'm not your son!" I jerked forward in a desperate attempt to free myself. It only caused the ropes to tighten against my back, ribs, and skin.

Brown laughed. "I never said you were, you imbecile. And speaking of sons, your old man's lucky he croaked when you were a fetus, so he never got to see the waste of a life *his* son lived."

"I know what this all is," I stated with confidence. "You wanted me to kill my own great-grandfather, so my great-grandmother and grandparents had no choice but to give in to your demands. You're disgusting. You're using me to blackmail my own family."

Brown's laughs got even louder, to the point where a piece of crumpled paper on the table seemed like it was trembling. "And exactly why would I do that?" he sneered at me. "It makes no sense, kid. I could blackmail them with my gun, you idiot."

I turned my eyes toward his neck, finally dodging his merciless gaze. "So, why did you bring me here?" I asked.

"I didn't *bring* you here," Brown replied. "I may have wanted you here, and you being here is quite a delightful surprise to me, but I didn't open the portal to bring you here."

I was confounded. What Brown was telling me didn't make sense. Of course he was the one who brought me to the past. It had to have been him.

"Figure it out, kid," scoffed Brown. "You're smart. You're a *geek* and all. Well, that was until your friend Larry saved your sorry little ass. But is he *really* your friend?" Brown's smile was the widest I had ever seen it. His crooked, plaque-infested front teeth—a dentist's worst nightmare—were in full view.

My heart was beating out of my chest. Blood rapidly drained from my face. *This whole time, Larry was a traitor?!* I wished that what he was saying was just a threat and had no element of truth to it. But then, I thought about the last thing I remembered before I was transported to 1974 with the rest of the group—my final few seconds in 2022. Before everything went to black, my very last memory had been Larry reaching into his pocket to grab something. *No, please, dear God. Just be a coincidence.*

As I paused, Brown cackled. The ear-splitting noise he made could've easily come from a drunken hyena.

I inhaled abruptly, nearly choking on the stale air as it entered my parched throat. "You're saying that Larry was behind this?" My voice cut out at "behind," but Brown still understood what I meant.

"Now you get it, you foolish nincompoop. Yes, Larry was the one who opened the portal—the guy you've been eating Polish dumpling things and going to concerts with. What a dumbass you are."

I have been living a lie. "Why would he do this to me?" I screamed in a harsh, rasping tone.

"It was all part of our plan. We carved out a trap, and you fell right into it. We've been watching you closely. We knew you were desperate to be popular and would leave your only *real* friends in a heartbeat if you had a chance. What was that fat kid's name again? Noodles?"

"Pasta," I hoarsely squeaked. My world had not only fallen apart—it was disintegrating.

"Yeah. You dumped his sorry ass in a heartbeat. What a great friend you were to him." Brown cackled yet again. "Anyway, my 2022 self had Larry pretend to be a transfer student to your school and pose as your 'friend.' And you got caught hook, line, and sinker. It was a huge-ass ego trip for you. I had him convince the Krikorians' son to invite you to that party, just so I could set a trap outside."

"The Kobras!"

"You bet. I paid off Skyler Bonilla and his wannabe 'street gang' on those pathetic bicycles. That bozo is nothing like his granddad. He has no street cred—he just wants to get stoned all the time. But he was just who we needed to cause a diversion. That way, Larry would be able to trigger the portal to bring you to me in my prime, and you would never suspect it was him all along. The original plan was to have just you and Larry go through the portal, but your little sister had to complicate things with that pitiful meltdown of hers, and she and those other *sexy*, new friends of yours decided to come along for the ride. But you're the only one I want. I gave you the assignment to kill your great-grandad on purpose. I knew you were gonna chicken out and call the cops, so I used it as an opportunity to separate you from the others. It's so poetic. You will be dead, and those sweet, innocent, boy band-loving girls will never know it was Larry who was on *my* side the entire time."

"But that still does not answer my question! Why *me?* What do you want from *me?*" I was steadfast in my pursuit of learning the whole truth.

But Brown wouldn't tell me. "That's for me to know and for you *never* to find out. I think we're done here." He turned to his guards. "Boys, please bring him to the Science Room."

The two burly men unfastened me from the chair and lifted me. They dragged me out of the room before reapplying the tape to my face. *Please, God—there must be a way out of this hell.* There just had to be.

35

OPERATION GREEN DRAGON

The narrow streets of Chicago's South Side were lonely in the dead of night—save for a couple of police vehicles. A van toward the front of this ensemble was piloted by Officer Nick Sargento, a young ex-Navy SEAL, only three years out of the academy. Special Agent Al Cannella sat next to him, with Special Agent Manny Santos and Sergeant Jerome Perry in the second row. In the back two rows were the four Fresno teens: Maddie Thomas, Hannah Preston, Kylie Hernandez, and Larry Travers—as well as Kathryn Brown.

"I hope we got enough troops to take Brown and his cronies down," Sargento said. He had survived the bloody Tet Offensive in Vietnam, yet the unique and present danger Brown posed still scared him to his core.

"I'd never imagine we'd been doing it with last-second notice at one in the morning," remarked Perry.

"Same here," Sargento replied. "I was watching *Brady*

Bunch reruns when I got the call that Operation Green Dragon was a go."

"Operation Green Dragon," Perry said, still in disbelief that those words were coming out of his mouth. "After eight years of talk, it's finally happening." He briefly turned to Kathryn, sitting by herself in the van's rear, behind the teenagers. "Thanks to Kate over here, we finally know where he's stationed."

"But that don't matter if we're outnumbered," Sargento uttered nervously.

"We dispatched every single person we possibly could," said Al. "Chief Marshall has been on the phone nonstop. Governors Walker and Bowen are sending in *both* the Illinois and Indiana National Guards. And since his hideout is in Gary, there's now undeniable proof that Brown's crimes crossed state lines, making his operations a clear federal issue. President Ford is on this too and is sending the army over. The question isn't whether or not we'll get help—the question is if it will come in time. Who knows, Brown might leave the hideout as he likely assumes that we're coming for him. He has access to that network whatchamacallit after all."

"The *Internet*," Kylie corrected him.

"Yes, that," Al noted. "So, he probably knows that we're coming."

Kathryn, who had been quiet thus far, piped up. "I know Aidan. He ain't going nowhere. He's not gonna take that risk of leaving and exposing himself outside of the territory he knows—he's gonna stay and fight. He probably already called all his men to the headquarters. He knows where we'll be coming in, and they'll be there to greet us. He's not going to hide. He's gonna try to kill us all, and *then* he will hide."

"Not if we kill him first," replied Larry.

"I sure hope you're right," said Hannah.

"So, what's the game plan when we get there?" barked Al. It was clear he was losing his patience.

"We have to come up with something that's gonna catch him by surprise," said Larry. "If we just go in there cold, we'll get annihilated."

Even though they didn't say so, everyone agreed with him.

"I think we need to cause a distraction," suggested Kylie.

At the word "distraction," all eyes looked at Kathryn.

"Seriously?" the estranged mob wife responded. "And how exactly am I going to *distract* him?"

"I don't know how, but you're our only hope," Hannah answered. "Just think of something."

"She happens to be right," Al stated. "We're gonna let you out a few blocks away, so they don't see you coming out of a cop van. Then I'll radio the rest of our men and tell them to wait. You'll go in by yourself, do whatever you can to capture Brown's attention, and get him to ignore his inter-network surveillance monitors. At that moment, we'll storm in. Whatever you do should be long enough to stall things to the point where the military can arrive. If they can supply more armed manpower than Brown has *and* get inside in time, we stand a chance. But that's a big *if*."

"So, in other words, we're going out on a huge limb here," Sargento observed.

Perry nodded. "I don't even think this qualifies as a limb. We're going out on a *fingernail*."

36

KISS ME, KATE

Sargento stopped at Second Street—four blocks away from the Greenies' hideout—and let Kathryn out. Any closer would have tipped Brown off.

The brunette beauty walked down the trash-filled roads of the industrial park in her stiletto heels. If only she knew how the night would unfold, she would have brought a change of shoes.

Kathryn found the paint thinner factory with ease and started her descent down the ghastly labyrinth of stairs, corridors, and ladders to Brown's lair. In no time, she had entered the locker-lined hallway, which Brown had dubbed "The School of Hard Knocks." She noticed that instead of the usual one Greenie guarding each "classroom," there were *four*, in some cases *five*. She was right. He was really putting all hands on deck.

But there was one room in particular that had nearly a dozen guards watching over it. Kathryn surmised that it was

Brown's prized Science Room, smack-dab in the middle of the hallway adjacent to the boiler room. She didn't exactly know what her husband used it for—he never let her go near it, let alone inside. The door was closed shut but had a tiny window. She squinted, attempting to peer through it from a distance, and was barely able to discern three figures and what appeared to be a makeshift hospital bed. Two were standing on the side of the "bed," aiming what appeared to be long apparatuses at the third person, who, as Kathryn detected, was strapped to the bed-like device, unable to move. Even though she had never met him, she knew he must have been Charlie.

"Step away from the operatin' room, m'lady," a heavily accented guard ordered her.

"Sorry. I thought my husband was in there," she lied.

"He's where he always is, sweetie pie," another guard said, pointing toward the room at the end of the hallway. "Now go along, would you."

Kathryn, fearful for Charlie and his friends, continued walking down the hall. When she reached the boardroom, Brown's gravelly-voiced henchman awaited her. "Greetings, Dragonette," he grumbled. "Here to see your *fear céile?*"

"*Is maith bhean í ach níor bhain sí a broga di go foill,*" she replied. Her Irish pronunciation was not the best. She was half Italian, after all, something for which Brown constantly berated her.

"Access approved, honey-bun." He opened the door.

Kathryn walked into the room to see Brown sitting at his

favorite end of the table, looking at his computer module. Five henchmen were beside him, also fixated on the monitor.

"They seem to be lost," one heavily tattooed Greenie observed. "They're going in circles around the building."

Kathryn examined the computer screen from the corner of her eye. The cops were still a few blocks away, waiting for her to create the diversion.

Brown, holding a packet of paperwork, smiled widely at his men. "They've come close before, but they'll give up. I don't think those kids remembered that much about the directions. Just watch. The cops will arrest *them* for leading them on a wild goose chase. It all goes full circle, my friend."

Kathryn came rushing over to Brown. "Aidie dear!"

Brown, annoyed, turned to her. "Kate, gimmie a second. Can't ya see I'm in the middle of something here?"

"Oh, you'll be in the middle of something very soon!" Kathryn replied romantically.

"Darling, now's not the time," he replied. "I'm hard at work here. I can't believe these kids really think they can find me."

"You're worried about a bunch of kids? What got into you, honey?" Kathryn was a better actress than she had thought.

"These are not just kids. Well, I guess they *technically* are."

"Look, Aidan, I'm really sorry about before," said Kathryn. She referred to their fight the previous night where Brown had viciously attacked her in a drunken stupor for no apparent reason. "I didn't mean to get upset because I felt like you're never home and care more about your work than me. I was wrong and just want to make it up to you."

Brown smiled. "You can make it up to me in about ten minutes. I just gotta make sure these coppers are off my tail."

"Please! Don't make me wait."

"Come on, Kate. I love you, but I'm working now. Patience is a virtue." Brown winked at her.

Kathryn didn't give up. "Pretty please!" She channeled her inner Audrey Hepburn.

"Okay, five more minutes," Brown relented. "Then I'm all yours."

"Please with a cherry on top!" Kathryn should've gotten an Oscar for the hell of a performance she was giving.

Brown looked intently at the GPS monitor. He analyzed the several blue circles that represented the cops. None of them appeared to get any closer to the headquarters. He sighed. "If you insist," he said to his wife.

Kathryn grabbed Brown by his chest and furiously kissed him on his lips and neck. It wasn't something she particularly wanted to do, as he was a psychotic, abusive creep—but if it would help to take him down, it was worth it.

The guards watching the monitor with Brown walked out of the room in amused disgust, closing the door behind them.

The couple continued their "romantic interlude." Kathryn, who was forcing all the action, removed her blouse and threw it upon the table, exposing her pink brassiere. Brown was still looking at the computer screen.

"What's the matter, Aidan dear?" she cooed. "You don't

wanna look at your pretty wife?"

Brown stammered. "Uh, of course I do!"

Kathryn kept kissing him progressively harder, trying to keep his eyes off of his cop tracker. When he was finally fully absorbed by her formidable charms, she slyly reached for the computer's electrical cord and jerked it out of the outlet. The power shorted out, and the screen went black.

Brown didn't seem to notice as he took off his shirt. "It's been a while since we did this—man does not live by bread alone," he said, stirred by his own comment.

"That's for sure!" Kathryn exclaimed while pushing Brown atop the table. She proceeded to climb on top of him, kissing him even more frantically.

"That feels good!" Brown cried out. "Keep going, baby!"

Kathryn kept kissing him for another thirty seconds. Once her husband was distracted enough, her eyes quickly turned to the table. She immediately reached her right hand into the fabric of her blouse, revealing a tiny pocket-like compartment. Wasting no time, she gingerly grasped the object she had concealed—a small cylindrical syringe. It was filled with a nearly lethal dose of ketamine—or as it was known on the streets, *Special K*. Unbeknownst to Brown, Kathryn had stolen it from him following their violent fight the previous night. She had been holding onto it for self-defense, just in case Brown attacked her again—she didn't plan to use it *offensively.*

Using a sleight of hand technique she learned from a street magician in her hometown of Bay Shore, Kathryn concealed the Special K syringe tightly between her index and middle fingers while continuing to kiss and caress Brown. Then when the time was right, she twisted her fingers, dislodging the syringe's cap. She let it fall to the ground, as given its size, it made no noise. Then, keeping her face on his, Kathryn placed her right hand on Brown's arm. She had studied biology before meeting him, so she knew where the cephalic vein was by touch. Once the needle was in the right location, Kathryn abruptly smashed the plunger fully down, emptying the contents of the syringe. Brown instantly fell limp and rolled off the table's edge. Kathryn waited to hear a thud.

"Aidan!" she screamed. She quickly gathered the tiny plastic cap from the ground and placed it back on the needle—before placing the syringe back into her secret blouse "pocket." Then she opened the door, startling the army of guards outside.

"Help!" Kathryn yelled to them. "Me and Aidan were, well—in the middle of something—and all of a sudden he just passed out cold! You have to do something! Help him!"

Dozens of guards immediately rushed into the lair to attempt to resuscitate Brown. A guard began to administer CPR. Kathryn continued her flawless acting as she ran down the hallway. She shouted to all the guards in front of the "classrooms." "Aidan just blacked out! Please help him!" At once, all the guards abandoned their posts and stormed the lair as well. Her plan, so far, was working like a charm.

Kathryn ran back into the boardroom. "Is he okay?"

"He's not responding," replied the Greenie who was feverishly trying to rouse him. "He's breathing, but he's out cold. It's almost like he's been drugged."

Nervous that they were on to her, Kathryn quickly dismissed the comment and pleaded, "Just please help him!"

She saw that a guard noticed the monitor was off and was about to plug the power cord back into the outlet.

"Forget the monitor!" Kathryn yelled to him. "Aidan might be dying!" She squeezed her eyes together, sending forth a torrent of crocodile tears.

Though most of Brown's henchmen took her histrionics as sincere, one large man was suspicious. "He seemed fine today," he said as he ignored the comatose Brown and instead gazed at the computer.

Kathryn kept sobbing, increasing her volume. "I haven't gone at it like that with him in a while. I think I exerted his heart too much."

More guards heard the ruckus and piled into the boardroom. After a minute or so, the hallway, generously stocked with guards just before, had emptied.

A wily, tousle-haired guard forcefully nudged Brown trying to wake him without any success. "Hurry up, get a medic!" bellowed the guard. "Get both of them!"

"The medics are busy doing experiments on that boy," replied an enormous, red-faced man. He was none other than Dan McCreery, Brown's most senior Greenie and the person he mistrusted the least—as he *trusted* no one.

"That can wait!" begged Kathryn. "Please! If Aidan dies, it's my fault! And we're all doomed."

Seeing he had no other option, Dan summoned the

medics into the lair. The two severely underqualified men rushed into the room and began tending to Brown.

"I can't watch," Kathryn screamed as she made her way to the boardroom's exit. She cleverly slipped out through the door and down the hall, all the way to the entrance to Brown's Science Room.

The "school" was completely deserted. The dozens, if not hundreds, of guards had all left their assignments and flocked to their ailing leader. The Greenies' blind, one-sided loyalty was clearly on display. Brown, who saw them as nothing more than a bunch of dumb and obedient lackeys, was like a god to them. They worshipped him. Their entire life revolved around appeasing him. With their dear leader's status uncertain, the men pretty much felt lost, with no direction or purpose.

Not taking anything for granted, Kathryn barged through the thick wooden door, for the first time ever. With the medics gone, Charlie was alone in the room, brutally battered and tied to his gurney. The chloroform had just about worn off, and he was almost fully conscious. Kathryn quickly untied the teen before removing the tape from his mouth and eyes.

Now free, he groggily sat up. "Who—who are you?"

"I'll tell you later," Kathryn said. "First, let's get you the hell out of here so we can give that worthless piece of shit, Brown, a taste of his own medicine!"

37

GOLIATH

A sea of vans bombarded the blocks surrounding the factory. Everyone had arrived—the FBI, the police, and the military support.

The four friends were still patiently waiting in the safety of their police van.

"Kathryn's been in there for like thirty minutes now," Al said to the group. He was getting restless. "I wonder what in the world she is doing."

"Playing chess?" Larry sarcastically replied.

"Well, what are we waiting for?" asked Sargento, fondling the pistol holstered to his belt. "Let's bust this joint."

Once the commanders gave the green light, the cops and military began to pour into the hideout. The four teens helped lead the way, giving them directions through the dark, unforgiving maze. Sargento and Perry, assisted by the most experienced soldiers, protected the girls and Larry at the front of the pack.

The group pushed on through the asbestos-lined cellar before encountering a lone, defenseless guard. He frantically tried to reach the control center with his handheld CB radio—but there was no signal on the other end. Sargento knocked him out with a single blow and entered the password Kathryn gave him into a keypad, opening the next corridor.

The forces continued their descent into the void. They saw a few more guards along the way, but because all the senior Greenies were busy aiding Brown, they were entirely left to their own devices. Caught by surprise, they were similarly knocked out cold by the nearby soldiers and policemen.

The Operation had soon reached the ladder which led down into the upper part of the hideout. At this point, no more guards seemed to be in sight. However, when the troops had reached the so-called "School of Hard Knocks" entranceway, they spotted a quartet of Greenie guards blocking it.

"Oh, crap," one of the Greenies said, not yet realizing just how many soldiers they were. "They got everybody and their mother coming at us."

Another guard frantically shouted into his CB, "Code Goliath! Code Goliath!"

Unlike the previous guard's message, this one got through. Kathryn's diversion was only good for so long, as the control center was back up and running.

The Greenie at the other end of the signal tried to keep his composure. It wasn't easy. This was the first time those two words had ever been uttered over Brown's radio system.

"Installing defense mechanism number sixty-six!" he barked. His message was broadcast onto the hideout's loudspeakers for everybody to hear. "This is Code Goliath! Repeat, Code Goliath! The safehouse is under attack!"

38

TRUST NO ONE

The strange, pretty woman looked candidly at me. I saw the sympathy in her eyes. They looked exactly like the set of caring sky-blue eyes that belonged to my mother, who I dearly missed and was convinced I would never see again. The woman was around the same age my mom was when she had me. Aside from her hair color, she looked very similar to a picture of my young mother holding me as a newborn infant—which I kept on my bedroom nightstand.

I was thankful beyond belief that she freed me—but there still was a part of me that thought she was just another one of Brown's elaborate schemes. I had now come to trust no one. Hell, this was the same point of view that had gotten Brown so far in his criminal career. After I learned what Larry, or should I say, *Benedict Arnold*, did to me, every possibility was on the table.

I placed my newly untied legs in front of my body and gently lifted myself up onto them. It was the first time I had stood since I was in the restaurant. As soon as I was on my feet, the loudspeakers blared. "Code Goliath. Code Goliath." The message repeated at a pitch that would have made a rock concert sound softer than a lullaby.

The woman instantly grabbed my arm. "Hide," she whispered, dragging me along. I followed her without hesitation through a hidden door. It was a side entrance to the boiler room. "They won't find us here," the woman said in a barely audible whisper, once we were sealed inside the musty, unlit chamber.

What is going to happen to me?

"I'm here to help," she said quietly. "I know that you come from the future. The year 2022."

"Who—who are *you*?"

"If I told you, would you listen to me?"

I wasn't sure if her intentions were good, but I had no choice at that moment. After all, if it weren't for her, I would still be tied up like a human bundle of sticks. "Just tell me," I said.

She paused for a second. "Kathryn Brown. I know. Yes, I'm married to *him*, but I'm on your side now. It's hard to believe, but you have to."

"I can see why," I said, recalling my school paper. "He was an animal to you."

"*Animal* is putting it lightly. I wasn't a person to him. I was just a *thing* for him to look at. And that was when he was in a rare good mood. Most of the time, I was just his human punching bag."

I remembered seeing that she had a black eye. *If I ever see Brown again, he is dead.* I had no tolerance for domestic violence.

"I tipped them off," Kathryn continued, whispering directly into my ear. "I told the cops where Aidan is, where we are. They're coming. Some of the military's with them too. I managed to shut his security system off for a while. Well, until now."

She paused for another second. The "Code Goliath" messages were still booming.

Kathryn went on. "I stalled Brown and his men. I distracted them so the Operation could enter the hideout without them noticing."

I didn't ask Kathryn precisely what she did to distract Brown. I figured it was better left unsaid.

"Well, that's good," I replied. "But I have news for you too. Larry. He—he is working with Brown. Brown told me himself when I was in his lair with him."

Kathryn's look intensified. "Well, that's *not* good. The police have no idea. Last time I checked, he was with them."

"For all I know, he's leading them into a trap."

"But I can't say I am surprised," Kathryn said with an expression that was a combination of anger and disappointment. "When I first met him, I had a feeling I'd seen him before." She abruptly stopped talking for a second before resuming. "Now I remember where. I've seen him talking to my husband—talking to Brown."

I then remembered my brief meeting with Janusz Kazlowski,

my great-grandfather. He was sure he had seen Larry before as well. It all made sense now. Of course Janusz had seen him. The Greenies were in his restaurant all the time—and Larry was *one* of them. *What a scumbag that "Larry" is—if that's even his real name. He's gonna pay for what he did to me and the girls.*

"He's actually been here on several occasions," Kathryn continued. "For at least a few months now."

I thought back to my confrontation with Brown. He had mentioned that his 2022 self regularly traveled to the past. That's where he got all his "future," well, *present*, technology from. Maybe Larry had gone with him on these trips. I did some quick mental math. Brown would be well into his seventies in 2022.

I turned to Kathryn. "Have you ever seen Larry with, say, a seventy-something-year-old man who might look a little bit like Brown?"

She looked confused. "There are really no Greenies over forty. Most are either dead or retired by then. Mainly the former." She stopped. "Well, there is one old man I sometimes see in the lair. Aidan's Uncle Éan. He has the same eyes as him—it's scary. He holds down the fort when my husband's out on business. I'm pretty sure I've seen him with Larry before, but now that I think about it, I don't ever think I've ever actually seen Éan and Aidan *together*."

"That *is* Brown," I concluded. *There is no way anyone else has that exact same pair of bloodcurdling eyes.* "That's him from my time."

"And that explains everything," Kathryn replied. "Because they're the same person."

"So, 2022 Brown, or Éan, is going back in time with Larry. Essentially, he's using Larry to communicate with his 1974 self—just like he used him to bring *me* here." None of this answered the one burning question I had in my head. "But *why*? Why *me*? What is it about me that makes Brown want to pursue me so much and do experiments on my body? If it's not blackmail, what is it?"

Kathryn didn't have an answer. Despite being a full-blown Greenie on paper, she knew barely anything about official gang business. That, she told me, was between Brown and his very limited inner circle.

We stopped our conversation. Aside from the loudspeaker continuing to repeat the words "Code Goliath," I heard another noise. A more subtle noise. Footsteps.

39

RENEGADE

Brown began to regain consciousness. "Kathryn," he murmured groggily, with his eyes still closed. "Kathryn."

He opened his eyes. He was lying face-up on his lair's cement floor, a couple of feet away from the table he had fallen from. He had a mild concussion from the blunt force with which his head had hit the ground. Kathryn was nowhere to be seen. Instead, his favorite guard, Dan McCreery, was furiously shaking him by his shoulders.

"You're not Kathryn," Brown said to him as he sat up.

"No shit, Sherlock," Dan replied. He paused for a second so Brown could hear the "Code Goliath" message.

"Son of a bitch! I knew she was up to no good." Brown turned his head to see who was in the room and spied the two medics. "Why the hell did you leave that kid's side!"

"You were out for a good while, Dragon," the lead medic answered him. "Since you weren't responding to CPR, we honestly thought you had a heart attack or stroke and were going to die."

"I was drugged, you idiots! She must've jacked one of the needles I use to get high and gave me the *whole* damn thing."

Dan was panicking. As the closest thing Brown had to a second-in-command, he felt responsible for the Greenies' complete failure to keep tabs on Charlie and the hideout when Brown was unconscious.

Brown ordered his medics to go to the Science Room—they swiftly obeyed. "I swear. I should've listened to my future self about that woman," Brown growled as his inept lackeys rushed out of the boardroom.

Back in action, Brown commanded the dozens of guards crowding around him to retake their former places. Next, he ushered Dan to guard the door to the lair. That was the most important assignment, as he was the one who stood in the way between the good guys and Brown.

As the guards and medics exited, they saw that the police and military were flooding the hallways—they had already progressed halfway to the boardroom. The flock of cops and soldiers numbered at least in the hundreds. There was no way any of the Greenies could have entered the hallway without getting *crushed*. They quickly stepped back into the lair and re-alerted Brown.

In disbelief, the Green Dragon opened the door to see the commotion himself. He quickly shut it. "It's even worse than I thought!" he wailed. "They got the whole damned Chicago PD and the Army Guard with them. I'm gonna kill that bitch.

She must have given them the address—it's the only way!"

The guards were consumed by fear and confusion. For the many years they had been with Brown, crime was all they had known. Since joining the coveted ranks of the Greenies, being locked up was *never* an option for them. Their leader always knew how to outfox law enforcement, so they never got caught. Their hideout was heavily secured, six stories underground, and in a different *state* than the police were searching. They were safe to live as outlaws—until then. Justice was finally starting to prevail, and it seemed that their whole world was suddenly collapsing.

Brown frantically dispersed his men. He motioned for a few to stay with him in the room, a few to protect the door with Dan, and for the majority of them, mainly the lower-ranked and less experienced ones, to venture out to attack the cops and military. Essentially, they were, at least to Brown, the collateral damage he needed to cripple the attacking forces.

Back in the hallway, Sargento and Perry led the team further along, to the point where they were clogging a good two-thirds of the "school." The group of Greenies that Brown had sent out of the lair had caught up with them.

"Freeze!" Sargento yelled. "Chicago PD, FBI, National Guard, *and* the U.S. Army. The jig is up! Put your hands in the air, drop all weapons! No one needs to get hurt!"

"We can do this the easy way or the hard way!" shouted Perry.

The exiled Greenies, being severely outnumbered by cops

and military, complied with the orders. The officers collected their guns and handcuffed them, escorting each of them into an empty "classroom."

Seeing this, Dan, flanked by a few guards who managed to escape, flooded into Brown's room. He wasn't just losing his temper—his temper was gone. "We're no match for them! There's too many of them!"

His reaction didn't faze Brown. Instead, he *smiled*. "There is one thing they don't know about—the secret exit. It's our only choice right now. Sure, we'll have to sacrifice a bunch of men, but we can replace them all in no time. They're just a bunch of warm bodies at the end of the day. Our network is too powerful for the law to beat us."

At once, he ushered some of his guards out of the secret exit, telling them to go home and to meet him at the backup hideout at eleven o'clock the next night. When they had left through the concealed passageway, Dan turned to him.

"Can I go with them?" he asked.

"Danny Boy—I got a special job for you since you were *so* protective of the kid," he sarcastically derided him. "This is my way of thanking you for singlehandedly getting us into this disaster!"

"So, that's a no, right?"

"Daniel McCreery! You're gonna get your fat ass back out into the hallway and look for my *lovely* wife and that Charlie. I bet they're together—rats are attracted to other rats after all. Take half of these guards with you." Brown pointed at the two dozen or so who remained in the room.

"You're gonna need them."

"Do you want them dead or alive?"

"Kathryn could be either. I prefer to do the honors myself, but bring her whatever way gets her to me the fastest. But the boy *must* be alive. You better not kill him until the medics have fully experimented on his precious body and taken all the necessary DNA samples."

"Got it, boss," Dan said. "And what about Larry? What do you want me to do with him?"

Brown laughed. "Forget him. I have no use for that moron anymore. He's already served his purpose in life, and that was to bring me the boy. If you kill him, you kill him, and if you don't, you don't. I don't give a damn about what happens to him. He's just another waste of a warm body."

Since Dan had no more questions, he re-entered the hallway with his bevy of guards. He marched them down toward the police. The ambush of Brown's guards had set the Operation back a small degree. The majority of the police officers at the squad's front were busy fighting, subduing, handcuffing, and holding these guards. Behind the first row of officers, Dan spotted the four teens who had led the way: Maddie, Hannah, Kylie—and Larry.

Dan looked at the guards next to him. "Look who it is." He pointed at the kids from a distance. "Science experiment boy's sister, *girlfriends*, and Larry."

"Let's get 'em!" a guard eagerly barked.

"Was just gonna suggest that," said Dan. "Brown will do a number on them. He'll definitely be able to get the boy's location out of one of them. Probably the sister."

"That's if they even know where he is," one guard noted.

"Even if they don't, it would be *fun*," replied Dan.

The guards agreed. Dan and his men made a beeline toward the teenagers. Moving swiftly and precisely, they dodged through the sea of blue uniforms and hoisted the three squealing girls away from safety. Most of the cops were too distracted dealing with the other guards to notice, and the ones who *did* were too late to save any of them from the Greenies' clutches.

Another guard tried to lift Larry, but he was too big for him to secure in his grasp. He kicked his way free and back into the huddle of the cops, blending himself in. The Greenies didn't care that he got away. Brown said he was worthless anyway—and to them, whatever Brown said was gospel.

The guards carried the captured girls to the lair, where they were promptly seated at Brown's table and tied up as Charlie had been before.

Brown was still not satisfied. He glared at Dan. "I asked for my wife and Charlie Henderson, and instead, you give me Little Miss Sunshine, Betty, and Veronica!"

"Those are not our names!" Hannah cried.

"I never said you could talk, Betty," Brown scoffed.

Dan spoke up. "Boss, we got you these little *angels* because they might be able to tell us where Charlie is hiding."

Brown smirked. "True. Very true. And once he realizes his friends are not coming to save him, he'll give up, and boom— he'll be mine again!"

"I know my brother, and I know he never gives up, except when he plays Super Smash Bros. with me!" Maddie said. She was visibly tremoring, which caused Brown to laugh hysterically.

"Where *is* your brother, Madeleine?" Dan asked her.

"I don't know!"

"'You don't know' don't cut it!" Dan roared. "When Dan McCreery asks you a question, you answer it!"

Hannah whispered to the other girls, "I'm guessing that's Rick McCreery's grandpa."

"Well, now I see where he gets his looks *and* personality from," Kylie whispered back to her.

"Silence!" Brown hollered. "You better tell me where he is! Or else!"

"Or else, what?" Hannah challenged him. "Like Maddie said, we don't know."

"Yeah, Brown," jeered Kylie. "We came here to look for him, you idiot."

Dan was intent on torturing the girls until he got any kind of answer out of them, mainly because he wanted to prove his worth to Brown. But Brown knew that they were, in fact, telling the truth that they had no idea where Charlie was—and he didn't want to waste any time.

"They're not gonna help us," Brown said to Dan. He motioned toward the hallway, which was now seventy-five percent taken by the police and the military. "Go back out there with your guards and find them! I expect you to bring me the right people this time! Am I clear?"

"Yes, boss," Dan answered, doing what Brown commanded in leaving the lair with the guards.

Dan and his men were able to sidestep the front lines of the cops and sneak their way into the Science Room—but walking right past the boiler room door, they saw no sign of Kathryn or Charlie.

40

TRUE COLORS

Larry noticed that a lot of Brown's guards were disappearing. They were dropping like flies, but not all of them appeared to be getting arrested by the cops. This only meant one thing. Brown was ordering an escape through a secret exit which Larry didn't know about.

Continuing to blend in amongst the officers, he stealthily made his way into the Science Room, after Dan and the other Greenies had foolishly dashed out empty-handed. He poked around the gruesome chamber, observing the flimsy gurney on which Charlie had lain. Two long, pointy devices flecked with blood lay to its side. Being a football player, Larry liked to think of himself as having a high pain tolerance, but looking at the set-up made him sick to his stomach, especially knowing that the blood was Charlie's. Was this all Larry's fault? Was the blood on *his* hands?

He examined the room, thinking to himself. *If I was Brown's wife, where would I hide?* He pondered. Suddenly, the boiler room door came into his view. *That's it.* Without wasting any time, he opened the door.

The tiny space was completely dark. The only hint of brightness came from the small influx of the strobe light in the operating area—it was still enough to illuminate everyone's faces. Larry was greatly relieved to see that both Charlie and Kathryn were alive and, unlike the girls, away from Brown's lair.

"Thank God you're alive!" Larry whispered to Charlie, with the boiler room door still wide open. "Look, we need to be quiet. The cops are here, and they're getting the job done, but Brown's not going down without a fight. He's got all of the girls."

Charlie glared at him with even more contempt than he had Brown. "You traitor!" They were the only words he was able to get out.

"The secret's out, *Larry*!" Kathryn added. "We know your true colors. You're one of them, if not *worse*. Charlie and the others trusted you. We're not falling for this trap of yours."

Kathryn was about to shut the door in his face, but Larry, given his excellent reaction time, was able to hold out his arm to stop it.

"What are you talking about?" Larry replied, flummoxed. "I came here to *save* you."

"You're a monster," Charlie berated him. "You brought me here so Brown and his goons can do experiments on me and then boil my blood like soup."

Larry recalled the bloody surgical tools he had seen a

minute before. With the limited light, he could still see the gaping wounds on Charlie's arm—where medics had inserted the pronged tools. He took a deep breath. "Brown's full of crap," Larry said. "You know that."

"I—I thought you were my friend." Charlie was enraged and crying at the same time.

Larry looked earnestly at him. "I *am*," he said. "Look, Brown is lying. Hear me out."

"You better leave us alone," Kathryn fumed. "You're going down with Brown." She went to close the door again, but Larry once more grabbed it before she could do anything.

"Just let me in," Larry begged. "I can explain."

"Why the hell would I do that!" Charlie whisper-screamed.

"Well, the alternative is leaving the door open and *all* of us dying," Larry correctly pointed out.

Charlie reluctantly shut the boiler room door, finally letting Larry in with him and Kathryn. "Why would you do this to me?"

Larry inhaled again. "Look, Brown is half right—and half wrong. He's right that I brought you here. But I'm *not* working for him! He wants to get in your head so you won't let me save you."

Charlie refused to believe him. "That makes no sense! If you're not working for Brown, why would you bring me here?"

Larry rubbed his forehead. "It's about time I explained," he stated. "I'm not working with Brown. I'm working with Al."

41

A MATTER OF TIME

I didn't know what to believe anymore. "Al? The FBI brought me here?"

"Not really. More like Al in particular," Larry clarified. "He knows something that the rest of the Bureau doesn't—the existence of time warps. You see, there are these portals, or wormholes, between different times in history, like what we went through. Nobody yet knows who or what put them there, but what we do know is that there are a few people who can open them."

I was shellshocked. "But how?" I asked. "And why?"

Larry waited for a second to answer. "The *how* part, nobody knows for sure, at least as of now. We think it's due to a mutation of a certain little-known gene on Chromosome 12—that somehow allows a person's brainwaves to activate these time warps. Forensic evidence shows that whatever the difference is, it's especially marked in time-sensitive people's white blood cells."

I wasn't buying his explanation. "So, you're saying that there's a bunch of time wizards living among us, and we just don't know it?!"

"Not *wizards*," continued Larry. "Time-sensitive human beings. This is a matter of science, not magic. When you think about it, 'magic' is really only the word we use for something when there's no scientific explanation—yet." He paused again. "And as you saw, I am one of these people."

I was hearing a lot about time travel, but no one was telling me how I, or my family, factored into any of this. "But why—why use these powers on me?"

Larry sighed. "The truth is that Al is not really an FBI agent. He's actually a scientist working for a top-secret department of the U.S. government that makes the FBI look like mall cops. Manny is his personal assistant, who primarily serves as his body man. As you can see, he follows him pretty much *everywhere*. The government knows about these time warps but is keeping this knowledge under wraps for obvious reasons. We can't have the public find out about them. Otherwise, we risk the complete and utter destruction of the world."

I was taken aback by how casually Larry talked about the apocalypse. I still wasn't sure what to believe.

"Just think about it," he continued. "If people learned the truth, scientists would readily find a way to manipulate the human genome so *everyone* would be able to time travel. Billions of people time traveling at will would cause so many ripple effects that the world would cease to exist in a matter of *seconds.* Al and I are working hard to investigate the causes of these time warps—so we can ultimately destroy them and put an end to this madness, for once and for all."

Now I could see why Al was so adamant that I didn't tell Chief Marshall, Tom, Gallagher, or any of the *actual* law enforcement people about time travel. But Larry, like everyone else, wasn't telling me what *my* place was in all of this.

"But that still doesn't answer my question! Why me? What do I, a teenage *nerd,* have to do with this? And where does Brown fit in?"

Larry was delaying the inevitable. He finally broke it to me. "I was sent to your school by Al to *protect* you. The truth is, we believe you are the solution to restoring order to time and the world."

"So, you're saying I have your powers too?"

"No," he replied. "I'm saying that you're way, *way* more powerful than me. You've just lived a sheltered life and don't know about your capabilities yet."

So, Larry knew I could time travel all along? Why didn't he just tell me so that I could've gotten the group back home to our time safely? The answer was clear. It was because he wanted me in 1974 for some reason. But why? This didn't add up. "How do you know this about me?" I asked.

"Al's research is highly confidential. He doesn't reveal *any* of his methods to *anyone,* not even Manny, but what I do know is that out of the seven some-odd billion human beings on the planet, you may be our *only* hope."

It was still hard for me to wrap my head around this

information. "So, this explains why Brown was trying to experiment on me!"

"Exactly," Larry replied. "Al doesn't know why you're the way you are, but we know that some part of your blood DNA might be able to help all people time travel at will. Knowing Brown, he wants to use your DNA to make himself into a time-traveling super-human and change history to make himself the supreme ruler of the United States, if not the entire world."

"But if you knew this, why would you bring me to him? None of this makes any sense!"

Kathryn, who had been quiet this whole time, spoke up. "Yeah! I'm starting to think that Brown might have been telling the truth about you!" she yelled to Larry.

"Look," Larry responded. "Al told me that in order to defeat Brown, we needed you to be *here*. He and I had planned this mission for a while. What we initially had in mind was that I would pose as a transfer student at your school and befriend you. You would come to trust me. Al knew that Brown was going to bring you to 1974 at any moment, and since there was no way to avoid this, he wanted me to be at your side so I could protect you."

"But Brown did *not* bring me to 1974!" I stated. "*You* did."

"We estimated that Brown was going to act around Christmastime, so Al sent me to your side in September. That way, we had a couple of months to build a rapport and even prepare for our fight. But then, just a few days later, we encountered the Kobras."

I was starting to connect the dots in my head. I was a nerd, after all. "And knowing that we would have to eventually go to Brown anyway, you decided that going through the portal early was our only choice."

"Yes. They had us surrounded, so it was the only thing I *could* do. I happened to have a small canister of pepper spray in my pocket and used it to blind the gang so I could open the warp for us."

So *that's* why Larry reached into his pocket before my view faded. "What about my sister, Hannah, and Kylie? Does Brown want them too?"

"No. The girls were not part of the plan at all. It was just supposed to be you and me. But I had no choice but to take them too. The gang would have hurt or killed them if we left them behind."

"Do you think Brown knew that Al already knew that he wanted me—so he sent the gang to get us here by surprise?"

Larry hesitated. "I never thought of it that way, but it makes sense. Anyway, there's something else about me you should know." He paused. "Kathryn, remember you insisted that it was certain we met before?"

"Yes," she calmly replied. "I've seen you talking to Brown a few times."

"That's because we have." Larry was frank. "Al was having me pretend to be a member of another affiliate gang, to scope out some information on Brown's recruiting process, so I could prepare for when you, Charlie, came here. The truth is, I am actually this age in 1974."

I was thrown for a loop. It turned out that Larry wasn't time traveling to the past when he had met with Brown—this was his *present*. He instead was time traveling to the *future* when he came to my school. "So," I said, "you mean to tell me you're really a sixty-something-year-old man? Like your uncle Bill's age?"

"I'm *exactly* Uncle Bill's age—because I *am* Uncle Bill."

"This keeps getting weirder and weirder," I exclaimed.

"My full legal name is William Lawrence Travers II. I went by Larry as a young man and Bill as an older man. One of the ways time travel works is if you travel to a time where you also exist, only one version of you can be in the time. That's why you never saw Uncle Bill and me together. When he is in 2022, I—well, this version of me—is back in 1974."

His mysterious disappearance now made sense—as did the fact that he just so happened to have "Uncle Bill's" license on him so we could rent a car to travel to Chicago. I collected my thoughts before speaking. "So, wait. The morning before the game and the party, you were actually back in 1974? Because you were AWOL for quite some time, and I saw Uncle Bill, uh—future *you* at your house."

"Yes," he said. "That's one of the quirks of time travel, so to speak. Al calls it the 'twelve hour rule.' If you travel forward in time when you're still alive like I did when I went to 2022—the *past* version of you can only stay in the future for half a day at once. The same thing's the case when your future self travels back in time, as long as it's *after* you're born. Either way, if you stay a second longer than twelve hours, you automatically return to your original time, and you have to stay there for twelve more hours before you can time travel again. I knew I needed to be with you for the game and the party, and I obviously was right, so I had no choice but to disappear on Thursday night and stay in the past until late Friday morning."

"So, twelve hours in the future, you return to the past—twelve hours back in time and forward you're blast."

Larry chuckled at my unintentional rhyme. "I guess you can say that—but it's only the case if you exist in the time to which you've traveled. Since you or the girls weren't born yet in 1974, the twelve-hour rule doesn't apply to either of you. It doesn't apply to me either here because this is my *correct* time."

My skepticism was still at an all-time high. "But if you've never seen Uncle Bill, does he know you traveled to 2022? How could he have registered you for school?"

"You're forgetting that Uncle Bill *is* future me. He knows most of everything I know now. You do forget *some* information in forty-eight years, so we also communicate by letters. Every time we, well, the two versions of me trade off, we leave a note for each other on my, well, *our* iPhone in 2022."

"Now that I think of it, this is how Brown communicates with his future self," I said.

"But Brown is *dead* in 2022," Larry responded.

"That's not what he said," I told him. "Apparently, when he 'died,' he reinvented himself under another identity. When you were gathering intel on the Greenies, did you remember meeting an elderly man named *Éan*?"

"Yeah, Brown's doddering uncle," he replied. "What about him?"

"That's actually 2022 *him*," I said. "Well, it's at least what he told me. He could very well be lying. He did convince me that you were a traitor after all."

"I guess I'm not the only time traveler pretending to be their own uncle *and* nephew."

We heard what sounded like rustling noises coming from right outside the boiler room. Had somebody found us?

"I don't know about you guys, but I think we should keep our voices down," whispered Kathryn.

"Let's listen until we don't hear them anymore," I said. "And that's when we'll make a run for it and meet up with the girls."

"There's only one problem with that," said Larry. "Brown *has* the girls. And from what I can tell, he's making a run for it himself through a secret exit of some kind."

"But aren't the police and military here?" asked Kathryn.

"They definitely got Brown outnumbered," he replied. "But you're forgetting that it's Brown we're dealing with—the same scoundrel who's been evading them for eight years."

"Yep," she agreed, "I'm positive that he's still got a few tricks left up his sleeve."

The rustling noise appeared to have stopped.

"I don't hear it anymore," I noted.

"Then this might be our cue," stated Larry.

Kathryn placed her ear in the crack of the boiler room door

and waited for about fifteen seconds. "As a former outlaw," she said, "I know when the coast is clear—and the coast *is* clear."

Hand-in-hand, we bolted out of the boiler room, through the Science Room, and back into the hallway, blending ourselves in with the omnipresent police and military forces. An officer spotted us and motioned for us to follow him. We passed the adjacent two "classrooms," where dozens of Greenies were being detained. However, one thing was amiss—the door to Brown's former lair was flung wide open— the first time I had *ever* seen it that way. It was clear that the conniving mobster and many of his men had escaped through the back exit Larry told me about.

"We need to follow them!" I yelled. "They have my sister and friends!"

Larry looked at me with a sense of pity. "We can't. It's too dangerous."

"I have to agree with him," added the officer, who I would later learn was named Pellegrino. "We should get out of here alive first. Then later, we'll think about sending out a search party to look for them."

I was absolutely livid at both of them. "No!" I defiantly uttered. "I refuse to go to safety now. I didn't go this far just to watch Brown win and my sister and friends die!"

Larry looked at me and glanced back at the cops. "If it were up to me, I'd rather do what the police say. But at the end of the day, I'm this kid's protector." He nervously smiled at me. "If he's gung-ho on risking his life to go after Brown,

I'm sure as hell going with him."

Kathryn chimed in. "I'm going too. I want to see my husband—well, soon-to-be *ex*-husband brought to justice! As does the entire city of Chicago, *and* state of Indiana for that matter!"

With Larry and Kathryn making the case to them, Al, Sargento, and a large portion of the police-military forces reluctantly followed us into the deserted lair. However, a decent number of the cops had to stay back to watch over the imprisoned Greenies.

Kathryn, taking the lead, racked her brain for secret places Brown had taken her in the hideout. Finally, after nearly five minutes had gone by, she, helped by a few officers, removed a leather chair in the corner of the vast boardroom, exposing a depression on the wall. She gently tugged at it, and a rectangular passageway opened. All of us were relieved— but it had taken much longer for her to find it than we had anticipated.

After Kathryn had successfully located the Greenies' secret exit, we shuffled through, with the cops and military quickly following us. Leading the charge and moving as fast as my legs could carry me, I saw that I was in a labyrinth of winding corridors, similar to the hideout's entry maze. But these corridors were significantly wider, wetter, and far more foul-smelling. This could only mean one thing—I had led hundreds of brave young men and women into the *sewer*. Up ahead, I heard noises—voices that sounded distinctly like Brown and his associates.

"We're closing in on them!" I shouted to the police officers and soldiers who were behind me.

Kathryn was not as optimistic. "They sound too far away. At the rate they're going, they're gonna lose us soon."

We heard the commotion again. I then realized that the noises were not coming from ahead of us as I had thought. They were coming from *above* us.

"You hear that?" Larry said. "Those bastards are already making their way out of the sewer!"

"Yep," agreed Kathryn. "I knew Aidan would find a way to outsmart us. Unfortunately, due to where he is, he must've had at least a fifteen- to twenty-minute head start."

"If only you spent less time looking for that damn door!" Larry railed at her.

"Sorry," Kathryn said. "It's not like Brown ever told me where it was. He probably foresaw something like this happening. That creep plans for *everything*."

"What do we do?" I asked.

"We can't really do anything now," replied Al. "We can just keep going forward and hope there's some sort of roadblock up ahead, Brown stumbles, and we catch up to him."

"Not going to happen," Kathryn said. "'Stumbling' ain't in Brown's vocabulary. He's slick as a whistle."

Larry flashed a concerned expression. "To catch up with Brown, we're gonna need to throw a Hail Mary," he said, making a football analogy.

"It'll take more than a Hail Mary," Sargento remarked. "It's a full-on ninety-nine-yard pass."

I just couldn't envision the thought of Brown getting away with Maddie, Hannah, and Kylie. *Please help us all, God,* I prayed. I heard the noises from the Greenies fade further into the distance. They probably were already out of the sewer and beginning to make their getaway on the city streets. Brown was at large again, and the girls were with him.

42

HAIL MARY

Suddenly it hit me—I could *time travel*. I still didn't know how to do it, though. But it was why my friends and I were stuck in the seventies in the first place, and ultimately, it was the only thing that was going to get us out.

I anxiously looked over at Larry. We had lagged for a few minutes, allowing nearly all of the soldiers and cops to blaze past us in a futile quest to catch up with Brown. Per the orders of Chief Marshall, we were to be watched like a hawk at all times. Sargento and Perry, therefore, stayed very close to us as their colleagues marched forward.

Soon the entire cadre of armed men and women had passed by, and there was no one behind us. Sergeant Perry lightly gestured to us to hurry up, but he wasn't pushing the issue as he knew we were trying to think of a "Hail Mary pass" to metaphorically "throw."

Larry and I leaned against the wet brick wall to our right. Since we were a reasonable distance from the police and

military, and there was so much background noise anyway—
not a soul could hear us. "If only I could use my powers to
turn back the clock twenty minutes. That way, we could close
the gap with Brown and catch up with him."

Larry frantically shook his head. "That's impossible," he
replied. "Time traveling *at will* is not a thing. At least *yet*. No
one has figured it out. The only way people have ever been
able to time travel is by manipulating existing time warps. I,
and every other time traveler I met, can only open portals.
We can't *create* them."

I knew I was in over my head. I'd only known I could time
travel for about fifteen minutes, after all. But if I didn't try, I'd
let Brown win, and my sister, Hannah, and Kylie would die. "If
anyone can do it, it's me," I confidently said to him.

"Well, I guess it's worth a shot," he replied. "From what
Al has told me, you are the most powerful time traveler in
human existence. That's why Brown is pursuing *you* for your
white blood cells and DNA—not me and not any of the other
handful of time-sensitive humans out there."

"So, how exactly do you open a portal?" I asked Larry. I
had no idea.

"It's all about using your brain," he stated. "Think of
the particular time you want to go to—in this case, twenty
minutes ago. Think deeply like you never did before. Then
use your hands to *pry open* the air in front of you for lack of
better terms. Almost like there's an invisible door there."

I felt like my life had become a science fiction movie. I
mean, it pretty much had been. I did exactly what Larry said.

I thought hard about going back in time twenty minutes before desperately scraping at the air. Nothing happened. I tried again and again. Still, there was no portal. Maybe Al, Brown, and *everybody* got it wrong. Perhaps I couldn't time travel at all.

"It's not working," I groaned to Larry. "I guess you're right."

"You're not doing it correctly," he pointed out. "You're focusing on using your hands, not your brain."

But Larry had told me to use my hands to poke at the air! At that point, I was ready to accept defeat.

"The hands part really does nothing," Larry explained. "It's a *placebo*."

"Now's not the time to be speaking Italian," I scolded him.

Larry looked at me compassionately. It probably took him a while to learn how to open a portal himself. I had to learn it all in a matter of minutes. "What I meant is that when you wave your hands, it causes your brain to focus more on what you're doing, and thus, it sends a stronger signal. The stronger the brain signal, the easier it is to open a warp."

I took a deep breath. I thought as hard as I possibly could have. I remembered how intense my focus was when I kicked the game-winning field goal against Desert Valley. I breathed in again. I thought about my little sister and all the silly battles we had throughout the years. But ultimately, I realized how much I loved her and how I would do *anything* for her. I thought about Kylie, who had become one of my best friends in the last few days, and who'd taught me how to be so much more confident. If *she* didn't believe in me, I wouldn't have made that kick in the first place. And I thought about Hannah, who I was falling for. She was right on the track to becoming my first love. She kept telling me how we'd go on our date as soon as we went home. I was overcome with intense passion.

You're going down, Brown, I emphatically said to myself. I moved my hands. All of a sudden, it felt like there was a forcefield in the foul-smelling sewer air. It was like I was pushing against the force of gravity itself. A gust of wind whooshed down the wide sewer pipe, and a swirling vortex appeared a few yards directly in front of us.

"That's it!" Larry said. "That's the portal! Make it wider so everyone can fit through it!" He gestured to me, moving his hands out to the sides of his body.

I copied Larry's movements. Then, to my surprise, the portal opened up wide. It didn't look like a vortex anymore. Instead, it looked more like the famous *Cloud Gate* sculpture in downtown Chicago. I didn't quite know if my brain was doing it or my hands, but I didn't care at that moment.

Larry smiled, giving me a double thumbs-up. "That's it, bro! Now step aside and let the magic happen! But, whatever you do, make sure you go through it *last*!"

I thrust the portal forward down the sewer and straight into the platoon of cops and troops. I remained brushed against the wall the entire time, covering my shirt in all kinds of muck. Standing restlessly, I watched as the portal gobbled up everyone—except Larry and me—in a matter of seconds.

Then, when there was no one in sight, we walked several feet to the portal's edge. First, Larry allowed himself to be engulfed by the void. Then I dived in myself.

For a few seconds, everything was black.

I feared the worst. *What had I done?*

43

TWENTY MINUTES

The darkness stopped. I landed knee-first on the sewer floor.

"You okay, kid?" an Army reservist asked me. He helped me back up onto my feet.

"I see you been laggin' behind," a city police officer noted. "I thought you were in the front with the other FBI kids."

"Yes, sir," I answered, not wanting to draw any attention to myself.

I overheard chatter among the soldiers and cops alike. None of them had any idea what happened when I opened the portal. Some thought it was just another trick up Brown's sleeve to leave us in the dust, while others suspected a sewage treatment malfunction.

Kathryn, knowing that something was up—and rightly suspecting that it was my doing—rushed to meet up with Larry and me.

"Did it work?" I asked Larry.

Larry checked his watch and showed it to me. It was *exactly* twenty minutes earlier than when I had opened the portal. "You tell me," he said. I was still in disbelief at my newfound ability.

He then showed his watch to Kathryn. She didn't say anything—but she didn't have to. Her shocked expression said it all.

"Well, we're back in time now," I said. "Where's Brown?"

I heard a series of ear-splitting shrieks coming from behind me. I turned around and right behind our platoon—*there* was Brown and his Greenie guards. When I had sent us back twenty minutes, we were now only a few paces *in front* of them. The gang's head start had vanished.

"Freeze!" yelled Sergeant Perry. "Chicago PD, FBI, National Guard, and U.S. Army!"

"Noooooo!" Brown bawled when he saw that the good guys outnumbered him by at least five to one.

He tried to head back to the lair, but when he finally processed what had just happened, Perry and Pellegrino were close enough to seize him. Heading back wouldn't have done him good anyway, as the hideout was already taken by the cops and military who didn't go with us. Brown was sandwiched in—he had no place to escape.

"This can't be! This is impossible!" Brown started to cry. It was the first time I had ever seen tears actually come out of his eyes.

"Put your hands in the air! All of you!" ordered

Chief Marshall as the police and military surrounded the outnumbered Greenies. "Your days of running amok have come to an end!"

The murderous gangster was flabbergasted. "But—but how!" He wept. He pointed back toward the hideout. "You were all the way over *there!*"

I got closer to Brown. I wasn't afraid of him. Without all his fancy technology, he was just a petty thug—and on top of that, a coward. "What's the matter, Brown?" I called out to him. "I know what the matter is. You just got outclassed by a *teenager.*"

"Noooooo!" he screamed again. "This can't be happening. I *know* the future! *This* is not what happens!"

Larry and Kathryn had also come close to Brown to watch him finally being brought to justice.

"It is now, buddy!" Larry exclaimed. "My dude Charlie over here just changed the course of human history forever."

"You're nothing but a vile, disgusting murderer!" cried Kathryn to her defeated husband. "It's over! I've put up with your abuse for almost five years! I thought I could change you—how stupid was I! Enjoy your new life behind bars!"

Al, who stood next to us, was smiling ear to ear. He shot Brown a grimace. "Pellegrino, do the honors!" he barked.

Officer Pellegrino elatedly aimed his Taser gun at Brown's chest and pulled the trigger, sending a stream of electricity pulsing into Brown's body. He became limp as a dead fish, plummeting backward onto the sewer floor. It was a fitting end to the evil crime lord's career.

Pellegrino radiated excitement after seeing what he did to Brown. "I've been waiting to use this newfangled Taser thingamabob ever since it came out a few months ago!"

The rest of the cops immediately began to handcuff Brown and his men and drag them away into custody. They also untied Maddie, Hannah, and Kylie, who greeted me with big hugs once freed. I was extremely relieved that all of them were relatively unharmed, aside from being in great shock and distress.

"That was awesome!" Hannah proclaimed.

"You guys just came out of nowhere," noted Kylie. "How is that possible?"

Larry pointed at me. "It was all this guy," he said. "He used his time travel powers to turn back the clock twenty minutes and completely erase the lead Brown had on us!"

"Time travel powers!" Maddie remarked. "*This* I need to be filled in on when we're alone again!"

"We actually did it. We actually beat Brown!" I said.

"No, *you* did it," said Hannah. "My hero!" Then she grabbed me, pulling me in for a warm, tender kiss. It was wonderful. I had never imagined that my first ever kiss would be with Hannah Preston—in a sewer under the streets of Gary, Indiana, and after fighting a gangster—in 1974. But damn, it felt good.

Kylie offered me another hug, which I gladly accepted as well. She looked a little upset that I had kissed Hannah but nevertheless tried to hide it for the sake of the moment.

I then turned to Maddie and gently embraced her. *My*

baby sister, I thought. Thank God she was okay. No matter how hard Brown tried to tear my family apart, there was always a part of me who knew that he would fail. There was no bond between humans that was stronger than a family.

Chief Marshall, Al, and Manny all walked over to us. "Congratulations, kids," Al said as he shook each of our hands. "You beat Brown at his own game."

"Special Agent Cannella, I must say," remarked Marshall, "I thought you were off your rocker when you suggested throwing these young'uns at that malicious, egomaniacal mob boss, but somehow it worked."

Al shrugged. "Decades of experience means something *once in a while*," he uttered sarcastically.

I looked around, examining the sea of people, and noticed a familiar face not too far away from us. It was a young, blond man dressed up in an army uniform—my grandfather. I called out to him. "Paul! Is that you?"

He stepped closer to me. "Hey! You were in my restaurant a few days ago!" He turned his head and noticed my friends were next to me. "Don't tell me it was because you were infiltrating that gang!"

"Yes, we were," I stated proudly. "And now they're not gonna bother your family anymore."

"So, now you can ask Vicky, the waitress, out on a date," Maddie said.

Paul smiled at us. "I actually did. We're going to the movies this weekend. And thanks to you guys, those Greenies are gonna leave her alone for good!"

We said goodbye to him and followed Al to a manhole where we exited the sewer. As I pulled myself onto the street, I observed a seemingly endless line of police cars and vans, with their sirens blaring. Officers, assisted by the military, were hauling all the Greenies into them one by one. Farther ahead in the distance, we saw Brown, handcuffed and surrounded by four or five cops. He was awake and squirming like a worm—to no avail. *That monster is finally where he belongs.*

"The prison's gonna be very crowded tonight," Pellegrino said to us.

Journalists had arrived on the scene. We saw reporters interviewing Chief Marshall as well as the commissioner of the Chicago PD. But there was also a third person being interviewed, my grandpa Paul. I was able to listen in on bits and pieces of the conversation.

"You're a hero," the interviewer said to him. "The city needs more young people like you. What was it that made you volunteer to be part of Operation Green Dragon?"

"Well, the Greenies sure had it in for my family's restaurant. That business is my parents' lifeblood. They have worked so hard trying to provide a better future for my siblings and me." Paul paused. "But I had enough when I almost saw my own father die, in front of my own eyes. Their attempt on his life—well, it was the straw that broke the camel's back. So I joined the effort to take down Brown for my family's sake, but especially for my father."

"Is there anyone you would like to thank?" the journalist asked Paul.

"Yes, yes, there is," my grandpa replied. "There was this one kid, around the same age as me, who I met in the restaurant. He's actually here right now as he was part of the operation too. I want him to know that when I doubted that I could actually do something to change things, this kid—well, he just inspired me and gave me a lot of confidence. If I didn't talk to him, I never would have had the courage to put my life on the line and storm into Brown's stronghold."

I smiled. I knew that kid he was referring to was me. If only he knew I was his grandson.

My friends and I tried to get closer to him, but Al quickly ushered us away with fears the media would also interview us and find out our secret.

44

WHAT NEXT?

Maddie, Hannah, Kylie, Larry, and I stepped off to the side of the street, next to the entrance to an alleyway. We needed to take a breather from all the action that had engulfed us over the past few days.

"I hate to be a Debbie Downer," Maddie said to the rest of us. "Brown being in jail is nice and all, but how the hell are we going to get home?"

Larry turned to the girls, who still didn't know the whole story yet. "I got good news and bad news," he stated. "The good news is that both Charlie and I have the power to travel through time, so getting home is no problem."

The girls were more relieved than surprised, to be honest. The whole time travel thing made everything that happened to us make a lot more sense, after all.

"How long have you known this?" Hannah asked me.

"For like thirty minutes," I replied honestly. "Larry told me when Brown was getting away, so I turned back the clock to finish him off."

Kylie stared at Larry. "And the bad news is *you* knew this all this time."

Larry sighed. "The truth is I did, but I had a reason not to tell you. You see, Al and I work for the government."

"Al and *you*?" Maddie uttered. "But that makes no sense. Al would be like at least a *hundred* in 2022."

Larry realized the girls weren't with us when he had told us his secret. "That's another thing," he continued. "I am a time traveler *from* 1974. Well, I mean, I'm also alive in 2022, but I look quite different. I was born in 1956, so you do the math."

The girls were stunned. Larry had done a great job of pretending to be from our time.

He continued, "I learned about my powers three years ago when I was fifteen. I accidentally stumbled upon a time warp when I was out hiking with the Boy Scouts. I got separated from my troop, and the next thing I knew, I was in the year 1892. I was stuck there for three days before I figured out how to get back to my present. It turns out, all I had to do was think intently about a time, and if a warp was there, it was usually triggered. As soon as I got back home, I did some deep digging on time travel. Obviously, there's no Internet in the seventies, so I had to do what we did in Fresno—go to the library. I spent days, if not weeks, figuring out how to hone my special skills and trying to learn why I was the way I was. My local library wasn't cutting it, so I had to take a trip to the University of Alabama, where I read a dissertation on time warps written by some Turkish guy whose name I can't pronounce to save my life. One thing led to another, and I met Al, who eventually took me under his wing."

"But why travel to *our* time?" Hannah asked. "Did it have something to do with Charlie?"

"It had *everything* to do with Charlie," Larry continued. "Special Agent Cannella, or should I call him by his *actual* title, Dr. Cannella, is the world's foremost expert on time warps—and the people who can use them, such as Charlie and I. He was a student of that Turkish scientist. Al's known about their existence for nearly thirty years and was commissioned by the U.S. federal government to conduct extensive research out of fear the Soviet Union would access them. However, Al found that while the Soviets hadn't figured out time travel—Brown *had*. As we already know, that's how he had become so powerful and was able to elude the cops, well, until now, of course. Al's focus then shifted to using the knowledge he'd gained to find a way to beat Brown at his own game. The secret government agency he works for had him join the FBI's Chicago office so he could work directly on the Brown case."

"But what does this have to do with Charlie?" Maddie asked.

Larry explained to the girls the same thing he had told me in the boiler room. Al found out that I, a person who wasn't going to be born for another three decades, possessed a mysterious genetic mutation that gave me better control over the warps than any other known human had thus far. Because of this, Brown was planning to kidnap me and milk my blood and DNA in order to steal my powers for himself.

He explained the now-successful plan Al had devised, which was to use Larry's powers to bring me to Brown, bait him, and ultimately use my powers to defeat him. "We concluded that Charlie was the only person who could take down Brown, so it had to be done," he said. "Unfortunately, you three happened to be with us when the Kobras attacked—"

Maddie cut him off. "I'm glad we were, though." She looked at me. "We're family, and families stick together."

"Damn right they do," I agreed.

"So, as Al said, you need to leave before the press sees you," Larry noted. "Based on the rules of time travel, you will be in the exact same spot you were in on the date you're going to, so you don't need to worry about airfare or anything."

"Am I gonna be seeing you in 2022?" Kylie looked at Larry with disappointment in her dark brown eyes. Like the rest of us, she really enjoyed his company and was pretty bummed out to learn he was not our age.

"Of course," Larry replied. "I'll be there. Just to note, I am a little—well, *a lot*—older and go by Bill to most people, but aside from that, I'm the same loveable, easygoing guy."

The girls and I smiled. We didn't like that this was the last we'd see of him as a teenager, but it was reassuring to know that he would always be our friend.

"So, let's get this show on the road already," Hannah stated.

The five of us had one final group hug. Maddie, Hannah, Kylie, and I then said goodbye to Larry, who was obviously going to stay back in 1974.

The four of us stood in a giant circle holding hands. We made sure to stand in the alley, as far away from every other human being in sight. After all, we didn't want "The Four Disappearing Teens" to become a 1974 *Chicago Tribune* headline.

"Okay," I said. "Hopefully, I remember how to do this."

"*Hopefully*," Maddie snarked. She was starting to get back to her old, sarcastic self.

I thought about our last day in the present—September 9, 2022. It was around midnight when we were transported to the past, but remembering a scene from *Back to the Future*, I didn't want to go back to that exact time because I feared that the gang would be there. So, I thought intently about going back to September 9, 2022, at 9:00 p.m. That way, we had three whole hours to get out of the Krikorians' house and avoid the gang.

I unlocked hands with Hannah and Maddie to open my "air door," as Larry had taught me. Sure, enough, I made a portal.

"Holy crap," remarked Kylie, "that's awesome."

It is awesome, I thought. And what felt even more awesome-er was that we were finally about to go back home, to our old boring but safe lives.

"Well, here it is," I said. "I guess I'll see you all in 2022?"

"Yep, see you in 2022!" Hannah happily exclaimed. "And remember *tomorrow*, we're going to the Brown Cow, then we're seeing that Gina Carano movie!"

"Of course I remember!" I said. "How can I forget!"

A MATTER OF TIME

Maddie was the first to step through the portal, followed by Hannah, Kylie, and finally me.

My world faded to black.

45

2022

A few seconds later, I woke up. I had expected to be at the Krikorians' mansion, but I was someplace completely different. I was sitting in a plastic, black folding chair in the front row at some kind of event. *Is this another one of those boring Fresno city festivals my mom has dragged me to?* Directly in front of me, there was a podium with an official-looking seal of an eagle on it. Was it possible that I had jumped further into the future than I had wanted? *Maybe I thought of the wrong time?*

I observed my environment. Many men in suits, some even holding guns, and reporters holding cameras were surrounding me. I noticed that I was wearing a suit as well—definitely *not* what I was wearing to Krix's party. I observed the Washington Monument looming large in the distance. I turned around and saw the giant white mansion that Congressman Krikorian only dreamed of inhabiting. I wasn't only in D.C.—I was on the White House lawn. *Why would the president invite me to the White House? Was it because of something I did?*

Without getting out of my seat, I immediately searched for the others. Maddie was seated next to me on my right, wearing a *super* expensive dress—but there was no sign of Hannah or Kylie anywhere. However, I did see Larry, in old "Uncle Bill" form, as expected. He was sitting in the front row as well, a few seats away from me. Next to Larry-slash-Bill was a brunette woman around the same age as he was, if not a few years older. She looked familiar. *Is that his wife? I thought older Larry was single?*

To my left and Maddie's right were burly men with suits and guns. I deduced that they were the president's Secret Service. I was utterly confused about *everything*.

I whispered, "Maddie, how did we get *here*?"

She turned to me with an extremely annoyed look. Only two minutes back in 2022 and she was already back to the old Maddie. "Stop daydreaming, Charlie," she scoffed. "Jeez, even though you got a hot girlfriend, you're still a dweeb in my book."

"Hannah is not my girlfriend," I said in reply. "And we just had one kiss. Where is she—and Kylie?"

Maddie's expression changed to appall. "Wait till I tell Vanessa you cheated on her with *two* girls!"

I was even more confused. "Who's Vanessa?"

Maddie was about to snap. "I'm not playing these dumb games with you anymore. You better shut up because Mom's about to speak."

Why is she acting like this? I pondered the answer to that question for a few seconds before resuming our conversation, which was going absolutely nowhere.

"Why is Mom making a speech? And why are we in Washington, D.C.?"

Maddie still wasn't giving me any answers. "Look, Charlie. You're trying to be funny and epically failing. Don't you know you're an idiot sometimes?"

At that very moment, the crowd quieted. Then a short, sandy-haired man in his late-forties—who I had never seen before—took the eagle-sealed podium.

His voice boomed for everyone on the lawn to hear. "I'm pleased to welcome the President of the United States— Sarah Henderson!"

My mom is the president! What the hell—

46

HAIL TO THE CHIEF

My mom looked different from usual. She looked—well, *presidential*. Her suit was made by a designer brand, unlike the more basic ones she wore to her job at the mayor's office. She wore her hair down and cropped at her shoulders—shorter than it had been in a while. She stood at the podium flanked by a man who looked just like an actor I recognized from a few TV commercials. It must have been a coincidence. Next to them was a young boy, around seven or eight years of age. She gave the man and the boy a kiss before they left the stage to watch her speech. *Wait, she has a new boyfriend, and he has a son?* I thought. Or maybe that was her *husband,* and that was *their* son. I always wished I had a brother. Maybe I finally got that wish. The man and the boy sat down at two empty seats in the front row, with the Secret Service surrounding them.

The various reporters asked my mom several questions. I realized that this was a press conference—a *presidential* press conference. It lasted for a while. The media drilled her on a wide range of topics, from her economic initiatives to foreign policy. I dozed off for the vast majority of it—politics was never my thing. I noticed the "Soviet Union" and "USSR" were mentioned repeatedly by both the reporters and my mom. *Wait, didn't that thing cease to exist before I was born? What had happened?*

I was still bewildered that my mom was the President of the United States. Was I dreaming? It wasn't like my mom being president would be something I dreamt about. Yes, she worked for the mayor, but as far as I knew, she never wanted her boss's job, let alone the *presidency*.

Then toward the end of the conference, I heard a journalist ask a question that caught my ear. I instantly began to pay more attention.

"Josh Banks here from American Eagle News Network."

American Eagle, the clothing company? Do they own a news channel now? Everything I knew was wrong.

Banks continued. "There has been a lot of talk about a seemingly inevitable so-called 'Time Race' brewing between the Soviets and us. Madam President, the country wants to know, what is your position on taking up Secretary Krikorian's proposal and investing billions of taxpayer dollars on researching *time travel*?"

Krikorian? As in Congressman Krikorian? I guess he always found a way to power no matter the circumstances.

My mom laughed at the reporter's question. "Jesse is a great guy," she replied, "and he's done a lot for the

Department of State. It's been an absolute honor to have him serve as my top diplomat. I would not have appointed anyone else." Her expression suddenly became more serious. "But, with that being said, the answer is a hard no. The Secretary of State and I, despite being from the same party, agree to disagree on this issue. Let's face it—the overwhelming *scientific* consensus is that time travel is one hundred percent infeasible. I'm all for outpacing the Russians, but it's a terrible idea to waste Americans' hard-earned money on science fiction. Tell the Secretary to prove me otherwise, and if so, we'll have a conversation."

I obviously knew my mom was wrong, but I also knew there was no way she would believe me if I told her. I didn't know what to do.

I looked at Maddie to see if any of the time travel talk resonated with her. However, she seemed completely unaffected by it. I realized that she wasn't going to be any help here.

When the conference was over, I immediately headed toward Larry-slash-Bill. The men in suits were all over. As I got closer to him, he noticed me and made eye contact.

"Uh—hi, Bill," I said.

The old man smiled at me. "Hey, Charlie, how's it going?"

"Good. I just—uh, want to talk to you when I have a chance. It's pretty important."

The Secret Service agents looked somewhat suspiciously at me. I thought the answer was "no."

"Sure," old Larry surprisingly replied. "Anything for you."

He motioned to the agents. "Can I have a minute alone with the president's kid? We won't go too far." He pointed to an empty corner of the property, away from the crowd.

The Secret Service were not too thrilled at the request, but they relented. "Okay, Vice President Travers," an agent replied. "But make this snappy. We'll be keeping an eye on you two. If we notice one thing out of the ordinary, we're breaking this little talk up."

Vice President? So, *Larry* was my mom's running mate?

We both nodded our heads in compliance. An agent then gave me a thorough pat-down for weapons—which definitely caught me off guard.

I then followed Larry-slash-Bill over to the corner where he had pointed.

I spoke as low as I could, much like I had in Brown's boiler room. "Larry, remember me?" I said. "I'm back."

The vice president was startled—as if nobody had called him "Larry" in a *long* time. He immediately began to cry tears of joy and hugged me. "Welcome back, Charlie! I've been waiting for this day for forty-eight years!"

47

THE BUTTERFLY EFFECT

I was relieved for once. "Thank God you remember," I said. "Maddie seems to have no clue that this is an alternate reality."

"Of course she doesn't," Larry replied. "She isn't *time-sensitive* like us. Regular people who slip into alternate timelines have no idea anything changes because their mind is programmed to think they've lived in the new timeline their entire life."

I was thrown for a giant loop. I still didn't know most of the rules of time travel. "So, you mean to tell me that the past can be severely altered and no one, except for a few other people and us, will even have a clue?"

"Exactly. It's scary."

I was lost for words. I froze for a few seconds before continuing. "Uh—congrats on becoming vice president. But that and the fact my mom is president, exactly how did that happen?"

"Well, apparently, when Brown faked his death and changed his reality in the old timeline, he did not just become any Joe Schmo; he became Keith Byrd."

I was stunned. "Wait. As in FBI Director Keith Byrd? You mean to tell me he was Brown all along?"

"Yes, and a lot of Washington knew and let it slide due to his power and influence. By turning him in, we, well, really *you*, saved the country from a lot of corruption."

"But that doesn't answer my question." It sure appeared that I was saying that sentence a lot.

Larry went on. "Right after Brown was arrested, actually, on the same day, he committed suicide, ending any discussion of him escaping from prison. Paul Kazlowski, your grandfather, got a lot of the credit for permanently ending the Greenies. The media knew about the plot to kill his father, and since they obviously didn't know about *us*, it just made sense for them to paint him as the hero. The Kazlowskis, well, your family, became famous overnight. This made a political career for your mother much easier than in the old timeline. As for me, well, a lot of my early fame had to do with my wife."

Things started to make at least a little sense for me. "Wait, the woman I saw before, she looked familiar. She almost looks like an older version of—"

Larry stopped me. "Yes, now she's Kathryn *Travers*, my wife of forty-three years. She was the biggest hero of all as she was the one who disclosed Brown's location."

I just couldn't believe how changing the outcome of one seemingly small event made *everything* go differently. "So, you're telling me, us bringing down Brown caused all of this?"

"Yes."

"But wait, if the timeline was changed in 1974, how do Maddie and I still exist? My mom was also born after the timelines diverged. This does not make any sense."

"There's this thing in time travel called the *butterfly effect*. Basically, if one little thing in the past is changed, even if it's as minute as a butterfly flapping its wings, a ripple is caused, changing the entire future. Look at the people around us— almost every person you see under the age of forty-eight did *not* exist in the old timeline. In fact, every non-time-sensitive person conceived after September 1974 in our old timeline does *not* exist in this timeline. These people, as we time-sensitives call it, are *butterflied out*."

I thought about pretty much everyone I had known. Most of my teachers. The Garcia twins. Alang. Rick McCreery. Pasta. All of them were gone. Well, technically, they never even *existed*.

Larry continued. "Well, everyone except for a select few, of course, including you, Maddie, your mother, your father, and Maddie's father. This is where a corollary to the butterfly effect that I call, for lack of a better term, the 'butterfly net' comes into play. Since you and Maddie were instrumental in changing the past, your existence was saved in this new timeline. Therefore your parents' existences had to be saved as well."

"But what about Kylie and Hannah?" I anxiously asked. "They're in this world too?"

"Yes," Larry replied. "They also played a role in changing history, so they were saved as well—but they're likely in Fresno. And, like Maddie, neither of them have any idea the old timeline ever existed."

It was hard for me to process this. All the bonding between the girls and me during our time in the past was for *nothing*. "So, Hannah doesn't remember our kiss?"

"No. In fact, to her, it never happened. But you do happen to have a girlfriend in this timeline. Perks of being the president's son."

That must be that Vanessa person Maddie was talking about. I was upset—I didn't care that I had a girlfriend. I wanted to be with Hannah. I immediately got off the subject before I started to hurt more. "I see I have a brother too?" I asked Larry.

"Yes. In this timeline, your mother and Maddie's father divorced earlier than before, so she married a third time and had a son with him. Your brother's name is Louis, by the way."

"My mom's husband, Louis's dad—he looks familiar."

"Well, yes, in the old timeline, he was an actor. Derek Rogers."

So, my suspicion was correct. "You mean the guy from the tire commercials?"

"Yep. Let's just say First Gentleman is a step up from washed-up mid-2000s sitcom star turned Hankook spokesperson."

"This world is just weird," I remarked, stating the obvious.

"Get used to it, man. It's *your* world now."

I felt empty. My former identity was erased from the

face of the earth. Yeah, I had the same name and DNA—but aside from that, I was a *completely different* person. I quickly thought back to my first day of senior year—well, in my old life. I *wanted* this. I wanted to be a different person. *Be careful what you wish for.*

I was on the verge of losing it. "So, you mean that seventeen years of memories are all gone? Like they never happened?"

"Like they never happened," Larry agreed. "But don't worry. You'll get new memories in this world. They'll all come to you in time."

I hadn't ever heard of such a thing. "New memories? Like how is that supposed to happen?"

"Based on what Al taught me, it depends on the person. So, your experience could be different than mine would be. But usually, they come to you in dreams. Trust me—you'll *know* when you're experiencing a memory."

I paused for a good ten seconds before I spoke again. "I just can't believe my whole life—the whole *world*—is changed."

Before Larry could respond, the Secret Service appeared in front of us.

"Time's up," an agent said. "Vice President Travers, you're needed for an appearance."

I threw my face into my hands. I had no idea what I was going to do—if there was anything I *could* do for that matter.

The men promptly hauled Larry away before he could say another word to me.

EPILOGUE

The interrogation room was dark—except for the lone spotlight that hung above the cold steel table. Special Agent Alphonse Cannella was alone, sitting at one end, happy as a clam at high tide.

"I swear. I've been waiting to say these next few words for all my life!" he growled. "Manny! Bring him in!"

Al's loyal, Spanish body man barged into the room carrying the disheveled prisoner. The struggling man looked like a shell of his former self. His orange jumpsuit was two sizes too big—it looked more like pajamas than a prison uniform. Heavy shackles restrained both his wrists and ankles.

"Lookie what we got here!" Al taunted him. "I guess a bunch of kids were too much to handle for the mighty Aidan Brown and his Mount Greenwood Boys."

"I—uh, they—uh, the sewer—!" Brown was tongue-tied.

Manny placed the handcuffed Brown down on the chair opposite Al. He promptly left the room and shut the door, leaving his colleague and the fallen criminal by themselves.

"What a pathetic showing that was!" Al roared. "You had the *easy* job! Isolate the boy, get his blood, and then get *rid* of him!"

"If it was so easy, why didn't you do it yourself, Al?"

"After all I've done for you, show me some respect, you idiot! You *know* that's not my name. Say it! Kerimoğlu—Alkan Kerimoğlu."

"Fine, Al*kan*." Brown was sweating bullets. "We'll get him the next time. Just stage an escape, and I'll get my whole band of thugs back together again. It's not like they have any other place to go."

"There is no *we*!" Alkan put his hand two inches away from Brown's face, causing the former mob boss to flinch. "There will sure be a next time, but it won't be with *you*! You're all talk and no action. A true *dead* weight."

Alkan reached into his pocket and pulled out a cat's eye marble. He placed it on the table and flicked it off with a single tap of his index finger.

Brown was pleading for mercy. The sweat had visibly drenched his jumpsuit.

Alkan continued. "You were supposed to be the *dragon*— the Darth Vader to my Emperor Palpatine. I was the brains behind all of this. All you had to do was act tough, yet you still failed miserably."

"The what?" Brown's voice became like gravel.

"Oh, that's right. I forgot that you're the 1974 Brown. But it's not like the 2022 Brown even exists anymore!"

Brown did not respond.

Alkan smiled. "I don't need your ass anymore. The one thing you got right is how to treat your henchmen. At the end of the day, they're just disposable pawns."

Aidan Brown's eyes widened as Alkan brandished a long syringe filled with a clear, viscous liquid. He pointed it at his neck.

"No one will suspect a thing," Alkan stated. "They will all

think you just put your poor self out of your own misery."

The gangster tried to free himself from the shackles. But it was too late.

In one fell swoop, Alkan slammed the needle into Brown's jugular. Then he carefully pressed the plunger forward as the poison gushed into the base of his neck.

"Good riddance!" he trumpeted. "You were *never* anything but a wannabe Whitey Bulger!"

Brown's lifeless body slumped off the chair and onto the stone-cold floor.

Alkan adjusted his fedora and stroked his chin. "Watch out, boy, *time* is on my side," he remarked coolly. "On to Plan B."

———————◆———————

END OF BOOK ONE

CPSIA information can be obtained
at www.ICGtesting.com
Printed in the USA
BVHW032113090222
628564BV00004B/38